Worth the Ride

Ann Clay

Worth the Ride
Gumbo Love Series
Copyrighted ©2018 by Ann Clay
All rights reserved.
ISBN-13: 978-1981460526
ISBN-10: 1981460527

Cover image from fotolia.com Author: bst2012

Book Cover Design by Nikisha Logan

DEDICATION

This book is dedicated to all the followers of the Brooks family. The journey of this family reminds me how important it is to appreciate and admire a unit that through all things life can throw at you, can love, respect, and have each other's back at all times.

There is real power in a family with faith, commitment, and true love. May you find something relatable in your own family.

Also, I can't say enough about the people around me; always loving, supporting, and encouraging me. My greatest hope is that you gain something from my stories. I am and always have been about true love, family, and friends. This story and how we got to this point, hopefully encompasses all three.

ACKNOWLEDGMENTS

I've been so fortunate to have such great reader support. You guys have stuck with me during this entire journey with the Brooks family. Your encouragement has help create an awesome experience, for which I'm eternally grateful for.

My love and admiration for my family and friends has kept me ground. A great big 'thank-you' to my children, Nikisha and Brian.

A huge shout out to all the book clubs. You rock!

Thank you to my sister-girlfriends and author-mentors who always have my back.

And more importantly, I acknowledge my maker, for He continues to bless me better than I deserve.

It is with humility, that I thank you for allowing me to be a part of your days and nights.

Happy Reading!

CHAPTER 1

Trish brushed the back of her gloved hand across her forehead to dab the excess sweat there. She lost her footing, and went sailing in a downward spiral from the landing, which was exactly two steps from the floor of the stall. The pitchfork in her hand flew and, depending on where she landed, would surely end up either on her head or chest. Groping behind her, she desperately searched for anything that would break her fall, and when she touched rough fabric, she was relieved. She was all too happy to hold onto a fistful in each hand.

Landing against the solid wall of a man's chest, she was surrounded by strong massive arms. She relaxed as hands gently held her up before placing her back on her feet.

She turned, ready to praise her rescuer, only to stall after meeting cool, dark eyes glowering from beneath a worn cowboy hat. Her breath caught in her throat as her eyes lifted past his prominent chin, tempting lips, strong nose, and yes, very cool eyes. The flying pitchfork landed near his boot. He casually glanced at it as it landed with a thump. His cool gaze quickly returned to her.

"You should really watch what you're doing. You could have hurt yourself."

She probably could have regained some sense of control once she made it to his furred heavy brows, but his booming voice ripped straight through her and she practically fell backward again. He reached and grabbed her yet again. The heat of his touch and not the crash near their feet startled her. Trish yanked her arms free and frowned. While she appreciated his concern, she refused to be reprimanded like a child.

"Thank you, I'm fine. Now if you don't mind?"

"But I do. Who are you, and why are you in my barn?"

Fighting the effects of this man's overpowering presence, and staving off the tremors from just hearing his voice, she stuttered. The answer was at the tip of her tongue. It practically refused to come forth. She brought her hand to her neck, hoping to calm the leaping on the left side of it. Wrong move. His eyes followed her hand and then trailed to her lips where he paused before bringing his attention back to her eyes.

"Mr. Denver Baldwin?" Her voice trailed off as she gazed into his face. His expression didn't change. Instead both of his hands went to his waist as he glared down at her without another word. "I'm, Trisha Brooks, the vet resident from Texas A&M."

The instant she revealed her identity, she witnessed a small transformation in his appearance. His jaw tightened and he drew his lips into a straight line. The fire in his eyes grew dangerous. The air felt stifling between them, nearly suffocating her where she stood. Though still fueled by electric sparks, heat pushed from pit of her groin and traveled up, completely washing over her. She dropped her lids, trying to stave off the jitters now creeping up her back. *Woo, girl, he can't scare you.* She lifted her chin, this time higher than she should have.

"That doesn't explain why you're here, Trisha Brooks." He moved his feet apart and waited.

"Aww, I spoke to a Mr. Craig Rogers, who cleared me to…"

As she spoke his name, Craig waltzed into the stall, slowing when he saw them. Both she and Denver looked his way at the same time and the man stopped dead in his tracks.

"I see, Boss, you've met…"

"Exactly when were you going to clear this with me, CR?" Denver removed his hat before he turned his thorns on the middle-age man with heavily tanned skin. Trish was glad to relinquish the rancher's attention to anyone but her. She took that moment to gain her foothold, moving several steps back. The attempt only drew his eyes back to her and she continued to stare as Craig answered his question.

"You needed the extra hands, so I didn't see no harm. We could always send her…"

"No! Please, I need these hours for my grade. I promise I will do my part."

Trish hoped the plea didn't sound pitiful, but she was at her wits end to secure an intern position. She'd waited too late to apply for any of the other facilities on the list. Just barely keeping up this semester, she spent a lot of time in the lab, more than she'd planned to, and had lost track of time. She struggled to get the hours needed to meet her class requirement.

Removing the gloves from her hands, she held out her right one to him. "If we can please start over. Trisha Brooks, third year resident at Texas A&M Veterinary Medicine Center."

When it looked like he would leave her hanging, he reached for and cupped her hand in his. It was calloused, warm, and sent a bolt of lighting up her arm until the heat reached her face. She gasped. He glared at her as though he wasn't going to cut her any slack. When he finally released her hand, she instantly felt the cool, which left her uneasy. He had yet to utter a single word.

Craig stepped forward. Neither she nor Denver looked his way. The air between them steadily grew with uncomfortably thick. Trish prayed silently that he would move on, release her, but it was as if he knew he held her captive, He was testing to see if she would break first. She'd be damned. Yes, she needed the hours and this was the last site. If she bailed now, she would have to retake this class. She wasn't that dumb or stupid so she waited.

"Look, Den, we need the help so stop giving the girl a hard time."

The word 'girl' didn't sit well with her. She narrowed her eyes toward Craig. In response he held up his hands.

"Little lady, I'm just trying to help you out."

She turned back to Denver, ready to blot if she needed to. She'd met challenges far worse than having to retake a class. Her family thought she'd gone absolutely mad when she decided to come to Texas, let alone study to become Vet. Her narrowed gaze now centered on him. She fought to contain the emotions riling to the surface. She didn't want to burn any bridges if she didn't have to.

"Do I stay, or will I have to retake this class Mr. Baldwin?"

Nothing was more annoying to her than his continued attempt to unnerve her. She had to admit he was doing a good job at it. He stood before her sucking up all the air, even the stench of horse muck in the stalls. She'd already spent two hours of her day cleaning his damn stalls. She hated to think she'd wasted her time.

A few more seconds ticked by before her rattled nerves couldn't stand it any longer. She dropped the gloves in her left hand. They fell to her feet and she moved to pass him. His calloused hand wrapped around her arm, squeezing it slightly and halting her progress.

"You can stay, but…"

She yanked her arm away and moved into his space to challenge him and set her own demands before he dictated his.

Big mistake!

This method worked with her brothers, who were far bigger than him, but her molten legs gave way. Denver tightened his grip, reaching with his hat-filled hand to steady her, and flattening the hat against her back.

"Whoa." He frowned. Instantly, his indifference shifted as the dark pools of his eye squinted and pierced straight through her. He held her captive for a long moment. Craig's voice interrupted the private conversation of unspoken words.

"Are you okay, Trish? You can't be too careful. A lot of things can trip you up in a place like this."

"Ah, yes, I'm fine. Thank you." She continued to stare into Denver's concerned face. Her whispered reply made the point.

Releasing her, Denver stepped back. He placed his hat back on his head. "CR is right. Are you sure you're ready to work in a place like this?"

"I'm sure." She brushed her hands down her soiled denims. The surge between them continued even though they stood apart. Her aching feet throbbed like hell in boots she swore she would never wear. She ended up borrowing them from her lab-mate, Kim. Although they hurt like hell, she was thankful her friend had talked her into wearing them. Her shoes, good shoes, would be destroyed by now and it had only been, yes, two hours. For now, she ignored the pain and concentrated on the man in front of her.

Denver seemed okay with her answer. He took several steps backward before turning and heading for the galley door. Just before he moved through the exit, he turned and directed an order to Craig.

"Make sure she stays out of trouble. The last thing I need is to have to file an incident report."

Without looking at her again, he left them standing, staring at his back.

"Well, that went better than I expected." Craig lifted his hat and repositioned it on his head.

Trish huffed before bending, picking up her gloves and shoving her fingers through them. When she was done, she took several steps and picked up the pitchfork. She climbed the two steps back to the platform where she'd been before Craig and Denver had entered the stable.

CHAPTER 2

Denver moved quickly from the stables. The little spitfire that had fallen in his arms could have easily caused a disaster had he not been there to catch her. He could see it now: mounds of paperwork and for what reason?

Her taking a significant fall was not the only thing that had him seeing red. She didn't look like a woman who should be mucking his stalls. Her flawless face, even free of makeup, and her tousled hair with sprinkles of straw in it made her the most breathtaking creature he'd seen in a long while. Her snug denim shirt and pants hugged and complimented her curves. He'd tried not to stare at the flesh peeking above the tank showing under the open-buttoned shirt, but it was there for the showing.

She felt like soft, refined cotton in his arms, despite the stench of straw and manure. Her fragrance filled his nostrils with reverence. The man in him came to attention like a soldier given a direct command. He fought the urge to squeeze her against his body. Though the temptation was strong, he saluted his will to withstand the need.

Her little fiery gaze and sharp tongue clearly made him consider sending her on her way. She wasn't doing him a damn favor. He'd prefer to pay a hand to do the work rather than deal with her. Still he was curious. What made little prissy Trisha Brooks tick? The fact that she looked so out of place piqued his interest. What was she doing in a horse barn in Texas? And why did she want to be a vet? His curiosity had fueled his decision to let her stay.

He busied himself for an hour before going back to check on her progress. He'd smacked his hand with the fence mallet at least three times before he gave up on fixing the south end fence. He'd then attempted to stack the bails near the trotting path. He'd managed to get halfway done before quitting that chore as well.

Finally, he couldn't stand it any longer. Who was he fooling? He didn't care whether or not she'd made progress. He wanted to see her, to feel the way she'd made him feel. It'd been a long time since a woman had snagged his fascination with such ease. Hell, he'd been too busy keeping this ranch afloat to be concerned with women.

His father's sudden death bolted him straight into the operations of the ranch instead of managing business side as he'd done since finishing college. CR was there to help pick up the pieces. Together, things were getting done. But managing both ends took away much of his freedom.

Denver sauntered into the barn where he'd left Trish. When he entered, he heard her humming. He smiled. What on earth was there to sing about? Working a ranch was back-breaking work.

He stepped into one of the stalls. She was brushing Winter, his horse. He'd been the only one able to tame the animal and here Winter was as calm as kitten, eyes closed as she serenaded him while brushing his thick mane. He couldn't believe it. So he wasn't the only one to succumb to her charms.

He cleared his throat, bringing both the buck and the woman's attention to him. Winter glared with disdain, as if to say why are you interrupting us?

"That's my horse you're brushing."

"Really? I wasn't aware of that. He and I are making great progress, I must say."

"I would say so. Nobody on this ranch is able to get him to stand still to put on a bridle let alone brush him down."

"Oh, really? We had a little issue at first but we came to an understanding."

Denver walked up to the animal and patted him on the hind flank before moving close to where she stood. He felt the warmth of her body. His eyes moved from the stray hair in her face to her lips before rising to meet hers. He reached for the hair and lifted the strand to the top of her head. He felt her tremble.

Winter must have felt the energy as well. He bent his head and snorted air through his nostrils.

"Whoa, boy." He patted Winter's neck before looking down at Trish again. "What have you done to my animal?" His voice dropped an octave. It was unrecognizable to him. He grazed Trisha's hand lightly as he reached for the brush.

She would have stepped back but there was nowhere to go. She was trapped and her only option was to move into him. He watched the pulse leap in her neck as her chest rose and fell. Their gazes held. "I… I can't help that he likes me."

"That's funny. He doesn't like anyone. Did you drug him?"

"No, I didn't drug him. What kind of question is

that?"

He lifted an eyebrow, enjoying the ire he provoked in her. She filled his head with her scent and filled his blood with her nearness. He wanted to grab and kiss her until she withered in his arms. Instead, he stepped back. Winter bobbed his head and nudged him.

"Just making sure." He turned to Winter. "What's all the fuss about? I was just asking her a simple question?" He rubbed the horse's neck before moving from the stall. Trish followed him.

"He doesn't take too kindly to you harassing me, Mr. Baldwin."

"Please, drop the Mr. Call me Denver. Winter has no say around here. I run things."

"Is that right?"

"Yes. Exactly what are you expected to do around here, in addition to mucking my stalls."

"I hope to help out where I can. Mostly, I want to make sure your herd is healthy and to learn as much as I can about horses in this setting, for starters."

He admired her beauty. Her posture was straight. Her body was fit and lean. Everything about her seemed to call his name. He guessed she was about 5'8". She could be a model anywhere if she wanted to. Instead, she stood ankle-high in straw and manure in the middle of the mid-morning heat.

"I must admit you don't look the veterinarian type."

"And what does that type look like?"

She raised her chin and glared up at him. Her soft demeanor shifted. She roused her guard as high as the rafters. While his, it was certainly his opinion, he paused a moment before replying. He had no intentions of offending her, especially since he could use her help. He calculated how much money he could save by having a vet on hand, if it worked out, even if it was student vet. Three of his mares were pregnant and would give birth soon. Trish would hopefully spare his budget…if she panned out to be the kind of help he needed.

"I'm sorry, I just don't see you knee deep in manure or your entire arm up a horse to reposition a foal. Your hands--" He captured one and held it up. "--don't look like they've seen a hard day's work. Ever."

He watched, expecting Trish to jerk her hand from his. She didn't. Instead, she studied her hands as if seeing them for the very first time. When she looked up at him again, she tilted her head to one side.

"I use gloves. A lot. But don't let these looks fool you, Mr. Baldwin."

"I guess we will have to see. And it's Denver."

She turned and headed toward the door. He noticed she limped and reached for her before she was out of reach.

"Did you hurt your leg or foot?"

She hesitated before answering. "No, why?"

"Sit." He pointed to a bail of straw. She sat and he knelt in front of her.

He raised her pants leg to the top of her boot. "Are these yours?"

Trish frowned, moving her foot from his grasp. "Yes. Why?"

"How long have you been wearing these?"

"Not long."

He raised a brow and waited. She sat up even straighter. "They belong to my teammate. She let me borrow them."

"They don't fit. The worst thing you can do is wear boots that will bust up your feet." He picked up her foot again and observed the leather decorative boots. They were more for fashion than working. He glanced at her. "You might want to go to Charlie's. He has boots that would suit you better here. He has some reconditioned ones. You won't have to worry about breaking them in."

"Wearing someone else's boots? I don't want nobody's cooties."

He raised his eyebrows again. "These aren't yours. What's the difference?"

"The difference is I know Chris. Her feet are clean."

He stared at her for a moment without a word, and then replaced her foot on the ground.

"What?"

Denver stood and shook his head. "They're your feet. But if you don't get a decent pair, you're going to ruin them. If I were you, I'd take those off." He pointed to her feet. "Before you don't want to wear any shoes at all."

"I'll go to Charlie's when I leave here." She stood and gazed up at him. She didn't move, waiting for something. Her gaze, from what he could tell, stopped right at his lips. He licked his bottom one and confirmed his assumption. She hurriedly looked away.

"Tell him I sent you. He'll likely give you a discount."

"Price is not an issue."

Her comment made him take a closer look at Trisha. Yes, clearly her now-soiled denims didn't come from Brown's Country Store. And her expensively manicured hands indicated that she came from money. He'd never known anyone to toss it in his face so casually. Watching her closely he could tell what she said was a fact.

He headed back to Winter. He might as well ride him down to the pasture to check on the hands digging a drain. He'd come to the stables earlier looking for CR to check the crew's progress.

"What time will you be back tomorrow?" he asked

without looking back.

"Six, if that's okay with you."

He did turn at her response. "That's mighty early. Have you already worked out what hours you will be here?"

"Just tentatively. I have a class and lab late morning, so I'll have to come early to get my hours in."

"Okay, that will be fine." He nodded and tilted his hat. "See you tomorrow."

Trish waved. "Have a good one."

"Yeah, you too."

She turned and limped through the doors. He waited several seconds after she disappeared before patting his horse on the back. He reached for the blanket and saddle, draping them across the stallion's back.

"You traitor. How do you explain your actions, man? You're girl crazy, you know that?"

The horse snorted as Denver led him from the pen and through the side exit. "Admit it. You like that woman."

Winter's head bobbed up and down. They made their way to the worn path leading to the pastures. He mounted Winter and before trotting off, looked toward the main gate. A steel gray car sped toward the main road. It suddenly stopped and did a three-point turn, heading back towards the house. He turned Winter around and slapped the reins on the side of his neck.

"Hhaaattt!"

CHAPTER 3

Trish turned the car around and headed back for the stable. She'd been so preoccupied with Denver Baldwin that she'd walked off without her backpack. Luckily, she remembered it before getting halfway to the lab. Of course, her license and apartment keys were in it, but her books and phone as well. She stopped and hopped out of the car, almost stumbling when she saw Denver seated on Winter just at the bend in the road.

Good Lord, when was she going to stop tripping over herself? She pressed her hand to her chest. She tried to recover her wits but they just weren't behaving. She felt dizzy looking up at him. The sun created a halo above his head. He looked extremely dangerous, sexier than any man she'd ever seen. And she'd seen her share of Texas cowboys.

They didn't hold her attention long because all they talked about was cattle, horses, and their mommies. Gee whiz. Yes, she was in school to be a vet, but she didn't want to talk to someone who couldn't at least carry a decent conversation about anything else.

She missed home and shopping and culture. She swore she would scream if she saw another steak. In fact, she'd all but stopped eating meat. She would kill for some fresh seafood, especially a dish of her mother's etouffee. The smile that thought brought to her face faltered when his voice broke into her thoughts.

"Miss us already?"

"Um, I forgot my bag. I left it on the ledge." She didn't want to give him the idea that he'd turned her world upside down. It wasn't like he didn't already know, of course.

"Okay."

"See you later."

"Sure thing."

She hurried in and was out in a flash, hoping like hell that Denver was on his way already. He made her a walking disaster. She slowed as she passed him. He looked down on her like a towering god. He tilted his hat and she did all she could to hold it together.

Winter blew air at her when she moved in front of him. Trisha looked back before getting back into her car. She stopped at the fork in the road before she pressed down the turn signal.

When she reached her apartment, Butcher Monroe was leaning against the rail leading to her front entryway. She groaned inwardly. He was the last person she wanted to see. All she wanted right now was a hot shower and something to eat.

Butcher, who in her opinion was stuck on himself, had no idea what the word 'no' meant. In her opinion, he simply thought it meant try harder. She didn't have it in her to be out right mean and nasty to him, like she'd seen so many women do. Her mother would skin her alive if she behaved that way.

Taking a long breath, she fortified herself for the encounter. She stopped several steps away from the husky brown-eyed man.

She smiled. "Hey, Butch, what are you doing here?"

He looked at her with piqued interest. "You look like you've been rolling in the hay with a bull. Hot damn!"

See, this is what I mean. She groaned inwardly again. *Oh, boy, I hate this.* She worked hard to keep the smile on her face.

"I wouldn't say that exactly. Again, why are you here? I'm sort of in a hurry. I need to take a shower."

She fanned her hand in front of her, starting from her head down to the boots, which were killing her feet.

"Yeah, uh. I wanted to see if we could grab a bite."

"I'm sorry Butch. I'm exhausted. Not this time." She should have said not ever, but again the soft side of her spoke. Her mother would be so proud.

"I can always wait on you, 'cause I'm in no hurry, you know."

Trish shook her head from side to side and bit the inside of her cheek to contain the scream ready to surface. She stepped back as he took a step forward. They did this dance a few times before she lifted her hand toward him. With no patience left, she glanced up into his face.

"Really, Butch, I'm too tired."

He'd already closed her hand in his rough palm. He gave it a light squeeze.

"Okay, sugah, next time. You get yourself cleaned up, you hear."

She withdrew her hand, hoping she hadn't snatched it too quickly from his grasp. By the look on his face, he hadn't noticed her sudden move. His lopsided grin eased into place and his eyes sparkled with glee. In the few encounters with the man, he seemed to be good natured. If nothing else, it was the one trait that might attract people to him. Trish smiled.

"Thanks for understanding, Butch. Talk to you later."

"Sure thing."

He watched as she headed to the door. Once safely through, Trish turned to find Butch smiling into the face of a woman from her building. She frowned. Her feelings should have been hurt but she was too exhausted to give it a second thought. Instead, she walked to the elevator and with weary steps, entered the galley.

****

Trish nonchalantly flipped the pages of her manual, not really seeing or comprehending anything there. She stared at the same three sentences she'd written more than hour ago. She hadn't added or deleted anything, not even the references she needed to complete her class assignment.

Instead, her concentration centered on the man who made her body tingle just thinking about him. His luscious lips and sensuous eyes had occupied her thoughts since leaving his ranch. As if she'd summoned him, her phone chimed. Baldwin Ranch appeared on the display screen. She'd saved the number to her contacts after the ranch hand agreed to let her earn her hours there.

"This is Trisha Brooks," she answered, almost a little too quickly.

Her heart sped, forcing heat up her neck and face. She set up in her bed, almost flipping the laptop over.

"Hello, Ms. Trisha, Craig here. I didn't get to say my farewell before you left today. I just wanted to check on you. Hopefully, we ain't run you off and you'll come back tomorrow."

Trish's body deflated on hearing Craig's voice. She closed her eyes, silently listening to him, wishing it was Denver on the other end of the line. They thought the work was much harder than she'd bargained for. She smiled. In actuality, the day hadn't been bad at all.

She'd not expected to muck the stalls all day but she had to start someplace. She was willing to do just about anything to make sure Baldwin didn't give her the boot. This close to the end of her journey, retaking this class was not an option.

"Sorry, Mr. Craig, I didn't get to see you before I left. It was my understanding that you were on the far south side of the ranch. And I will be back tomorrow, that is, if I've not been given my leave."

"You worked out the hours with Denver?"

"Actually, we did not, but if it's all the same with you, I'll come the same hours as today. I have classes late mornings. So, I should be there the same time as today."

"Good. Then we'll see you tomorrow."

"Yes, I will see you tomorrow."

After she clicked the end button on her phone, she held the device to her forehead and silently counted to ten. Then she glared at her laptop and took a long breath.

"Okay, girl, let's get this done."

She stroked the keys, added words that until a few minutes ago were a distant thought. She paused when her phone chimed again. Her heart raced at seeing the Baldwin Ranch number once more. Trembling fingers hit the talk button.

"This is Trisha Brooks."

"Trisha, I've left you a list of things I would like you to do when you arrive tomorrow."

Denver's deep voice snagged her concentration and she missed all he said.

"Is there a problem?"

Trish nearly knocked over her laptop and the huge manual at the edge of the bed.

"Aw, no problem. Got it."

"Great. I won't be here in the morning but might be back before you leave."

She dropped her head to her chest. Something about not seeing him made disappointment flutter in her stomach. She realized her mission was to get her hours, not to look at his gorgeous eyes all day. She retrieved her laptop before responding.

"Okay. Maybe I'll see you tomorrow."

"Have a good evening, Trisha."

"Thank you, Mr. Baldwin. You have a good evening as well."

"Trisha?"

"Yes." She straightened as if reprimanded.

"Please, there are no formalities here. It's Denver."

Denver's voice, full of brass, sent fire through her veins. Her heart thumped hard and the warm sensation crept to her face.

"Of course. And most people call me Trish, if you don't mind. Good night, Denver."

"Better. Good night, Trish."

She held the phone to her face, even after she heard the line disconnect. When it chimed again, she startled.

The device nearly slipped through her fingers and she glanced at the display and smiled.

"Hi Daddy. I miss you."

"Hello, sweetheart. How's my favorite girl?"

Trish slipped back onto the pillow. She was definitely daddy's girl, and although thoughts of Denver still lingered, she gave her father her undivided attention.

CHAPTER 4

Denver placed the phone back in its jacket but his hand remained on it for a long moment before he moved back to his over-crowded office desk. It hadn't been necessary to call Trish, but his need to hear her voice overpowered his minimum control.

He could have left instructions with CR. She didn't need to know his early morning plans. He had to inspect a new herd from last week's auction and he wanted her to know his absence had nothing to do with her.

Trish had turned his world inside out the entire day, causing him to nearly forget his plans for the next few days. Had he remembered, he wouldn't have promised to be here in the morning. He also had other motives. He wanted to hear her raspy voice.

Pushing his tired body into his worn leather chair, he rubbed the tense muscles in his neck. Sighing heavily, he dropped his chin and willed his mind to focus on the transaction report in front of him. Denver glanced at the brass clock, noting the late hour. His thoughts drifted to the time piece that had belonged to his father.

His heart grew heavy. His parents had him late in life. They didn't think they could have children again, not after trying for many years. Melvin, ten years older than his mother was in his fifties when they learned she was carrying him. Beatrice had lost two babies, twins, nearly twenty years before Denver was conceived. They were still-born. The tragedy nearly broke his parents both mentally and physically.

This ranch had been passed down to Melvin, and after Denver was born, he was determined to make sure his heir, his son, kept the ranch in the Baldwin family, to Denver's dismay. Denver's original plan was to escape as far away from Texas as he could possibly go. But after graduating with an MBA, his father's failing health, forced him to reconsider that idea.

The year after he returned to the ranch, he began to keep his father's books. He attended to all the buying. He'd hired and managed the hands. And no sooner than he could wrap his head around the aspects of the business, his father fell terminally ill. Denver had found himself doing both the operations and management of the ranch.

His mother helped as much as she could. Until his father died, Beatrice had been relegated to caring for their home-life. And she didn't mind. In fact, she took great pride in 'caring for her men,' she would always say.

Denver sighed again. He picked up a sheet of the report and forced himself to concentrate on the rows of neatly aligned numbers.

He would have gotten further if not for two reasons. One, Trish filled his every thought and had lit a fire he couldn't put out. And, two, his stomach growled.

He'd picked at a cold supper earlier. The stew had grown cold because he was at the other side of the ranch until dark. All the hands stayed until the ditch had been completely finished.

Denver wandered to the kitchen and dug through the refrigerator. He stumbled across a bowl of fried chicken from the day before. He pulled a thigh from the bottom and pulled a beer from the door. He headed back to his office and consumed the cold, but tasty treat. He washed it down with the cold brew as he finished all but two pages of the spreadsheet.

His body ached so he showered and dropped face down, completely naked into his bed. Face buried into his pillow, visions of Trish reappeared. Her perky lips tempted him. Remembering how she melted in his embrace made him stir. His breath caught in the folds of his linen at the mere thought.

He flipped onto his back and stared in bewilderment up at the ceiling. Perhaps it was better that he not be here in the morning. In fact, he might actually stay away until he was certain she was gone. He didn't need the distraction. He had too many other things on his plate. Trish was temporary and would move on soon. He had responsibilities. He couldn't afford to lose focus, not for any reason.

Fighting his urges, Denver fell into a fitful slumber. When he awoke the following morning, he believed he'd been run over by a truck. He silenced the 4:00 a.m. alarm at least three times before he rolled out of bed and into the frigid spray that beat his back like a wayward storm.

After tending to a few chores, he climbed into his truck and took the winding road leading to the highway. He looked down at the dashboard and eased his foot off the accelerator. Flying like a bat out of hell was not necessary. It would at least an hour before Trish turned into the gate. And though he planned to stay away until she was gone, she still weighed heavily in his mind.

****

As the morning slipped into early afternoon, Denver grew antsy to return to the ranch. His plan, although intentional, was not setting well with him. He wasn't in high school or college, yet this girl-- this woman--had him feeling like he was back in school.

When he pulled through the gates, he frowned, slowing his truck to a crawl as he passed Trish's sedan. *What the hell? Why is she still here?*

He parked in his usual spot and shifted into park. He bolted from the truck, scanned the area for his ranch-hands before rushing towards the barn.

What if something was wrong with one of his mares? Surly someone would have called. What if something had happened to her and no one had discovered her alone in one of the stalls? Things unimaginable crossed his mind, fueling him faster towards the opening. His heart quickened as his eyes adjusted to the dim light inside.

Her humming caught his attention first. Heart still racing, he slowed. His search ended at in the first stall. She was humming to a disgruntled stallion the ranch-hands called Lightning. Most of the time Lightning had been left outside in the corral because he refused to be stalled. And now here he was, being bewitched by a cooing Trish.

Denver stopped completely, his mouth agape. His eyes studied the situation in disbelief. Who was this woman? And what was she doing to his animals?

His heart quickened when she turned in his direction. Her humming ceased. She tilted her mouth into a huge smile and his once speeding heart stopped.

"Hi," she greeted him.

The brush in her hand fell to her thigh and she

straightened to her full height. Denver didn't know when or how, but he moved and stood inches away. He stared into her upturned face.

"Hi, Denver."

She tilted her head to one side and her eyes glowed in the dim stall. She was even more breathtaking than he remembered.

Every fiber of his body went on high alert, sending him the unnerving need to touch her. Giving in to his desire, he dragged a finger down the side of her cheek. She closed her eyes and leaned into his hand.

When he found his voice, it sounded raspy to his own ears.

"What are you still doing here? I thought you had class."

He gazed into her beautiful face, wanting badly to pull her into his embrace.

She fluttered her lids and met his gaze. When she finally responded he released the breath from his tight chest.

"I came back. This…" She looked at Lightning before finishing. "This young man was having a fit when I left earlier. Out of concern, I came back after class to check on him."

Denver shook his head. "What are you doing to my herd?"

"What?"

The confusion clearly written on her face made him step closer. She looked so innocent and content.

"You do know this horse hadn't been stalled in over a year. He refuses to be caged. And no one, I mean no one, messes with him except me and sometimes CR. Once again, I'm asking, how are you seducing my herd?"

Trish stepped back but remained in his reach.

"I guess I have the magic touch. They seem to like me."

The animals weren't the only ones affected by her. Something intense and uncontrollable drew him to her. So much for his plan to stay away until she was gone. In a way, he was relieved to find her still at the ranch. Horse witch or not, he was happy to see her.

"What were you singing a little bit ago?"

She smiled broadly. "Oh, it's a Cajun lyric my uncle taught me as child."

Cajun? He realized he knew nothing about Trish, other than she was a third-year vet resident who needed hours for her internship. She'd filled out an application. CR had taken it on himself to collect and keep charge of her. It was her second day, though it seemed like he'd known her a long time. He wanted to know everything.

He lifted his brow and, though he wanted to dig deeper, he decided to save it for another time. He tapped Lightning on back and the stallion turned and shook his head from side to side in protest. "This spot is only big enough for two us," the look said. "A third party is not welcome." Ignoring Lightning's objection, Denver returned his attention to Trish.

"How long are you staying?"

"I'm heading out in a few. I'm meeting my study group for a instructed led session in about an hour."

Something fluttered in Denver's stomach. Hope died at her response. He glanced across the stall before meeting her gaze.

"Well, okay. I'll let you go."

"I'll be back in the morning." She perked up as if she knew he needed to hear her say so.

He nodded. "Great. I'll see you in the morning."

"Yes."

He paused a moment longer before giving the stallion one last pat and turned on his heel to head for the door. He took one last look back and found her watching him. He nodded and left.

CHAPTER 5

Lightning was the perfect excuse to return to the ranch after class, especially since Denver had not returned before she left mid-morning. Trish stayed as long as she could in hopes of seeing Denver, even if only a glance before she high-tailed it back to the university. She'd cut it extremely close, especially given the drive was more than 20 minutes away. Deflated, she rushed to class, slipping into a seat, just as instructor began to speak.

She'd happened on the stallion standing alone and bucking a fit on the far side of the corral. When she opened the gate, the wood frame was immediately snatched from her hand by one of the three hands on the ranch today.

"Exactly what do you think you're doing?" She met Glen's intense glare. She frowned when he blocked her path through the gate.

"He'll hurt himself if he's not stopped," she hissed through clenched teeth.

"He'll be just fine. I can't let you in there. Denver will have my hide if you get hurt messing with that crazy kid."

"What's his name?"

"Don't make a difference, you ain't going in."

"Please, just his name."

"Lightning, and he's off limits so you can just move on." He stood his ground.

She eyed him closely, seeing he had no intentions of budging. She pretended to head back to one of the three barns near the corral. She stepped through an open door and watched until she saw the man round the path then headed back. She looked from one end of the path to the other before easing the tongue of the gate up. She hugged the length of the fence until she was several yards from the bucking creature.

She hummed as she slowly eased toward the animal. When she was in arm's-length, the chestnut-colored Lightning snorted in her direction to warn her not to come any closer. She ignored his protest and slowly extended her hand until it was inches from its silky short coat. His breathing was erratic and the stench of his sweaty coat was suffocating. His light-colored eyes darted in her direction.

"I'm not going to hurt you, promise," she cooed. "I just want to make sure you're okay. Deal?"

As if Lightning understood and valued her concern, he turned to face her. Both stood unmoving for several seconds before she extended her hand further. Had she thought about it, she would have grabbed a tart apple as a peace offering. Too late to make the gesture, she held out her hand, palm open. He sniffed from where he stood.

"It's okay, boy. I won't hurt you. Come closer."

Again, as if he understood, Lightning moved toward her, and as calm as a foal. He dipped his head until her hand brushed up the white line of his face. This could be a dangerous situation if the horse decided he didn't like her or her invasion. She moved carefully.

"There. You're such a fine stallion, if I must say so myself." She patted his neck. "What's all the fuss about? Nobody's paying you any attention?"

Trish patted the animal, moving slowly around him to make sure there were no injuries she could see by the simply looking. Lightning seemed to adore the attention because when she attempted to walk away, he nudged her in the back. She giggled.

"Behave. I'll be right back."

And as she walked from the corral, he followed her to the gate, but didn't attempt to pass through the opening. Trish rushed to the pail of apples, grabbed two to reward him, and walked back to where he stood waiting.

"Here you go."

He accepted both pieces of fruit before snorting. He then took off, his clippity-clop kicked up dust in her face. Fanning her hands in front of her furiously to avoid choking down the dirt, she backed away. She watched him gallop around the fence several times before neighing several times. He then proceeded to the far end, away from her.

"Well, be that way," she whined. "I'll come back and will see just how much of a smarty pants you can be."

When she returned, she found a halter hanging from a hook on the fence. She eased the gate open to avoid spooking her new-found friend. He glanced over his back as she approached. When she neared, he took off.

"Now, is that any way to be?" Lightning turned and began to crow-hop, a move she knew meant that she should probably keep her distance.

"Fine. I'm out."

She turned and headed back to the gate, the halter

dragging the ground. She heard him approach. She dared not to run. Not knowing a lot about his temperament, she remained calm, but she was determined to make it to the gate as quickly as she could. Luckily, he approached her and nudged her as he'd done earlier. She released a breath of air, thankful she wasn't in danger. She turned and touched his nose.

"Be a good boy and let me place this on you, okay?"

Without a fuss, Lightning allowed her to slip the halter over his head. She mildly pulled to tighten the leather strap.

"Let's go." She clicked her tongue to urge the horse forward. The clip-clop behind her didn't quit until he tromped the layers of stray on the stall floor.

"Whin-em," he responded once fully inside the stall.

Trish released the halter and began to hum as she reached for a dandy brush atop of a barrel. She continued the song her Uncle Clem had taught her when she and her brothers visited his cattle and horse farm when she was a girl. This was after he'd stop his worldwide musical tours. The renowned jazz icon doted on her and her three brothers.

Their trips to country had initially made her consider her current career choice. Her family thought she would enter the family business, like all three of her brothers had. It wasn't until her advance biology class her senior year that she had made her choice to leave home and attend veterinary school in Texas. She shocked her family and friends when she announced her big move.

"Girl, who wants to smell like stinking cows?" Brandi snorted.

"Are you sure about this, honey?" her mother asked.

"I know this sounds out of character, but it's definitely what I want to do. You'll see. I'll be good at this."

At first, giving up the stilettos and fashionable attire were a bit much. But now, almost done with her years of hard work, and having learned what she needs to know, she sees what she can contribute. She's even more determined to finish what she'd started. She smiled with satisfaction. She pushed herself. She wanted her family, especially her father, to be proud of her.

She brushed Lightning's slick coat in a flicking motion with one hand as she stroked his forelock with the other. The bright-colored mane hung forward between his ears. She continued the serenade until she heard footsteps and eventually felt Denver's presence.

Her breath caught in her chest at the sound of his voice. When she glanced into his dark face, her entire body lit on fire. Her humming ceased. She pressed her lips together several times to restart her vocal cords. He removed the brush from her hand at Lightning's protest, moving into her space. Something about the warmth he brought made her want to moan. Instead, she straightened and kept her focus on the man and not her wired senses.

His attack on her questionable skills to manage his animals went uncontested. She responded with a light heart. When he revealed that Lightning hadn't been stalled, she glanced at the stallion. That gave her time to regroup. And when he asked her about the tune she hummed, he looked as perplexed at the news as she felt.

The comfort she felt being near him wouldn't last long. She had to meet her study group. Even though she needed the study time, she longed to change her mind. She'd done well on her mid-term, but this upcoming test would make or break her final grade.

His disappointment when she said she had to leave

soon made her anxious to return in the morning.

Sighing regretfully, she watched Denver leave the barn before she, too, patted Lightning on the rump and headed for her car. Once outside, she looked around. Denver had vanished in thin air. His truck was parked in its usual spot but he was nowhere in sight.

****

Trish did her level best to concentrate on the equine health study guide. This course in particular would be beneficial for her work at the Baldwin Ranch, especially since Denver had several mares ready for delivery.

She had yet to find out much about Denver. Other than learning that the ranch had been in the Baldwin family for years, she didn't know about his passion for horse ranching.

In her research, she'd discovered that he'd been a scholar with duel degrees. The fact that he was single could only mean he was married to his work and happy with that arrangement. Question after question about Denver made it impossible to think about her study guide.

She'd done her share of dating, if you wanted to call it that. Pizza with a group of people clearly didn't qualify as a true date. That's what she'd done since arriving in Texas. And, no, Butch didn't count.

Her peaked interest in Denver made her think there was a lot more to Denver than his tall dominating physique and earth-shattering gaze.

Earlier in the day, she asked around about him. Based on the answers she got, he was a very private person. Most of the people she talked to answered her questions with, 'you really should talk to Denver about that.'

If she played her cards right, she just might get a chance to do that. She was dying to know what made Mr.

Baldwin tick. For a quick second, she chastised herself. *Why would Mr. Magic Eyes be interested in me?* She glared into space, totally ignoring the classmates around her. She and Denver had nothing in common.

"Earth to Trish. Are you paying attention?" Chris, her lab partner asked.

"Yeah, sure." She thumped the mechanical pencil against her nose. "Ask me again."

"Get it together, Missy. We want to ace this test. Got it?"

"Yep, got it."

CHAPTER 6

His plan to skip out on seeing Trish, didn't work. And as bad as he'd wanted the plan to work, he was pleasantly surprised to find her in his stable. She'd managed to seduce his animals. Even the hands seemed awestruck by her beauty and especially by her willingness to fit in and pull her weight. Denver had to shut CR down when he went on and on about how many stalls she'd mucked.

"Hell, Den, it would have taken me all day to clean them many stalls," he bragged.

"That's because you have to take a dozen breaks in between, not to mention the snack breaks you claim to need throughout the day."

"Now that's just downright lowdown, Den. You sure know how to cut a man."

"Listen, it's only been a day. She's trying to make an impression. Let's see how long her enthusiasm lasts after a couple of weeks. I give her two weeks before she runs like a scary-cat. This kind of work can break a man, if you know what I mean."

"Well, I guess it will remain to be seen."

"That it will."

He dismissed CR's attempt to showcase the little spit fire he'd admired. There was something to be said about her willingness to work. She didn't goof off and she picked up her tasks fairly quickly. He smiled when he found that she'd actually cleaned all the horse-bits with perfections. He'd purposely not left instruction on how to clean them. He was pretty sure he would find spots missed.

He liked what he saw. But he wasn't a good judge. He'd not dated regularly since his college days. And speaking of college, Trish was still in school. She was just a tad too young for him. Besides, he had a hell of a lot more to do than daydream about a girl...a beautiful and tantalizing young woman. He admitted her skin was as smooth as silk against his calloused fingers. He rubbed his hands over his groin at the thought.

"Damn, Den, get your mind out of the gutter and off of this girl."

His father and mother had had about the same age gap as he and Trish. It didn't stop them from having a full and very successful marriage, despite his father's sudden death. He picked up his parent's wedding picture from the edge of the mantel. They looked so young and so in love. Speaking of Beatrice, she was scheduled to return soon from a visit with her sister in Arizona.

He pressed his head against the framed picture, remembering her return. "Oh boy, I can see it now." He replaced the picture and headed to his quarters on the far end of the house. With his interfering mother in the picture, there's no telling what would happen next. She would likely try to convince him to hire Trish on as the resident Vet after she graduated. Not happening!

****

As promised, Trish showed up bright and early. He saw her from his bedroom window as she talked to CR. He'd already made a list of assignments for the week. He'd given them to the overseer. His own plans for the day? Finish the fence on the far west side of the property. He needed it in place before the herd arrived in a few days.

After breakfast, he filled his canteen, grabbed his hat, and took the ATV. With his tools loaded in the short bed, he headed down the back path towards his destination. He started right away.

By the time Glen arrived, the sun was high and hotter than a broiling grill. He removed his hat and wiped his brow with his shirt sleeve.

"I'm here to give you a break for a while, Boss. You can catch some lunch."

Denver nodded as he returned his worn hat to his sweat-drenched head. He'd lost track of time, but looking around, he'd made great progress. He took a long swig from his canteen. "Okay, Glen, thanks. I'll be back in an hour or so. I have some things to take care of in the office."

"You have been out here all morning. I'll finish up. CR has already put up the tacks and rigs."

Glen reached for a plank and picked up where Denver had left off. Denver patted him on the back and headed to his three-wheeler. Slipping onto the seat, he looked back.

"No more than two hours, Glen. Then I want to you to head in."

"Yes, sir. Will do."

When Denver reached the house, he tried his best to not look for Trish's car. She was long gone. Even though he didn't want to admit it, he'd hoped she was still around. Who was he fooling?

He washed up in the mud room, rinsing his hands and head in the wide sink. The cold water refreshed him. Wiping his face with the towel on the rack, he moved to the kitchen and found his lunch in the warmer. He thumbed through his phone for messages as he ate. Once done, he went directly to his office.

He'd not forgotten about Trish. He did everything he possibly could to keep her far in the back of his mind. The phone jarred him and, picking up the phone without looking at the caller ID, he tucked the device between his ear and shoulder.

"Baldwin Ranch."

"Hi, sweetheart." His mother's cheery voice sounded eager. "Did you miss your Momma?"

"Hi, Mom. When are you heading back?"

"I'm landing tonight. Your Aunt Grace is driving me crazy. I love my dear sister, but I got to tell you, I'm ready to come home. Can you pick me up from the airport?"

Denver rolled his eyes at his mother's so-called annoyance with her younger sister. The two couldn't go a day without talking on the phone. For some reason, when they got together, Aunt Grace didn't like his mother bossing her around. Grace made it clear, 'just cause you're the oldest don't mean you can boss me around.'

"Sure, Mom. What time do you land?"

When he picked her up from baggage claim, she talked non-stop until they pulled into the driveway.

"Anything exciting happened while I was gone?" She didn't wait for him to come around and open her door. She bolted from the passenger side and was up three of the four steps to the wrap-around porch.

"The new herd is scheduled to be here soon."

"Anything else?" She looked at him over her shoulder.

Denver picked her single piece of luggage from the trunk and followed her. Apparently, someone had talked. He couldn't imagine who. He moved past her at the door and felt her eyes on him.

"Should there be, Mom?"

"Quit playing, boy. Craig let the cat of the bag. So, is she pretty?"

He stared at his mother for the longest time before answering. He'd make sure to give CR a piece of his mind in the morning.

"Well?"

"I suppose so, Mom. She's an intern trying to earn hours to complete her session."

"Are we keeping her? I can't wait to meet her. If she's everything Craig says she is, she'll do a good job."

"Mom, please. The girl is just here earning hours. After a few months she will move on."

"I guess we'll see."

He groaned. "Why me?"

"What was that?"

"Where would you like me to put your luggage?"

"Take it to the laundry room. I'm pooped. I want to be up bright and early tomorrow. What would you like for breakfast, son?"

He could tell from that devilish look on his mother's face that she was up to something. He would have to be four, maybe five steps ahead of her to make sure she didn't interfere.

CHAPTER 7

Trish pulled the covers over her head. The day had been long and exhausting. Her body ached from the top of her head to the ends of her red polished toe nails. After helping CR move horse-bits to the new stall for the incoming herd, it took all the rest of her energy to get through the twenty-page exam. By the time she answered the last question, she didn't think she could move.

But she pushed on she had a three-hour lab.

Trish picked over supper and just barely got through the reading assignment for class after she finished her hours at the Baldwin Ranch.

Speaking of the ranch, she didn't see Denver one time. She was told he was putting up a fence on the west end. Her gut said maybe he was avoiding her. No worries. At this point, she only cared about completing her hours.

She'd stifled a wide-mouth yawn and continued her reading assignment until the letters were no longer legible. She placed her head down for what was supposed to be a moment but fell fast asleep. She had to peel pages from her face when the morning alarm sounded. She dropped her fist on the snooze button. Nine minutes later when the snooze chimed again, she groaned loudly.

"Go away!"

She turned over but within seconds, her eyes flew opened. She couldn't afford to be late. She kicked the covers off and dragged her tired body to the bathroom. Fully dress with her bag and breakfast bar in hand, she sped from her apartment's parking lot.

When she reached the Baldwin Ranch, she rushed towards the barn and glanced at the house. She'd gone three or four steps onto the dirt path when the side door opened. Her heart stumbled. The thumping rang so loud in her ears, she was sure others heard it as well.

"Excuse me. Trish, is it?"

A woman's voice greeted her and she turned swiftly. She was almost afraid to look back to learn who the voice belonged to. What if it was Denver's woman? She thought 'woman' because she knew he wasn't married. In slow motion, she looked the direction of the voice.

She nearly froze on seeing a woman who was for sure his twin. His mother perhaps? The woman beckoned her. The woman's smile grew as Trish moved closer to the porch.

"Yes, ma'am."

"Come in. Craig is inside having breakfast. Come join us." She held out her hand. "I'm Beatrice Baldwin."

"Mrs. Baldwin, it's nice to meet you." A sigh of relief washed over her.

Her hand was folded into the small but warm hand and Mrs. Baldwin pulled her close. She wrapped her arms around her neck.

"It's nice to meet you, honey. Around here we give hugs."

She allowed the woman to embrace her and instantly

liked her. Mrs. Baldwin hugged like her mother did. The familiar feeling almost made her weep.

"Thank you." She pulled away slightly. "I have a bunch of chores to get to. I'm sure…" She looked down into the woman's face. Her eyes were light in color and very clear.

"Nonsense. Not before you get some breakfast."

"I ate a breakfast bar on the way here." Trish protested. Her fear was that, behind that door, was Denver. All she needed was him staring at her mouth as they tried to eat. "Really, I'm fine."

"Child, get in this house, I insist."

Begrudgingly, Trish followed. It was her first time stepping foot into the Baldwin's residence. She'd only been in the barns and tack sheds. The kitchen huge with a long granite bar in the center pleasantly surprised her. She was certain she would see or hear Denver. Instead, she heard CR's greeting.

"Good morning, Trish. How are you today?"

She smiled broadly, looking from him to Beatrice Baldwin. Both nodded their approval.

"I'm well, thank you."

"Know it was a long day yesterday, but I see you survived."

She chuckled. Her hands balled the ends of her denim shirt in their grasp.

"Yes, sir. Did Denver leave me a list of chores today?"

She looked beyond the man sitting, stuffing his face with bright yellow, fluffy eggs.

"Don't worry. It's not nearly as long as it was yesterday."

"Sit dear. What will you have to drink?"

She glanced at Beatrice's warm smile. "Just water, please." She slipped onto the nearest stool, her eyes still searching for any sign of Denver.

"Don't worry. Den is out finishing that fence. He has to get it done in the next few days or so." His mother placed a cool glass of water in front of her.

Hearing this eased her rattled nerves but disappointment raised its ugly head. This would be the second day she would not see him. Perhaps she'd take one of the horses out for a ride and somehow lose her way--toward the west end of the ranch, of course. As that thought took root, Beatrice began a series of questions.

"So, tell me a little about yourself, Trisha. Where are you from? What made you go into the veterinary field?"

"Please call me Trish." She swallowed a bite of a delicious blueberry muffin.

Trish took a long breath and told Denver's mother she was from New Orleans and the baby after three very overprotective brothers. A little more than an hour later, and after not completing one chore, she'd nearly told this kind woman her complete story. In turn, Beatrice shared a story of her own. She told her how Denver had been their surprise baby.

Some of the questions his ranch-hands hadn't answered, his mother was all too happy to share. She enjoyed talking and eventually Trish had to make an excuse to get to work. CR left as soon as he finished his breakfast. And Trish knew she would have to leave by mid-morning.

Her hope of seeing Denver was nearly dead until a few minutes before she had to leave. He sauntered into the covered area where she, CR, and one of the part-time hands were busy sorting the tacks to be used for the new herd.

She froze in place when his gaze sought hers. The energy between them was obvious, because everyone found an excuse to move on to a different part of the ranch. Standing from her squatting position, Trish set her feet apart to better support her wobbly balance.

"Morning."

He tilted his hat as his eyes ate her whole with an intense stare. Once his hat was back in place, he dropped his hands in front of him.

"Good morning, Denver. I've completed the list of things you wanted me to do today. I should be leaving in a few."

"Great. You had a busy day yesterday. There wasn't much to get done today."

She nodded. It was true. Everything she'd done so far has been a learning experience for her. She looked down at her feet.

"New boots?"

His question brought her attention back to him. With a half-smile, she nodded.

"Yes. Well not really. New to me, but they are reconditioned. You were right. They're more comfortable."

"Good. Well, I won't keep you. I need to do a little office work."

"Sure. I'll see you tomorrow?"

She watched, eager to learn his answer. Yes, she would be here tomorrow. She just wasn't sure she would see him.

"Yeah, sure. Bright and early. Have a good rest of your day."

"Thanks."

He stood for several moments before turning and making his way toward the house. Trish felt the sparks leave with him.

She swayed. "What a ride." She sucked a breath.

"Oh, boy." She lifted her hand and brushed it across her forehead. "Wow. What are you doing, Denver Baldwin?"

Trish grabbed her bag and headed to her car with far more pep than the previous day.

CHAPTER 8

Denver climbed the stairs two at a time and headed straight for the window overlooking the driveway. He'd finished the west fence in record time. The boards Glen had pre-cut were in the last batch, making his task go much faster. His rush was twofold. It ensured the fence was done today and, more importantly, he wanted to get back to check on his meddling mother. He was sure Beatrice was up to her usual antics.

He was relieved to discover that she'd gone to the market. Earlier, she'd tried her best to lure him into the kitchen for one of her special breakfasts. He convinced her that he had to finish the west fence. And with a wrapped sandwich and a carafe of coffee, she sent him on his way.

Trish's arrival caused a bit of anxiety for him. Finding the intern huddled with the men, fully engaged in the prep work reassured him.

He moved the sheer curtains back slightly. He saw her move past her car and head toward the corral. He had to pull the drapes back a little further. He watched her hike up to the fence while that two-timing Lightning galloped over and greeted her like she was his long-lost friend.

"Damn traitor." Trish leaned in and hugged Lightning's neck, kissing him on his head. Lowering herself to the ground, Lightning poked his head over the fence. She patted it and said something. He bobbed his head in agreement. Denver shook his own head and released the fabric. So much for Denver being the only person who could handle the wayward horse.

He descended the stairs and walked across the corridor that separated his quarters from the main house. He heard his mother's voice, so he turned in the opposite direction. He had been headed out to talk to Trish. Instead, he walked into office and closed the door softly behind him. Minutes later, someone knocked.

"Yes."

His mother waltzed in. She looked younger than her seventy-three years. Her bright yellow and white daisy sundress made her skin look radiant and fresh. She placed a frosted mug on his desk.

"I see you made it back. Did you have a chance to see Trish?"

Denver hesitated before answering. He picked up the mug and took a large gulp of the fresh lemonade. "Yes. She was working with CR. She should be leaving in a few minutes."

"Well, she just left. I think we should invite her back for dinner. I can't imagine being so far from home and a home-cooked meal."

He watched and waited. He knew there was more to come.

She continued, "I mean, the girl's family is all the way in New Orleans... You know if it were you whose family was in New Orleans, you would be greeted, fed, and sent home with leftovers."

"Mom, I'm sure Trish can manage. She doesn't look like she's starving to me. But you're going to do what you want anyway. Who am I to tell you differently?"

"You're exactly right. I will. You just better be on your best behavior. I told her to come back for supper tonight and I expect you to be here, understood?"

Again, he didn't respond and waited for more instructions. He leaned back into his chair and folded his arms across his chest. For all he knew, she might try and make him wear some get-up you only wore to a wedding or funeral. He would not cooperate, even if she threatened him or took to one of her spells to get her way.

"What do you think I should fix? The poor girl could stand to put some meat on her bones. She's as skinny as a rail. I think I'll make my meatloaf and garlic potatoes. You think she eats meat? I mean we are in Texas, after all. My goodness. I'll do a large mixed salad just in case."

He watched her as she rattled on. She'd walked to the bookshelf before turning back to his desk, not caring if he was listening or whether or not he responded. She'd already made up her mind. All he had to do was wait to hear how he fit into her plans. When she finally looked at him, her smile widened.

"She'll be back at 6 o'clock. Clean up and don't be late. You hear me?"

"Yes, ma'am."

"Good. I better get started. You need anything before I go? You want some lunch?"

"Lunch would be great, Mom."

"Okay, but not a big one. I'm making my blackberry cobbler and maybe a cake too."

****

47

Denver knocked out much of the paper work he needed for a meeting with his lawyer. Ankit Bertolli was scheduled to come by in the morning to finalize the payments for his new acquisitions. He rubbed his chin. It was coated with an evening shadow.

He groaned. He would probably have to shave. Once was enough in his opinion. But he'd do just about anything to make his mother happy. She'd been his rock when things got stressed right after his father died. She'd been the strong one, delaying her own grieving to make sure the family business didn't miss a beat. She'd picked up the bookkeeping duties in order for him to take on the tasks his dad once had.

Denver showered and shaved and slipped into a pair of low riding jeans and a Dallas Cowboy T-shirt. Instead of work boots, he slipped into the pair he wore for other meaningful occasions. Walking across the corridor towards the main house, the delicious aroma met him before he reached the French double doors leading to the kitchen.

He frowned when he heard the high-pitched laughter. Once in the kitchen, to his surprise, Trish and his mother were cuddled up next to each other, covering a three-layered cake with milk chocolate icing.

His breath caught in his throat as he watched her take a swirl of the creamy mixture with her finger and stick it in her mouth. Her lips formed an 'o'. She licked her bottom lip with her tongue. The simple jester stirred him so he quickly looked away.

They seemed oblivious to him so he cleared his throat. They both turned and faced him. Trish, her finger between her lips for a second time, stood up straight. Her eyes grew wide. Like a kid caught with her fingers in the cookie jar, she giggled. She was breathtaking. Her face bore a hint makeup and her hair flowed down her long silky neck and draped onto of her red strapless tank top.

Her hip-hugger shorts rode her curvy hips and stopped mid-thigh. Long shapely legs didn't seem to end. Her feet were incased in a pair of wedged heeled sandals. Who was this beauty? She looked nothing like the young woman he'd seen several days now in an oversized denim shirts and rugged jeans. His shocked expression didn't go unnoticed by his mother, of course.

"Close your mouth, Denver. You'd think you'd never seen a pretty girl before." She turned towards Trish. "She's a beauty, isn't she?"

The comment must have made her uncomfortable. She immediately glanced away. He continued to admire her flawless appearance. *So, this is how you roll?* He admired her curvy hips and rump.

"I suppose she is."

He checked his gawking and reminded himself that Trish was too young for him. Besides, he couldn't see her doing the back-breaking work of a rancher's wife.

This kind of life was no joke. It took a special kind of person to actually live it without a complaint. From the look of her well-manicured hands, she really hadn't seen hard work. She had worn gloves no matter what she was doing--except the times she was bewitching his horses.

He shifted and noticed the transformation on Trish's face after his comment. "Hello, Trish."

She sent him a tight smile. "Hello, Mr. Baldwin."

Yep, she didn't like his comment. He thought they'd dropped the formalities. He'd wait to see if she stuffed her face with his mother's meatloaf before he made amends for his shortcomings.

"It's nice to see you. Hopefully things are coming along fine."

Her eyes narrowed when she spoke. "School is better than I can explain."

Instead of making the situation more awkward than it was, he turned his attention to his mom. "Need me to help with anything, Mom?"

Her eyebrows rose. "We got this, right, Trish?"

The silly grin returned. She nodded her head up and down. "Sure do."

"Dinner is just about done. Table is set and as soon as we finish this beautiful cake, we'll eat.

All he could do was nod and move past them. He reached into the refrigerator for a beer, held it up in salute and went to the den. Happily, away from his distraction, he dropped into the leather chair and reached for the television remote. Mindlessly he flipped through several channels before settling on ESPN.

CHAPTER 9

Trish wanted to slap Denver Baldwin's mouth because she wasn't buying his nice-guy act. *Humph! You're not fooling anybody, Mister.* She turned away when he passed directly in front of her on his way to the refrigerator. She picked up the spatula and continued icing the cake.

She could have made an excuse when Beatrice Baldwin invited her to dinner. Lord knew she could stand to study a little more. However, the woman's insistence gave her a chance find out more about Denver.

The weakness she felt whenever he neared wasn't a bad thing, but a burning thing she just couldn't shake. He filled her thoughts constantly. Yet he didn't seem interested in anything except making her uncomfortable.

She bet he got a laugh out of making her tremble at the sound of his voice. He always seemed to be watching her. She knew her tremors gave her away. Nothing she tried made her believe he was the least interested in her. Nothing he did made her think he would pursue her, let alone be around her for more than a few minutes. He always showed up a few minutes before she had to leave.

And the whole sham of having to finish the fence seemed a little suspect, which was why she decided to dress a little edgy tonight.

From the look on his face, he definitely noticed her. His eyes told the story. Perhaps it wasn't the right one. *Was he making fun of her?* The thought ticked her off.

She refused to let him ruin her good mood. If nothing else, she would enjoy a home-cooked meal she hadn't prepared herself. Trish missed her mother's cooking and although Diane had made sure all of her children could cook, meals just seemed to taste better when someone else prepared it.

Judging from the buttery creamy frosting she'd tasted, Mrs. Baldwin could throw down. Beatrice told her when she entered the kitchen, "I sure hope you like meatloaf." Was she kidding? Trish loved meatloaf. Second to seafood of course, her mother made the best meatloaf ever.

They moved to the dining room, placing the covered dishes in the center of the table. Denver appeared as if summoned. He held the chair out for her first and then did the same for his mother. He also offered grace. The words touched a special place in her heart. *DAMN! I'm supposed to be mad at him.*

She peeped at him from lowered lids just before he completed the prayer. His head was bent and his hands lay flat on the table. At the closure he said. "Amen."

"Amen," she and Beatrice said in unison. He passed the meatloaf to her first. She added a chunk to her plate, and then passed it to Beatrice. Denver took his share last. They did the same with every dish on the table before they began to eat.

"Hmm. Absolutely, delicious." Trish hummed.

And it was no lie. Beatrice was definitely in the same

league as her mother. Trish tried to pace herself even though she wanted to devour her whole piece. Her etiquette instructor would be so proud.

"I'm glad you like it. It's one of Den's favorite."

Was she insinuating something? Instead of responding Trish glanced at Denver. He looked more than happy to let them do all the talking. He caught her gaze and wouldn't let it go. She lowered her lids and continued to eat.

Again, Beatrice initiated a conversation.

"Do you cook? Den here seemed to think so."

Trish looked at him. He drew her with his magic energy. A small smile lifted at one side of his mouth. She set her fork down, pressed her napkin against her lips and turned her attention to Beatrice.

"Yes, ma'am. I can cook. In my family it's practically required."

"How many siblings did you say you have?"

Trish suspected this line of questioning was for Denver's benefit. She played along, though she'd already shared her family's story with Beatrice earlier.

"Three brothers, all older than I am."

"You said they all played professional ball, right?"

Okay, what was she doing? Trish didn't see this helping her cause. If anything, it would likely run Denver away if he was the least bit interested in her. But she played along.

"College. The youngest, Traekin came the closest to going pro. All of my brothers decided to join my father in our family business."

From the corner of her eye, she saw Denver put his fork down. When she glanced over, he'd raised his glass to his lips. His eyes pierced directly through her. The sight of him made the vein in her neck leap. Her heart thumped in her ears.

"Isn't that something, Den? You two have a lot in common. Both dedicated to the family business. Isn't that right, Trish?"

At that very second, she wanted to slither beneath the table. There was absolutely too much attention on her. She cleared her throat, hoping the knot there would release once she spoke.

"Uh, would you like me to bring in the dessert from the kitchen?"

It was time to change the subject and she couldn't think of a better way. Beatrice placed her napkin on the table and pushed back her chair. Denver started to move, Trish guessed to help his mother with her chair.

"I got it Den. Just sit and finish your meal. You too, Trish. I'll be right back."

She left the room, leaving an awkward pause in the space between them. Trish pushed what little food left on her plate from one side to the other.

"You'll have to forgive my mother."

"For what?" She refused to look at him, afraid he would see how nervous she was now that they were alone.

"I don't want you to be uncomfortable."

"What makes you think that I am?" she spate a little forcefully.

That lopsided smile fell into place. It was contagious so she joined him. Only her smile changed to a low chuckle. She fidgeted with the napkin in her lap.

"I like you, Trish."

Her head flew up.

"I mean, you know what you want. You're extremely dedicated to your work, even if is mucking the stalls. You put a lot of heart into what you do."

"Oh."

All the air slipped from her lungs and the weight deflated her. He'd poked a hole even if he didn't know it.

"I don't mean it like that. I mean... hell I don't know what I mean. I don't want to distract you from the goals you've set for yourself. I just hope what you learn here will somehow help you in your endeavors."

His explanation sounded lopsided, but she guessed she understood what he was trying to say. Exactly what she was thinking? He didn't have time to invest in her. She suddenly lost the excitement for the dessert she'd helped prepare. And as she was about to excuse herself from the table, Beatrice reappeared with a tray of plated desserts.

"Here we go. If I remember, you wanted to try both the cake and blackberry cobbler." She set a small plate with both treats on them in front of Trish.

Trish tried hard to smile her appreciation for Beatrice's thoughtfulness. "Thank you. They both look scrumptious."

Trish picked up her spoon and took a bite from each item. She was disappointed--with Denver, but not with the dessert. She kept her head down and took one bite and then another. The portions were modest, so it didn't take long to consume what was on her plate. Satisfied with the entire meal, she shifted in her seat.

"Oh, boy, I'm stuffed."

"You're welcome to take whatever you want home with you."

"Thank you, I mean for everything. It's special that you invited me into your home."

"Nonsense," said Beatrice. "You're always as welcome here as if it's your own home."

Trish wondered if Denver felt the same way. In a couple of sentences, he had already given her the boot.

He glared at her from the other end of the table.

"That's wonderful of you, Beatrice. And to show my appreciation, I want to clear the table and clean the dishes."

"No, honey, that's…"

"Please. Allow me. My mother taught me to carry my weight, even if it's a gift."

She stood and began to collect items from the table. "You sit and relax." Trish directed the comment to Beatrice. "I'll bet you've been in the kitchen all day."

Beatrice smiled. "Okay, have it your way."

Denver stood and started picking up dishes from his end.

"I'll help, Mom. Really, you sit and chill. It won't take us long, right Trish?"

She paused in the midst of picking up an empty tray. This energy held a different feel than the one he'd crafted earlier.

"Sure. No time."

CHAPTER 10

Denver felt like a heel when he saw Trish deflate. He hadn't meant to quash her mood. The happiness on her face made her eyes bright. It was a smile he'd not seen before. Yet something he said, or perhaps didn't say, changed her whole demeanor.

The questions she answered regarding her family piqued his interest. The fact that she'd strayed from what might have been expected of her said a lot about her. Tradition seemed relatively important in their family business. Everyone had stepped in to play their role in making the business successful. She'd taken an entirely different direction. Or maybe not.

He realized he didn't know yet what their family business was. Her becoming a vet could be part of a bigger plan. Who was he to interfere with that?

Certainly his priorities were here, with his own family business. Any woman he took an interest in would have to be here, where he'd put down roots. There was no budging in that regard.

Considering she might be too young for him, he also

had no guarantee she would stay in Texas. Her family was in New Orleans. From the sound of things, they were an extremely tight unit.

Wait a minute. This can't happen, no matter what. He was not looking for a relationship, at least not yet. He still had a lot to do. His focus was on positioning the ranch to do business nationwide. He didn't have time for anything else.

He helped Trish clear the table. They worked in silence at first, placing dishes in the dishwasher, emptying leftovers into containers. When he couldn't stand it any longer, he reached for Trish, pulling her within inches of him.

"Listen, I don't know what I said that punctured your happy mood, but it wasn't my intent. I promise."

Those beautiful light eyes looked up at him. Heat from nowhere crawled up his back and filled his face. The fierce energy between them created a bond neither seemed able to break. Everything else he'd planned to say was lost. He stared into her face.

Denver gave into his urge and cupped her face. Her eyes fluttered closed. The smooth curve of her jaw rested in his palm and he bent his head and touched his lips to her brow. Trish trembled, forcing him to wrap his other arm around her. He pulled her close.

He groaned the way a man who'd not been with a woman in a long time would. It didn't help that she snaked her arms around his waist. The move was his undoing. Lifting her face, he touched her lips with his once and then again. Her kisses were sweeter than the chocolate icing on his mother's cake.

He pressed a little harder and her lips parted. She gave him just enough room to capture her bottom lip between his. His agony grew stronger as he explored deeper. And she allowed it.

She squeezed her arms around his waist. His pleasure nearly made him forget where they were, who he was. All doubt about her vanished.

Trish parted her intoxicating lips even more and she melted against him. Neither seemed capable of coming up for air. Instead, they continued greedily until breathing was necessary.

Unwillingly, he lifted his head. Hers fell back into his hand. Her easy surrender stirred his groin. Yes, it had been far too long since he'd had a woman. But he wanted to believe it wasn't the absence of women that made him weak. It was Trish. She evoked a yearning only she could satisfy.

When she finally met his gaze, the sweetest smile lit her face. He kissed the corner of her mouth before loosening his embrace. They stared at one another for several seconds before he released her.

"We're supposed to be on kitchen duty, Miss."

"We are, aren't we?"

"Hmm. I think we abandoned that duty."

She stepped back. He experienced the lose immediately.

"Then we better get to it. I have to be back early tomorrow, remember?"

She turned but looked behind her. He wanted to damn the dishes tonight. Somehow, rational thought kicked in, and they finished their chore.

His mother had already pre-packed a to-go bag for her. It sat on the counter. After they were finished, they walked side by side, stealing glances at each other, back to the den.

His mother lounged in his father's chair. She looked up from the television and smiled. "All done?"

"Yes, ma'am. And unfortunately, I have to go. I have an early day tomorrow."

His mother looked from Trish to him. He wasn't about to take that bait. "I'll walk you to your car," he offered

"Okay."

His mom stood and briefly hugged Trish. "I enjoyed you, sweetheart. We have to do this again soon."

"Next time I'll come early to help you with the preparation."

"Okay, you've got a deal."

"Again, thank you so much for your hospitality."

"Drive safely."

"I will. Good night."

"Good night."

Trish followed him through the kitchen. He stopped long enough to pick up her bag and stepped aside for her to lead. Once they reached her car, he opened the backseat driver's side door. He placed her food inside then opened her door. Then he pulled her into his arms.

"I'll follow you home; make sure you get there safely."

Her eyes danced in the night light. "There's no need. I'll be fine."

"That may be true, but I'm doing it anyway."

"Why the change?"

"You have to ask?"

"Yes."

"I've been running from this feeling I have for you. It started the first day you fell into my arms."

She laughed. "Yeah, I almost broke my neck. I was sure you were going to send me packing."

"I thought about it."

"You did?"

"Yep. But I'm glad I didn't."

"Me, too."

He gestured toward her car. "Get in. And make sure you do the speed limit."

"Boss during the morning. Not at night, Mr. Baldwin."

He lifted his brow. Instead of arguing with her, he pulled her door open wider so she could slip into the driver's seat.

She pulled out to the road as soon as he was in his truck and behind her.

He was impressed when she followed the speed limit. Before long, she pulled into a vacant spot in front of a gated apartment complex. He pulled behind her and got out, his engine still running. He helped her with the bag, holding it as he pulled her close with one arm, capturing her lips.

He kissed her strongly and fully but didn't linger "Good night," he said before he released her. "See you bright and early."

"Yes. Good night. Sweet dreams."

Funny, there was no chance of that, but he didn't tell her so. Instead he kissed her forehead and got back into his truck. He didn't move until she was through the lobby doors.

The drive home was short. In fact, he didn't remember turning onto the road leading to the ranch. Trish consumed that much of his attention. He entered the rear door and heard his mother call, "Den?"

"Yes, ma'am."

"Trish make it home okay?"

"Yes, ma'am. She'll be back early in the morning."

"Good night, son."

"Good night, Mom, and thank you."

"She's such a nice girl."

He shook his head and eased down the corridor to his

quarters.

CHAPTER 11

Trish turned down the dusty road on two wheels. Her restless night made it almost impossible to cooperate with the determined alarm. She didn't have time for her usual pampering or the breakfast bar that she normally consumed on her short ride to the Baldwin Ranch.

"Ugh," she complained once she pulled her car in the same spot she'd used all week.

She grabbed her phone, stuffed it in her top pocket, and rushed to the stall. Mucking was at the top of the list of things to do. In her haste, she didn't see CR and nearly ran smack into him.

"Whoa." He stepped aside.

"Sorry, I'm a little bit behind this morning."

She ignored his grunt, but looked at him when he said, "The boss wants to see you." He pointed to the covered slab where Denver stood with his back to them.

She eyed CR before moving in Denver's direction. She walked slowly, tucking in her shirt. She brushed her hands along her hair. His hands were busy twining rope. That ceased when she neared. She assumed her shower wash gave her away. As he turned in her direction, she met the eyes that had haunted her all night.

"Good morning. CR said you wanted to see me."

Denver dropped the wad of jute to his side and studied her face. Judging by his looks, she would say he got the same amount of sleep as she did. Trish drew a huge breath of air and held it.

"Good morning."

He stepped closer. With him, came all of his maleness and his heat.

She thought her world would collapse. God forbid. What would happen if he touched her? She wasn't sure she would survive it. He made her woozy and out of control. *Please don't touch me Denver. I mean it.*

He must have heard her thoughts because he raised his hand but let it fall back to his side.

What? Hold me, please. Put me out of my misery. She demanded inwardly. The mixed feelings had her spinning inside.

Denver must have also heard those words screaming in her head. He whispered breathlessly. "If I touch you Trish, I'm not sure I'll remain in control."

She swayed at his words. How would they keep their feelings from the crew, from his mother? Perhaps it was a mistake. She should have just stayed her distance. She needs these hours. It was too late to start over. She refused to start over. She had to stay focused. And she was doing a piss-poor job of it.

"Don't worry, baby. We can do this. I won't interfere with your work or your hours. There's no need to be concerned, okay?"

She nodded and swallowed the hard knot stuck in her throat. Heat crawled up her thighs. The sensation had no time to fully combust. It started all over again.

She nearly panicked when Denver reached for her. When he moved his hand back to his side, she calmed her nerves to a low simmer. Had he touched her, she was certain to fall completely apart. He glanced around before bringing his attention back to her.

"I have a meeting today in the house and then I will leave to finish some business at the bank."

"Okay," she responded in a whisper.

"I'm trying to tell you I may not get to see you the rest of the day. I really want to. Maybe I can come see you later if you have time.

Trish blew out a sigh of relief. She too glanced around before she spoke. She didn't want to jeopardize her decorum with the crew. She still had to get in all of her hours.

"Sure. I'll be studying but I can take a break."

"What time works for you?"

"Six, maybe seven."

"Let's make it seven."

"Okay, I'll see you then."

He did reach for her hand and squeezed it. "Don't overdo it today, okay?"

She nodded. Denver dropped the jute on top of a stack in a wire crate. He turned as he stepped up on the porch. He tilted his hat in her direction and headed into the house.

Wheeling from their encounter, Trish finally turned on her heels and marched back to the stall. She hummed as she worked. Her stomach protested due to her missed breakfast, but she finished in time.

She took a short break to brush both Winter and Lightning before she finished her last assignment for the day. She had one last paddock to clear. Several of the incoming herd were designated rogue. Denver wanted to keep them separate from the others, at least for a little while.

When she finished, Trish walked to the side entrance of the house and knocked. Beatrice came to the door.

"Hi Trish, it's great to see you. Look at you. You must have been a busy bee."

"Yes, ma'am I was. Just wanted to say hello before I head off for the day."

"Thank you, honey. You know Denver left a couple of hours ago."

"Yes, I know. He told me he would be out today."

"Well, good. Now did you eat something?"

"I'll have a chance to pick up something at home. I have to get cleaned up before I report to my afternoon lab."

"You're welcome to come back for dinner."

This time Trish was firm in her reply. She didn't need to tell Denver's mom that she'd already had that part covered.

"Appreciate the offer, but I have other plans for tonight. I'll see you tomorrow."

"Sure. Have a good evening."

"You, too."

She punished the road the same way she'd done earlier that morning. She prayed the entire way. A ticket was the last thing she needed. Her father would be upset. She'd been known to be late a time or two. And her concerned family had made a bet that she wouldn't make out in Texas without someone helping her. Well, she had a lot to prove. Thus far, she'd been winning big time.

A shower, then food, and her final lab for the week flew by. Trish knew exactly why. Her prayer for the day had been, 'Oh Lord, make this day go by so I can see this man I'm so crazy about. Help me get this day over with.'

She really hated wishing her life a way, but...

It was customary in her house to fix a little something when company visited. She pulled together a couple of snacks and dug into her lesson. Surprisingly, Trish devoured the six chapters she had to review, anticipating a pop quiz in the morning. She finished the syllabus list well before seven.

She stretched her arms above her head and stifled a yawn. Her sleepless night set in. Her excitement about Denver's visit stayed in her mind and gave her a boost of energy. She'd worked hard to keep her nerves calm and had done a pretty good job up to now.

She tidied her apartment--another one of her mother's strict rules, never invite company into a dirty house. She then, headed to the shower. What she'd picked out to wear was a far cry from her previous evening's outfit.

Slipping into linen walking pants, she pulled her hair up into a tight knot. She glanced at her phone and sent a few text messages so she wouldn't be interrupted. Then she turned the ringer completely off and took a long breath. Her timing was perfect. Her doorbell chimed.

She took one last peek at herself in the tall mirror in the hallway. Placing her hand over mouth, she blew into it and could still smell the refreshing mint on her breath. Trish brushed her hands down the pants and headed for the door. Checking the peep-hole, Denver's handsome face came into view, stealing every ounce of nerves she had left. Shaky hands pulled back the bolted lock and then she opened the door.

"Hi, beautiful."

I can get used to seeing your handsome face, she thought. In one hand he held his worn hat. In the other was a bouquet he held out to her.

"Hi. Please come in." She accepted the arrangement of

mix flowers. "These are beautiful, thank you."

She stepped aside to let him in.

His broad shoulders passed directly in front of her. His aftershave left a whisper of citrus aroma in his wake. He turned and waited until she closed and locked the door before he pulled her into his strong embrace. She went willingly, enjoying his massive arms around her. She dropped her head back in anticipation of his soft lips. The hand clutching the flowers fell to her side. She wasn't disappointed when he covered her mouth and took her breath away.

"I'm glad you're here," she whispered into his mouth.

"I've missed you, today."

CHAPTER 12

Denver's heart quickened when he saw Trish's face. He'd waited all day to see her again. When she melted into his arms, his vitality surged. The day and all of its drama were forgotten as he tasted her sweet, luscious lips. He held her close, but not too tight, even though he really wanted to. He needed her, today, right now.

Her surrender gave him something he'd lacked for a while: a way to forget all the things that had not gone right in his day. She felt right pressed against him. She eased his doubts and fears. Telling him she was glad he was here made it even sweeter, because for once someone wasn't trying to make a fool of him. He dropped his head into the fold between her shoulder and neck, worshiping the comfort it brought him.

He savored the moment, trying not to let the weight of his day creep into this special greeting. When she eased one arm around his waist and squeezed him, it was his undoing. He closed her to him even tighter. They stood that way for a while before he pulled away and looked down into her face.

"How was your day?" He moved away a little further.

She watched him and smiled, which made his heart melt. Rising on tiptoe, she pecked his lips and pulled completely out of his embrace. In the process, her hand glided down his arm and grabbed his hand as she turned. Leading him to the couch, she sat and patted the spot next to her. Placing the bouquet on the coffee table, she reached for his hat and placed it beside the flowers.

"Tell me." She placed her hands on top of his, which were now resting in his lap.

How did she know, he wondered? Was it in his eyes, was it the way he held her and wouldn't let go. He sighed, gauging his tone and trying to decide exactly how much he would reveal to her. They'd only known each other for a short while. And she was still his employee... well sort of. Yet he wanted more if she was willing. Lowering his gaze, he took a moment to gather his thoughts.

"There's a hold on the auction I won." He glanced away before he continued. "Ankit and I spent the majority of the day trying to sort through the whole thing. Apparently, another bidder claimed he'd out bid me, but his bid came long after the bidding for this lot was closed; a bid, mind you, that was only a few hundred dollars more. I would have definitely countered the offer had it been on the table in the allocated time."

She squeezed his hands, he guessed to encourage him to share what was bothering him. She'd not spoken a word. She only listened.

"It's a good investment and it would bring some much-needed revenue to the ranch." He looked away. "I have a lot riding on this deal. I've already extended some contracts for late fall. They are tied directly to this purchase, so it's a little disappointing."

Trish slipped onto his lap. She loosely draped her arms

around his neck, placing her forehead against his. Then she kissed the bridge of his nose.

"This will work out. I know it will. You've got what it takes to make this all pan out. Don't worry."

She caressed his jaw and he closed his eyes. How did she do this? How did she know? How did she know this was what he needed the most, reassurance.

His lawyer, Ankit, had told him the same thing, but in the pit of his gut, doubt troubled him no end. Her confidence in him meant everything.

"What can I do to help?" she asked.

He opened his eyes. He saw the sincerity in her gaze.

"You've already done it. Thank you."

"Good, because now I'm going to feed you." She grinned. Her smile was contagious.

"You can cook?"

"Shut up, man." Trish bumped his shoulder with a loose fist. She punched again him. "How about something drink?"

"A shot of whiskey?"

"I don't have whiskey but I do have beer."

"What are you doing with beer?"

"Do you want one or not?" She placed her hand on her hip.

"Sure, why not."

He started to get up. She held up her hand to halt him.

"Nope, sit tight. I got you."

Denver leaned back on to the sofa and watched Trish disappear. She returned and handed him a coaster and a frosty can. She left again, this time she returned carrying a tray. She placed a mitt on the table and the tray on top of it.   The mouthwatering aroma of the fare neatly positioned on the tray made him smile. His stomach also reacted. He hadn't eaten earlier. She handed him a fork and a napkin.

"Help yourself."

"Are you planning to join me?"

"Of course. Do you think I'm going to poison you or something?"

"Nah, I don't think so."

She pulled a fork from her shirt pocket and held it up. "See?"

He said a brief blessing and then plowed into the tasty delights.

"This is delicious."

She covered her mouth with one hand to talk after she pushed a sweet meatball into it. "Glad you like it."

"I do."

They talked comfortably as they ate. He felt more relaxed than he had in months. He withstood her constant touching on his arms and leg. Did she know she was driving him crazy? She shared more about her family. She seemed rather fond of her uncle, the famous jazz musician, Clemons Boudreaux.

"Your family is musical? Does that include you?"

She smiled shyly. "A little."

"And how little is a little?"

"Bass, drums, and keyboard."

"Whoa! There's nothing little about all of that."

He glanced around her neatly furnished apartment but didn't see anything musical around. Not even a radio or PDA. Nothing.

"Do you still play?"

"When I find the time."

Again, he looked around and hoped his nosiness wouldn't be too obvious. It was.

"The spare bedroom is my music room. Want to see it?"

"Maybe later, but first, tell me what made you want to be a vet?"

Trish tilted her head to one side. "I wanted to do something to honor my Uncle Clem. My brothers already secured my father's legacy. Yes, we all are musicians, and we had something in common with him. However, Uncle Clem was very fond of animals. He spent the better part of his life performing, but in his later years he moved to the country so that he could have as many animals as he could. It was how he grew up as a boy. When his mother died, his dad, my great-great uncle sent him to the city, New Orleans, to live with his sister."

"So, was he a vet too?"

"Not on paper, but many of the parish folks went to him when their animals weren't well."

"I see. Do you plan to go back to New Orleans, or to his country...?" He held out his hands to refer to the place she hadn't given a name to.

"I don't know, exactly. I'm still trying to figure that out. I mean, there is a need for vets in the city. There is also a need for Equine Vets in neighboring parishes. There are ranches with horses that participate in the many parades and equine events. I've thought about being a mobile vet, not tied down to one place. I don't know."

She hunched her shoulders. He watched her closely. Her reply didn't answer his burning question. He decided to come straight out and ask her.

"Had you considered staying in Texas, staying here?"

"The thought did cross my mind. I have about six months before I have to make a hard decision."

Not wanting to put pressure on her, he changed the subject.

"So, I've asked a lot of questions about you. What do you want to know about me?"

"How long has this crew worked for you? They're very protective."

"How so?"

"Well, I tried to find out things about you." She shifted. "I tried to find out if there was someone significant in your life." She laughed. "When I asked Glen, he just grunted and walked away."

"Do you still want to know?"

"I do."

Denver covered her mouth and kissed her soulfully. Before long, the back and forth dance of their lips led to hands and arms searching for spots that made them moan. When he found the strength, he released her mouth and dragged his lips to her ear.

"I guess that's my answer." He stared down into eyes blazing with desire.

"No, this is."

Trish boldly slipped her hands up his shirt, circling her arms around his waist. Denver wasted no time pulling her onto his lap.

CHAPTER 13

Trish shifted in Denver's embrace. She couldn't explain her reactions to him tonight. Being his conduit had been natural, like they'd been here before, like they'd known each other's strengths and weakness for years. She'd been drawn to the rancher the moment she untangled her body from his arms the first day they met. Their chemistry had instantly ignited a flame only he could quench.

But a tiny voice in her head whispered 'caution.' Her mother had warned her to listen to the voice of her true self. Denver wasn't a high school or her college boyfriend. This man knew what he wanted…he was a grown-ass man.

When she considered her own wants, including where she would be this time next year, she had nothing. She was still figuring it all out. Yes, the attraction was strong, but was physical attraction enough? Did she even want to be involved with someone? All she wanted tonight was to enjoy his company and savor his sweet kisses.

After a moment, she realized that was a lie. She

wanted more. The only way to find out what would become of them was to throw caution to the wind. She understood. If she was not careful, her heart would be in jeopardy.

Denver seemed self-controlled, respectful, things she admired about him. That gave her the freedom to move at any pace she wanted. She tilted her hips and felt him stir beneath her. The sensation surged her need. She shifted once more. Denver quickly moved her back to the couch and turned.

"What are we doing, Denver?" She asked when he pulled away.

He watched her intently. Pinching the bridge of his nose between two fingers, he paused. The jitters in her stomach battled with the uncomfortable position of her bottom on the couch. She wanted to move but her nerves wouldn't let her. He captured her hand and touched it to his lips. He then squeezed her fingers, which forced her to gaze at him.

"We are new. New usually means time." He turned her hand over until it was on top of his. "I like you, Trish. I'm attracted to you. And I promise that if you're at all interested in what I have to say, then we will go at your pace."

Trish looked at the beige carpet near her feet. He tugged her hand and her gaze returned to his.

"School is important to you right now, at least it should be. So, there's no choosing. And I think, in time, you'll know what you want. We have choices; some are not so obvious at first."

She leaned into him once more and he wrapped his arms around her. They sat in silence, lost in their own thoughts. She felt his steady, strong heartbeat against her arm. She snuggled closer and tilted her head as she whispered, "I like this."

"I do, too." Denver smiled. "By the way, what else were you trying to pry from my men? Better yet, what did my nosy mother tell you?"

"You should be ashamed, Denver."

"How much information did she pry out of you?"

Trish grinned and looked away.

"From the looks of that silly grin, I bet she know the day and hour of your birth."

"No, you're wrong."

"Well, pretty close, I'm sure. That woman can talk the feathers off of a chicken without lifting a hand."

She liked this side of Denver. He could be serious, but he was also funny. And very protective of the people he cared about. She was seeing it firsthand.

"How old are you?"

"Thirty-three. And you?"

"Didn't your momma teach not to ask a woman her age?"

"No. She tells hers all the time. She doesn't mind telling people I'm her late baby. She will be seventy-three in a few months. Now, quit stalling woman. How old are you?"

She lifted her chin. "Let's just say, I'm the legal drinking age. How about that?"

He didn't say anything but a large grin reappeared on his face. He bobbed his head up and down. "Time to get you drunk."

"I don't think so. Trust me. I've tested those waters already. It wasn't fun."

"So, you admit to overindulgence?"

"Man, where I come from, everybody drinks. Even the bishop of our congregation drinks."

She winked and he leaned back in surprise. His

response made her laugh out loud. He was amusing her and she rather enjoyed it. They relaxed a while longer as he answered her many questions. Sometimes he shared information without her asking.

"So why ranching if you earned an MBA? Surely, you wanted to work in a big corporation. Most people with those credentials do. What gives?"

"I considered moving away. If I was going to stay in Texas, I would have had to move to Dallas. But I was more interested in some place like D.C. or New York. I wanted to go someplace where no one knew me."

She frowned. "Why."

"In a way, I didn't want the responsibility my father intended for me, to take over the family business. And I almost did it." He paused briefly. "Along the way, his health deteriorated. He tried to do both sides of the business, running the operations and managing the books--"

"Like you're doing now?" She interrupted.

He nodded and continued. "Yes, but my father was well into his seventies. So out of duty, I came home to help with the finance side of things until we could hire someone we trusted."

He stopped speaking. For a very long time she didn't think he would continue. Even after she'd caressed his hands, he remained stoic, unmoving, seemingly unaware that she sat so close to him. With one hand, she turned his face to hers. She ran her thumb down the side of his cheek. He swallowed and she could see his Adam's apple move.

"My dad passed unexpectedly. We all had to scramble to keep things afloat. At the time he had more than thirty ranchmen and their families depending on us. Every cent we had had been reinvested into the business. He'd cashed out his insurance policy to make some investment moves."

Trish had often heard her father and brothers at the kitchen table discussing business and the risks. The things they often talked about, had she really been in tune at the time, would have frightened her. But as a teenager, she only worried about her allowance and how close she came to her credit limit. She realized that had her father not been smart and made sacrifices, she would not have had her carefree life.

Her heart filled at his story. The story revealed the kind of man he was. And she really liked that kind of man. Dedicated, responsible and passionate about others.

He had yet to tell her anything about his love life. It was the one aspect of him she was most interested in. So, as he continued to share with her, the very next story made her sit up. "I had twin sisters who were still-born."

Her gasp interrupted his story. She couldn't imagine having lost a sibling. She remembered the time her brother, Trae, had come home from college unexpectedly. The family thought for sure they would lose him. He'd lost his will to live. She never in her life wanted to experience that again.

"The loss nearly broke my parents apart." He continued. "My mother blamed herself that the girls didn't make it. She took it hard. My father on the other hand, consumed himself with work. They'd become strangers living under the same roof."

"What happened?"

"My mother was ready to leave. In fact, she did for a short while. She lived with my Aunt Grace in Phoenix for about six months. Aunt Grace finally put her out." He chuckled.

He looked off in the distance before he continued his

saga. Then he gave her the most intense stare she'd ever experienced.

"My father was a broken man. He'd not only lost his two daughters, but he'd lost the woman he'd loved since seventh grade. When she showed up on the front porch after she'd been kicked out by her younger sister, he swore that he would never let her off the ranch again. Eventually, they grew close again, and it was then that I was conceived."

She smiled, relieved to know his parents cherished that kind of love. It was every girl's dream.

"I promised myself, Trish, I would never commit to a woman who I didn't love enough that my own life would not matter without her."

A chill ran up her spine. Had he heard her thoughts?

"So in thirty-three years, you haven't found that woman? Not once?" she asked without a second thought. She wanted to know.

"No, but the truth is, in the last five years, Baldwin Ranch has been my wife. It needed me the most. I did what I had to."

"And now?"

"And now, I think it's time. I want someone to share my life with, to begin a family with. And I don't want to wait until I'm my father's age to do those things," he added.

"So I'm clear, what does that mean?"

He chuckled.

She glanced away. His response irritated her a little. Was he passing time until his special woman came along? Did he think she would be his lay until then? She was nobody's good time. She had way too much to do. And not even the most handsome cowboy in Texas would stand in her way.

"Trish, it wasn't just a happenstance that you showed up in my barn, sweet lady."

Now she was ticked. She leapt from the couch, picking up the remnants from their small meal. She gathered the empty beer cans and stomped toward the kitchen. She was certain a brush fire followed in her wake.

CHAPTER 14

"What the hell?"

Denver watched Trish snatch things from the table and march out of the room. He waited a minute then stood and followed her. He had no idea where he was going. They'd been in the front room of the apartment the entire time.

He passed a short walkway and heard slamming dishes. He rounded the short wall and found her in the small, but neatly arranged kitchen. Her back to him, she froze, he guessed because she heard his footsteps. He didn't understand how since she was making such a racket.

He walked behind her and wrapped his arms around her. She stiffened. A far cry from her earlier responses.

"Trish, what's wrong? Did I say or do something wrong?"

She swung around almost pushing into him. Positioning them closer probably wasn't her intention. She quickly stepped to one side.

"No."

"No, nothing's wrong? Or no, I didn't do or say something that upset you?"

She huffed and placed the cup in her hand on the counter. She deflated. He stepped back to really look at her. She didn't seem the flighty type, but she wasn't behaving like the woman he'd first met. When she didn't answer, he took it as his cue to leave. He stepped away. "I better leave," he said, turning away. "Thanks for dinner. Have a good night."

He thought she would say something but she didn't. He headed back to the front room, stopped and picked up his hat and strolled to the door. As his hand pulled back the lock, her hand touched his back. He looked over his shoulder and saw uncertainty on her beautiful face. Hat in one hand, door knob in the other, it was her move. "Please don't leave just yet."

He stayed near the door and gave her his attention. She wormed up to him, draping her arms around his neck. She slid her body up his front and he sucked in his breath. Even if he wanted to resist her, he couldn't.

Trish rested her face just inside his collar, pressing her lips against his neck. She trembled. He released the door handle and dropped his hat, using his now empty hands to pull her closer.

"I don't want you to leave."

"I'm here, baby."

"Tell me it's okay."

"It is." He dropped his head against hers. "What are you afraid of?"

"I don't know. That I can't be what you want, what you need."

"Let me worry about that, Trish. Trust me. I wouldn't be here if I wasn't sure."

She looked up, their lips mere inches apart. Her soft

breath kissed him and her eyes begged him. She moved closer and he met her lips, softly at first and then with hunger. He moaned before pulling away.

"We have time, yes?"

She nodded her reply.

"It's late. You need your rest. I expect you at the ranch bright and early." He raised an eyebrow.

She laughed. It was nice to see the change in her demeanor. Perhaps he'd been moving too quickly. He'd have to remember to ease the pace. She didn't know it yet, but she was exactly what he wanted, what he needed.

"You mean I don't get a break after feeding you?"

"Nope, more the reason I'm expecting you to be on time."

"Yes, sir. I will be on time."

"Good. Sweet dreams."

"Sweet dreams." She pecked his chin.

He wanted to kiss her again, but tempered the urge. Releasing her completely, he bent and retrieved his hat, placed it on top of his head, and tilted it down at her.

"Night."

"Good night."

He moved swiftly through the door and hauled ass to his car. His mother was right…again. Trish was going to be the one to totally undo him. He hadn't dated a lot, but the few who'd made it to his dinner table had been given a nice, but strict message from his mother: ranch life would break them. And of course, they listened.

In this case, Beatrice had made the dinner arrangements. Her confidence in this young woman meant she'd already given her approval. It wasn't going to be that easy though.

Trish had a lot to work out. School was a priority because it was important to her. That he understood fully.

He would do everything to support her.

Convincing her to adjust to ranch life was something totally different. The city girl still had a lot to learn. Running back to New Orleans was not an option. He sighed heavily at that thought.

"What are you doing, Denver McCall Baldwin?" He asked out loud. The radio answered him with Will Downing's tune, 'Tired Melody.' He parked in his usual spot and headed directly for his office. He was sure his mother would be up but she wasn't in either of her usual hanging places, the kitchen or den. Instead, the house was dark and quiet. He flipped on his office lamp and dug into the ledger open on his desk. He paused. Trish's sweet taste and sensational warmth still lingered with him. Consumed with thoughts of the woman he couldn't get enough of, he eventually forced his focus back to the books in front of him. The deed took great effort.

****

When he rose the next morning, he stopped in the kitchen at the coffee maker. It was preset to brew his java at same time every day. He filled his carafe and went straight to the tack shed. He wanted to get everything ready. Today, instead of mucking stalls, he was taking Trish with him to the south side of the ranch where the men had finished the ditch.

The crew had also released the spring to flow in that direction. While there, he would check to make sure the water had made it through. This plot of the property would serve as the initial holding area for the new herd until they were incorporated with the herd on the west end.

He turned on hearing CR. As far back as he could remember, CR had always been at the ranch, his father's best friend. At certain times of the year, the ranch had more men than the current crew on hand. Once the new herd arrived, he expected to have at least seventy men on hand.

"Morning, Den."

"Morning. I'm taking Trish with me this morning. You'll have to reassign her tasks."

"Sure thing. Anything else you need?"

Denver stopped and turned, an arm full of jute in tow. CR had been his confidant, the same as he'd been for his father. His dad had trusted him and now Denver trusted him the same way.

"Just hope the officials come through for us."

"I think they will do the right thing. We'll have that herd here early next week. And we're all ready for them."

"Yep." Denver continued loading the back of the three-wheeler.

"Are you sure she can ride one of those things?" CR pointed to the bikes.

"I guess we'll see, won't we?"

He watched the shit-eating grin on the old man's face as he nodded.

"You'll be surprised what this one knows and does. Did you know she changed the oil filters in that old tractor your dad loved so much? She said her brothers taught her."

Denver paused once more, chewing on what CR said. It piqued his interest even more. Remembering last night, he was learning this girl had multiple personalities.

"Is that right?"

"Yep. Might be nice to have a paid vet on staff, you know."

Denver briefly looked his way, not acknowledging his suggestion one way or another.

And, as if they had summoned her, Trish walked up,

her eyes brighter than Christmas tree lights.

"Good morning."

They looked at each other and then at her. CR spoke first.

"Good morning, Sunshine. Perhaps you already know you don't have mucking duties today."

"Really?" Her voice held a bit too much excitement. She caught herself and changed her tone. "Really, I don't mind."

"Humph, I mind. It stinks!" CR protested and left them both staring at his back.

"Good morning, Trish."

Just looking at her always stole his breath. This morning was no different. She did look refreshed. Her cotton shirt was neatly tucked into her belted hip-riding jeans. There was no way to hide her curves, even though she wore loose-fitting jeans.

"Today, you're going with me to the south end. Can you ride one of these?"

He pointed to one of the dirt bikes. Her face lit up and she wore the silliest grin ever.

"Are you kidding? My uncle owns a catfish farm in Rustin. It's one our favorite pastimes when we're there." She beamed.

Trish rubbed her hands down her thighs then rubbed them together, ready to get her hands dirty or something.

"Okay, pick one. And make sure it's gassed up."

He watched her attentiveness as she checked the vehicle. She stooped and looked under the straight bar before kicking the tires. She sat on the seat and adjusted the handle and break gears.

"Okay?" He dropped the canvas toolbox and a cooler with snacks in the corner of his cart.

"Yep."

He reached for the metal case, pulled down a hat and handed it to her.

"Here, see if this works. You're going to need something on your head."

Trish adjusted the ponytail until the hat fitted snugly enough to stay on. He then handed her a canteen filled with ice cold water. She accepted it, placing it along the hook on the inside of her bike's handle bar. She slipped her hands into a pair of hide gloves.

"Ready?"

"Lead the way."

He mounted his bike, put on his own gloves and started the vehicle and took off. Checking behind him to see she was right there on his tail. *Hmm, so you can ride. What else am I going to learn about you, Ms. Trish?* He entered a dirt path that eventually became a grassy path. He pushed his body up, feet on the paddles and looked across the pasture. Denver want to make sure the path they were taking was clear of fallen tree branches or any other blockage that might require them to go a different direction.

Seeing none, he revved his engine and accelerated.

Trish stuck with him. Before long the high grass scenery turned to a densely wooded area. The path was a little bumpy but all the seats on his vehicles had extra padding.

Again, he looked back for Trish. She was right behind him. She gave him a thumbs up. here.

CHAPTER 15

Trish followed Denver closely. While the freedom of being out in the open reminded her of the wonderful times she enjoyed with her brothers and cousins. This place was different and foreign to her. The last thing she needed was to be distracted. So she stayed close and followed directly in his path.

The scenery was breathtakingly beautiful. She eyed a patch of wildflowers off to her left. She would have to remember how to get back here. They would look great on Mrs. Baldwin's countertop. Trish was certain she would appreciate them.

The sun was high and hot already. Denver must have known it would be. She was thankful for the hat. She'd learned to wear long sleeves no matter the temperature, especially when she was outside. She'd also taken to wearing footless tights under her jeans. It was an extra precaution for ticks and the other unfriendly pests she'd already encountered.

She heard water before she saw it, even above the rattle of the ATVs. Denver slowed his bike and so did she, pulling to the right side of him. He stopped and dismounted the bike and came to hers.

"You're pretty good on this thing."

"Not really. I've flipped over once or twice. Was going way faster than I should have around a ravine. Gave my brothers a good scare."

"It sounds like you're a bunch of renegades."

She chuckled. "Not quite. But I'm not as prissy as you might think."

"Me? Why would you say that?"

"Some of your comments. But I can be a prissy girl if I want to be. Being in Texas, out in the middle of nowhere, leaves me little options some days. Not all the time though, mind you."

Denver lifted an eyebrow and she waited for a response which never came. He draped a neat roll of rope over his shoulder and gave her one. She did the same thing.

"Don't forget your canteen." He pointed to the jug hanging from the hook.

They walked in silence for a while and after five minutes they made a sharp left turn down a narrow path. He pointed to a rock, and held out his hand to help her climb it. He pushed up right next to her. The sun's burning rays didn't match the heat he brought when he stood next to her.

She wanted so badly to wind her arms around him but fought the urge. As if he read her thoughts, he looked into her face and draped his hand across her shoulder. Her canteen and jute were over the same shoulder. Following his lead, she slipped her arm around his waist.

"It's beautiful here."

"This is God's country, my love."

Did he just call me 'his love?' Her heart leaped. His

endearment touched the very fiber of her heart. To be his love would mean a lot of things. Right now, being here with him in this special place was a good start.

"It would surely seem so."

He stepped down ahead of her and reached for her hand again. On the other side of the rock, he led her down yet another path to a brook. Rocks were pre-positioned like a bridge to cross. He went first and encouraged her to follow.

"Come on, you can do it."

"I'm not totally convinced." She shook her head.

"Want me to carry you on my back?"

"No, of course not. Let's see if I can do this."

She adjusted the rope in one hand and the canteen in the other. She eyed each stone her feet touched. When she reached the other side, she squealed and leaped into Denver's waiting arms. Instead of releasing her right away, he pulled her closer, kissing her so sweetly she wanted to weep.

This was much better than mucking stalls.

When he stepped away, he led her again. This time they didn't stop until they stood under a rock that looked like an overhang. She reached up and touched the smooth surface of the rock, dragging her fingers down until they came to a small opening. Curious she slipped her fingers in it.

"I wouldn't do that if I were you," Denver warned.

Quickly she removed her fingers and looked at him for an explanation.

"Spiders and sometimes snakes hide in rock holes."

Trish jumped back from the rock and widened her eyes. She glanced down at her gloved hand. Denver laughed.

"Not very funny. Is that the truth?"

He grew serious and he stepped into her space.

"I will never lie to you, Trish. I promise."

Unsure of how to respond, she nodded. A man's voice interrupted their interlude. She looked to see not one, but two of the ranch-hands approaching them. So much for her hope that he'd brought her to the south side of his ranch to seduce her.

They had yet to use the ropes they carried. She wondered what they were for. She guessed she would find out soon enough. The two men greeted her warmly.

"Morning, Trish." They spoke in unison.

"Morning Reve, Jab."

They turned to Denver. "It's open on that end of the fence." Reve pointed.

"Okay, let's go see." Denver followed them.

She trailed closely. Since his little spider and snake comment, she wasn't taking any chances. She'd been warned when she first got to Texas about all of the loving creatures. Heck, she wouldn't have to worry about this had she kept her tail in New Orleans. Or better yet, went to a city school.

She soon learned the significance of the ropes. He tied one end of her rope to a tree and made a loop around her waist. She was confused. Neither Reve nor Jab had ropes. She looked from one to the other and then at Denver.

"I can't chance you falling, Trish. The sides are steep. Trust me, okay?"

"I do."

Reve and Jab climbed down first. Denver then instructed her on how to use the rope to make sure she didn't slip. They both went down together, but Denver did so without a rope. Once on the climb down, she understood. Her heart leaped the first time she lost her footing. Denver must have felt her anxiety because he moved closer.

"I got you, baby. Just keep moving."

She was all too happy to be on the bottom. She wanted him to pull her into his embrace. With the other workers there, it would have been too much. And he called her baby only loud enough for her to hear.

Reve and Jab were like her cheerleading crew. Reve patted her on the back once she was on the ground. "Good job, Trish."

"Thanks, Reve."

Jab nodded his approval and she smiled. Denver sent her a piercing look that only she understood. She gave him a thumbs up and he nodded as well.

The four prowled the opened area for about a half hour. She took several swigs from her canteen, welcoming the refreshing cool drink.

When they were done, they climbed back up the steep rock. Jab and Reve went in the opposite direction. She and Denver walked back to their rides. He put the toolkit back in his cart, took the rope from her and placed it with the others.

"Come. We have a few minutes before we have to head back."

He led her to a patch of wildflowers. These she could actually touch. She didn't have to wonder how she would get back to pick them.

"Oh, my God. I can stay here forever."

"Well, I couldn't let you do that, sweet lady." He pulled her to him. "The coyotes would have a field day with all of this sweet tender meat."

She placed her hand on his chest. "Why do you keep killing my buzz, man?"

"Just want to keep this to myself."

He kissed her, pulling her to the ground. They both

lost their hats and the sun kissed them warmly. Rolling onto his back, he pulled her on top without breaking their bond.

Trish straddled one of his thighs. She moved against his groin, which seemed to grow in size with each roll. His mouth took possession hers as one hand squeezed her right buttock; the other held her firmly against him.

She groaned, feeling the heat between her legs. Her body trembled. She wanted more but Denver's tight hold kept her from moving like she wanted. She tried to change their positions. He allowed it and she was now on her back with him straddling her and his knees on the ground. Their bodies nearly touched.

Trish attempted to pull him down. He didn't budge. She opened her eyes to find him watching her. The desire she saw layered there made her even hotter. How could she make him understand that she didn't want him to stop?

She pulled at his shirt, trying to get her fingers beneath. Her exploration ended when he kissed her even more deeply. She had no control of anything, not even her own senses.

"Den?"

He moved his lips to her neck. "Yes."

CHAPTER 16

Trish beneath him, tugging at his clothes, nearly sent him to hell and back. He moved his hands to her hips to keep her from grinding against his already aching erection. She managed to pull the tail of his shirt from his pants. Her trembling fingers burned hotter than the sun torturing them from above.

The one thing that stuck in his mind as she practically begged him with her touching and grabbing was his pledge to give them time to grow. At the same time, he wanted to damn the promise he'd made.

"I need you, Den."

She felt so good against him. *Damn!* He had to put an end to this. With one last, strong kiss, one that kept her from swarming beneath him, he was able to move. He lifted himself, bringing her up with him.

Their breathing was hard and rapid when he pulled away. Trish held fists full of his shirt in both hands. She wouldn't let go. He didn't want to let go either. He did not want to stop for that matter.

"We're both going to be in trouble if this continues,

baby."

She looked at him with that fire in her eyes. "You, maybe."

He mumbled. It was like her to come back with a smart answer. It was as if they'd been transported back to that first day in his barn.

"We better go, smarty pants, before you miss your class. Trust me. I wouldn't mind at all."

"That would be a bad thing, for us both."

He agreed. Getting her hours was the reason she'd ended up here in the first place. Productive hours didn't include rumbling through the fields with him.

He had no plans to give her special treatments either way. Everything she did while here would be a learning opportunity. He hoped it would be helpful in her field. Mucking the stalls didn't look like beneficial work, but the back-breaking task would get her used to the dwellings and pong of horses. It was a stench not easily tolerated.

Learning their surroundings might also help her determine if something on the land was harmful or could make the animals sick. He really hoped she understood his plan. Perhaps he needed to explain it. Just not today.

He took her on a different route back to the house. The scenery on this path was so different from the tall grasses and fields of flowers. It was all meadows, lush and close to the man-made river on the property.

He passed the piece of the property his father had given him to build his own home one day. It was supposed to be a place where he could live and raise his own family. Until Trish came along, he hadn't put much thought to moving from the big house.

He would have stopped to show her the place but they were already behind schedule. So he pressed on. Maybe next time.

Denver almost forgot there was a gravel road ahead that would kick up a lot of dust. He moved to a grassy area and decided to cut across to the paved path. In no time, they arrived back to the tack shed.

She dismounted her bike and walked over to him with her hat extended.

"Thanks, this might have saved my skin a hundred times."

"There are a few up here. Any time you need one, okay?"

"Do you mind if I head out now. I have to drop by the apartment before I get to my lab."

"Sure. You're here tomorrow, right?"

"Yes."

"What about tonight? Will I see you later this evening?"

She shuffled from one foot to the other. By her expression, he surmised that the answer would be 'no.'

"Um, I have an open house on campus tonight. It's the annual Large Equine Research Benefit. You know, you're welcome to join me. It starts at seven. Would you go with me, please?"

Now it was his turn to contemplate a response. He hadn't expected this, nor did want to intrude on her campus life. He wasn't sure he'd fit in her world. But what was the alternative? Wait to see her in the morning. He was leaning towards the latter when she interrupted his thoughts.

"I don't have to be there long. We can show our faces. I will introduce one of my professors. Then we can leave. It would at least let you see where I'm spending my time."

He'd been to the large animal clinic on campus more times than he cared. But having a student provide needed care for his animals cost far less than the local vet.

Attending events like this was how his ranch ended up on the referral list for interns, a part of their residency requirements. She had been his first referral, thanks to CR.

Trish spoke with such hope, how could he refuse? He touched her shoulder, eliciting a sweet smile from her. He hadn't agreed yet. Still, she did a little bounce to show her elation.

"Great, I'll meet you at the auditorium," she blurted out. "Do you need the address?"

"I'm quite familiar with where things are."

"Gotta go, but I'll see you later, right?"

"Yes."

He wanted to pull her into his arms and she looked as if she was expecting him to. He glanced around to make sure no one was watching and saw her do the same thing. She backed up several steps before heading to her car.

****

He spotted Trish the moment he walked through the door. He suspected she'd positioned herself there so he would see her when he entered. The room was bursting at the seams with people, some dressed casually, others in business suits. He'd forgotten to ask what to wear and had decided that the standard Texas attire, denim, button-down shirt, boots, and favorite hat, was appropriate.

As soon as he strolled her way, they locked gazes. She said something to the group she was standing with and then met him halfway. Rising on tip-toes, she met his lips with a soft but passionate kiss.

"Hi. I'm glad you're here."

"So am I." He scanned the room. "This place is packed."

He held her hand after they moved apart. Her spirited energy raced through him even when they weren't touching. Now that they were, her potency jetted through him like a raging storm. She squeezed his hand when she began to talk.

"This is one of our biggest events. There are way more people here than in the previous years I've been here."

"It's great. Helps the program, right?"

"Yes. Why don't we go and get some refreshments?"

She led the way and he followed closely. He accepted punch from a woman serving the red drink in clear cups. He took one sip and nearly went into a diabetic coma.

"They used all the sugar in Texas?"

Trish took a sip of her drink and grinned.

"Students have a tendency to overdo it, and I'm sure they're responsible for this syrupy beverage."

"I'm guessing you're deprived of that pleasure in your regular eating facilities."

"I wouldn't know. I refuse to eat at any of these 'facilities.'"

She lived in the resident apartments and he had sampled her cooking, which was awesome. A man she fed would definitely need to remain active. They moved to a cafe table and talked until a young woman touched her shoulder.

"Excuse me for a moment. It's time for me to introduce Dr. Easterwood."

"I'll be right here." He assured her.

"Okay. Be right back."

Trish walked up to the podium. "Good evening, everyone. My name is Trish Brooks. I am a third-year resident here at Texas A&M College of Veterinary Medicine and Biomedical Sciences. It is my pleasure to introduce you to our Clinical Assistant Professor, Dr. Leslie Easterwood."

She paused until the applauses diminished. She exuded

confidence as she continued. His heart swelled with pride. He would make sure to tell her so.

"Dr. Easterwood received her BS from Texas A&M in 1990, her MA in Animal Science from Texas A&M in 1993, and her DVM from Texas A&M College of Veterinary Medicine & Biomedical Sciences in 1995. Please help me welcome, Dr. Easterwood."

Trish moved from the mic and shook the woman's hand before returning to him where Denver stood. He wrapped an arm around her waist and smiled. The professor spoke, drawing their attention.

"Welcome ladies and gentlemen. Thank you for your continued support." A stream of applauses whipped through the room.

"Our Equine Community Practice Service oversees the majority of general medicine cases that presented to the hospital, including annual preventive care, problems related to the eyes, teeth and skin."

She pointed to Trish and a group of other students and staff.

"Our team regularly partners with our fellow clinicians in the Surgery, Radiation Oncology, Dermatology, and Internal Medicine Services to provide a team approach that we believe is essential to providing the best possible care for your horses. Please, talk to our staff and students. There's much to share. Thank you and enjoy your evening."

Trish looked at him expectantly. "Ready?"

CHAPTER 17

Trish's entire body had ached with need from the moment Denver had walked through the doors. Now she was ready for a little foreplay. The yearning rooted earlier when they'd tumbled in the weeds on his ranch. Her body had flared since leaving him.

She applauded her self-control. The only thing she wanted right now was to have her way. She hoped he was ready. She was.

His blazing eyes told her what she needed to know. She led him through the crowded room. They stopped briefly at the entryway.

"Where are we headed?" He pulled her close.

"My place."

"Did you drive?"

"No, I hitched a ride."

Denver opened his passenger door and waited until she was completely in. He then moved around the vehicle and slipped into the driver's seat.

"What you're doing is important work, Trish."

His comment came out of nowhere. She glanced over.

"Thanks, that means a lot."

"You were a natural up there. You're an excellent speaker."

Trish chuckled. "Thanks. My coach would be so proud. I've had a lot of help along the way, including my family. No shy person in the bunch, trust me. You would like them. I would like you to meet them." She turned in her seat.

"From all I've heard, I think I would like that." He looked her way then concentrated on the road again.

They pulled into parking lot and Trish waited until he moved around to open her door. Instead of stepping out completely, she reached for Denver. He willingly pulled her up as she stood on the nerf bar of the truck. He captured her mouth, his hat tilting back on his head. Locked tight in his arm, she lost her good sense in the wondrous song and dance of his tongue.

"Mm." She tightened her hold around his neck, pulling herself flat against him. A heat-wave shot straight up her thighs, making her want him even more.

Slowly, he pulled away, leaving her throbbing. It took a second to gain her composure. When she did, Denver helped her down from the side step. She stole a glance at his profile. He was tall, lean; his arms were as hard as rocks. Hand in hand, they walked to her apartment without a conversation.

"Beer?"

"Yes."

He dropped his hat on the edge of the couch and followed her into the kitchen. When she turned, he lifted and sat her on the countertop. He captured her mouth, trailing his lips down her neck, across to her ear, and then back to her mouth. She didn't protest and Denver didn't give her a chance to recover. He trailed kisses down her neck again. She dropped her head to allow him access. His hot mouth tortured her; his lips nibbled her exposed flesh. When his mouth ventured down to one breast, then the other, she felt heat beneath her cotton shirt.

She gasped as he journeyed downward until his face was buried between her legs. She parted them like the Red Sea and Denver blew hot air against her slacks as he held her thighs open. He held her tight to keep her from moving.

The shudder that rode up her body left her defenseless, vulnerable and unwilling to fight her lack of control. Instead she slumped against the sensuous pleasure until she had no strength to even sit up on her own. Denver's hands moved up in a nick of time.

He held her in place as he trailed kisses back up her front, covering her mouth again. He suckled until her center started to burn all over again. The cry from her throat was buried in his mouth. Somewhere in that fog, he'd pulled away. She didn't know when.

"Look at me, baby."

Trembling from head to toe, she slowly opened her eyes.

She wanted to press her legs together to ease the throbbing but couldn't.

"Trish," he whispered. His breath kissing her face made her lean toward him. He touched her lips lightly.

"Hey." He squeezed her arms and she raised lids so heavy she was just barely able to open them.

He smiled and she tried to mimic him, but like the rest of her body, her lips didn't cooperate.

"Here, let me help you down."

"No," she mumbled, not recognizing her own voice.

"Okay, I'll give you a minute."

"I don't want a minute, Den. I want you." Her voice

was a breathless whisper.

"You can have me whenever, wherever you'd like. Just let me know when you're ready."

His comment made her smile. This time her lips did rise. She was sure of it.

"Now."

"Not tonight, baby. We have plenty of time."

Trish knew what she wanted…Denver. She slipped off the counter. Denver helped until her feet touched the floor. She walked to the opening of the hallway and looked back at him.

"Come on," she ordered.

He hesitated at first, but eventually followed. She flipped on the hallway light and walked through her bedroom into the bathroom. She unbuttoned her shirt and jeans as she made her way to her final destination. She kicked off her boots, and peeled away her clothes, giving Denver the pleasure of watching her backside.

She opened the glass door to her shower, stepped in, and tuned on the water. She then released the ponytail at the top of her head and turned to face him. He stood and eyed her from head to toe. She was relieved when he did as she'd done. He kicked off his boots and peeled off his clothes.

His massive chest and well-defined arms led to a slim waist. A bugle saluted her with pride. His muscular thighs and legs were like giant trees. Looking at him made her hot with need. After a full appraisal, she lifted her eyes to his. Mistake.

CHAPTER 18

Denver shifted the bulge in his pants with his right hand as he watched Trish peel away clothing, one piece after another until she was completely naked. He grew harder looking at her petite waist as it rounded to her hips and plump ass.

He sucked in his breath when she moved into the shower and faced him. '*Oh, shit!*' He wasn't prepared for this. He'd thought if he gave her some release, as he'd done in the kitchen, it would buy him time. There went 'giving them time.'

Trish's sensuality called him by name. The way her body leaned towards him, the way she watched his lips, and her willingness to seduce him out in the open. He had not planned to go this route, not tonight.

Hell, he had to think this through. He had no protection, and he would never knowingly put her at risk. So, what was a man to do? Give her what she wanted, but still protect her. Once his clothes were off, he walked into the shower and closed the door.

"You're intent on having your way, aren't you, Ms.

Brooks."

She didn't give him time to put much-needed distance between them. She reached for his bouncing penis. He quickly captured her hands as she caressed him. He pulled them away, locking her buttery soft fingers in his tight grip. He backed her up to the corner of the shower which was big enough to accommodate them both, thank goodness.

"You're playing with fire. I must warn you."

"Duly noted." Her hair now stuck to her head, the curls extended to the middle of her back.

"I can't fully love you, tonight, baby. I don't have protection."

Denver didn't want her to think he didn't desire her. He would have to do what he'd done earlier, give her release and suppress his own. He wanted their first time to be when they could fully enjoy one another. He wasn't prepared to go the distance tonight.

"I've got you, Denver Baldwin."

He looked into eyes filled with unreleased desire. Her lips were parted and her lids half opened. Her full and high breasts heaved with her heavy breathing. She was luscious and ripe for the taking. He had no idea what her answer meant exactly, so he decided to ask. "Exactly, sweetheart, what does that mean?"

He placed a tender kiss at her ear. Surprisingly her response affected him more than he'd anticipated. His groin now bounced. He had to slow this down. He pressed his forehead against hers. Warm water beat his back and hind end.

"I'm on the pill."

Her answer was short and sweet. Yes! It would protect her from conceiving but not from anything harmful he might expose her to. He could tell from her reaction earlier, that she'd not been touched in a while, if at all. Deep down, he knew she wasn't one to sleep around. He had to make a choice.

"What if I'm the one you need protection from?" His voice dipped lower as he groped to remain in control. Again, he thought about how he wanted their first time to be special. Still, desire gripped him hard. His own lack of recent activity made this interlude a possible disaster if he didn't take his time. Denver welcomed her soft kiss on his chin. It was a nice way of reassuring him.

"I trust you Denver. I know you will protect me."

Yes, he would, even from him. He lowered her arms, allowing her to bring them up his back. They both groaned as their bodies touched. Arched against him, Trish pressed her lips against his wet neck. His hands trailed down her spine until they found her hips. He pulled her in until they were locked as one.

"I need you, Trish."

"I need you."

Her kiss sealed the deal. He shut off the water, forgoing the cleansing ritual. Drawing away long enough to open the door, he grabbed the towel hanging near the shower. He dried them both without a fuss from her and then lifted Trish into his arms. He headed back to her bed.

Once in, he eased above her and reached for the cool comforter. He tugged the silky fabric down by one corner. He dragged it as she lifted her body so that he could pull the folds beneath her. Hovering above, he ran a hand down to her hairy patch, summoning her to open her legs for him. She complied without a bother.

He caressed the folds hidden beneath soft hair and his fingers soon met moisture. She arched up, her hips moving to meet each stroke. He captured her mouth. She opened it willingly. Her submission excited him even more.

"Hmm. You're delicious, my love."

Her body moved beneath him and made him want to damn the foreplay. He was near his limit. Yet he couldn't. It would be their first time. He wanted to set the tone for their future encounters.

He removed his fingers and crouched on his knees as his mouth left hers. He nibbled his way down, watching her flesh fill with Goosebumps. He savored her soft flesh, taking his time as he eased his lips to her breast.

Holding them in his hands, he blessed each one with the moisture of his tongue, gently pinching the nipples with his teeth. Trish's body was fully engaged at this point, but he still had a ride to make. He got on with his task.

The center of her body quivered when he reached her navel. He kissed it, too, but it was the sweet scent of her V that caused him to rush on. He licked his way down until he tasted the nectar that instantly added more girth to his arousal.

"Mm!"

Trish whimpered. She massaged the top of his head. He used his hands to ease her hips up to get his fill of her. The heat of her hairy fold throbbed against his tongue. He alternated pressing it against her tip and slipping it inside of her. Holding her in his grip, he held her as she buckled under her first orgasm.

He used that time to move up and capture her lips, giving her a sample of her own nectar still fresh on his lips. At the same time, he pressed the tip of his penis to her opening. After waiting a few seconds, he pushed forward.

He snagged her crisp cry in his mouth and steadied his

body. He would not give her all of him at one time. Her fingers dug into his back. When they eased, he gave her more until he was completely submerged inside. The feel of flesh against flesh sent him to heaven and back. He'd always used a condom. To completely feel her brought another obstacle to test his control.

Trish didn't help much either. She tried to move her hips. His hands stilled her in place. He wanted her body to adjust to his entry. He moaned, trying to hold on so that he might give her as much pleasure as he could before he sought his own. Again, her hips moved as she squeezed his full erection with extremely tight muscles.

Denver lifted his mouth to her ear. "Not yet, darling. We've got plenty of time."

Her eyes opened and filled with tears. He kissed each one.

"I got you, remember?"

She nodded. Before long, they both were moving. Her hands were everywhere. Denver controlled the strokes...nice, long even ones. Every now and again he would deepen the dive. They both gasped each time.

Trish wrapped her legs around his waist, taking away some of his control. He gave her a long strong kiss when that happened and she relented.

When she lost the battle and went sailing off to her next orgasm, he increased his strokes to catch up. And as he finally got there, he saw bright lights behind squeezed lids. The room echoed with their loud cries.

Spent, and not wanting to crush her, he pushed off to her side and pulled Trish close. He draped his leg over her body and kissed the bridge of her nose.

"Are okay, my love?"

"Yes."

CHAPTER 19

Trish snuggled close to Denver. Her body still tingled vigorously and her heart raced like she'd done a five-mile run. She inhaled the fresh scent of their lovemaking. She bent her head and her face clung to the top of his wet chest. She rested there, listening to his strong heart.

She pressed her thigh firmly against his to suppress the throbbing between her legs. Their romping in the sheets left them half on and half on the bed. She wanted more.

She shifted her weight and he responded by holding her more firmly than before. "Where are you going?"

"No place."

"Good, I'm not done with you yet."

Just the intent of his statement lit a fire between her legs. She felt him rise against her thigh and immediately responded by rolling her hips.

"Really?"

"Really."

He pulled her on top, her knees now kissing the sheet and his shaft against her opening. She welcomed the heat, especially when he grabbed her buttocks with both hands and added pressure to their union.

"Hmm." She groaned into his ear.

He lifted her hip until he was able to guide his tip inside. He didn't stop until he was completely covered. She welcomed him fully.

It didn't take long to catch the rhythm of his movement beneath her. She lifted her upper body. Her hands rested on his chest. She moved her knees forward for deeper penetration.

Satisfied with her position, Trish moved with urgency, trying to consume every inch of him, hoping to reach every spot aching for just a mere touch from him. He allowed her to set the pace, making the ride worth her while.

Losing her own control, she bucked and turned on top of him until she could feel her body exploding. Giving into the sensation, she fell forward.

Denver picked up where she left off, using her hips to continue the up and down motions. She felt him shudder. He wrapped his arms around her, squeezing her tight. She collapsed, without an ounce of energy to move.

Sated, she had no idea who dosed off first, but she stirred when his hand moved to pull up the covers. Turning her face into him, she murmured, "I'm happy."

"So am I."

"Can I get you anything?"

"No. Stay with me."

She relaxed again until he turned and deposited her onto the bed. Facing each other, they communicated without words.

This was a big step forward. It definitely altered the dynamics at the ranch. For now, she was happy. She slid a finger down the side of his face, brushing it across his lips before replacing it with her kiss.

"Tell me more about Denver."

She shifted a little, making it more comfortable to be eye-to-eye. She admired his handsome features. His long dark lashes feathered his dark brown eyes which could sometimes seem so intense. When he spoke, his voice demanded attention.

"I'm a steak man, and unlike most ranchmen, I like mine medium."

"As in rare?" She turned her nose up.

"Yes, a little pink and without all that other crap people drown their steak with."

She frowned again. "You might as well leave the 'moo' in it."

He chuckled. "If it's good quality beef, from Texas of course, then steak tastes better when you don't overcook it."

"I like mine all the way dead."

He chuckled. The sound rumbled through her body. Everything about Denver thrilled her and she got great satisfaction from that sensation. Just sitting in his space made her toes curl. Feeling this way made her think about what her friend Brandi told her one night when they were talking about men. She told her to not to be afraid to test the loving, that is the physical side of it.

Brandi behaved like an angel around her family. But the girl was a freak. "Girl, I don't care how cute he is. If he can't lay this down--" She passed her hand over her hair. "--then, he's wasting my time," she said when they talked about the guys she dated.

"You're a crazy woman," Trish responded.

"Yep. But why waste all that time getting to know someone, and when he does the do, you're like, what the hell?"

Smiling inwardly, Denver had laid her hair, curled her

toes, and ripped her to pieces. His loving made her fiend for more.

Denver brought her back from her reverie with a question she had to ask him to repeat.

"What's your favorite meal?" He asked again.

"Anything seafood."

"Not here, my love. Maybe further south. Galveston is the closest you come to fresh seafood."

"Yeah, I know."

She frowned, but as quickly lifted her mouth into a smile. She was pushing it, she knew, but she'd managed to get what she wanted thus far.

"How about you join me when I go home to visit my parents?"

"It's not like I can just up and leave, Trish. I have a ranch to run."

Wrong answer. She didn't give his response a chance to register before her ire was up. She tried to move from his embrace, but he held her. He glared with stony eyes.

"I have a lot of people depending on me, Trish."

He softened his voice just above a whisper. It finally dawned on her. She couldn't just leave when she wanted to either. After entering the residency program, she had to plan in advance for any travel. Residents provided support and patient care for the equine ambulatory service on campus. She was on a pretty tight schedule herself.

Students in her class were encouraged to publish case reports or become involved in a research project during their internship year. It took time to participate in giving seminars and lectures to both small and large groups of students, faculty, and veterinarians.

She and her study group had been successful in exceeding their requirements in record time. Though she was behind her group with getting in her hours at first, she was slowly catching up, thanks to Denver. He'd agreed to her working three to four hours a day until she caught up.

Resident also alternated weekends doing surgeries, equine lameness, and emergency rotations. When she wasn't working in the clinic, she was penning her papers to fulfill her publishing credentials.

"Can we work on it, maybe give you time to make arrangements? Would you do that for me?"

He did as he always did before answering, He paused. Denver lifted to his side, propping his head onto his hand.

"I would love to. You'll just have to give me ample notice."

"Okay, that's fair."

"When were you home last?"

Trish dug deep into her memory because it seemed like forever. It'd only been a few months ago, May, Mother's Day weekend.

"Early May. I went home for Mother's Day. It was a very short trip, though."

"I see. So, you haven't had a break all summer?"

Trish pouted. She'd spent the past year consumed by study groups, research, and benefits. There were no breaks. She'd been focused on finishing her final year.

"No, I've been in summer school every year since starting. I'm doing double time on research and lectures so that I don't have to do an extra year."

"That's pretty intense. Why such an aggressive approach?"

"Honestly, I was homesick the moment I stepped foot in Texas. I couldn't imagine staying here longer than I had to."

"In a rush, were we?"

"Yes. That was then."

"And now?"

"Well, I got used to the red dirt, red ants, spiders, gnats, and the smell of nothing but animal dung, for starters."

Denver laughed so hard she thought she would have to give mouth-to-mouth resuscitation. He gasped for air between coughs. His face literally turned a hue darker. She shook her head, realizing the humor was on her.

"That's not very funny, you know."

He sat up and watched her.

"No, it is not. You're correct."

"About?"

"I'm sorry. Texas does take some getting used to. I've lived here all my life, and there are some things that…"

"You're making fun of me again."

"No darling, listen."

"Do you know how hard it is to keep my hair from bridling because I have to wash it every day, sometimes twice a day? I have to use a ton of lotion and moisturizers to keep my skin from tanning like leather?"

"Listen, I get it. But this ole girl, Texas, can get into your system and you'll never be able to get rid of her."

"Never. I don't care. I'm not extremely fond of Texas."

The air grew as thick as cotton.

CHAPTER 20

At first nothing moved, not even air. It was like something snuffed it all out. Denver slowly sat up. He turned his back and kicked his feet to the floor. Her hand on his back slowed his retreat but didn't stop it. "I better let you get your rest. You still have to get up early in the morning."

"Denver?"

"Yes, Trish."

He faced her, buck naked as the day his was born. Her awareness of his physic caused her to pause. Her eyes swept from his hips to his face.

"Um, I…"

"It's okay. I'll dress and get out your way."

She was on his tail, her hand reached the small of his back and he turned. She was faster than he was and ran smack into him. He reached around and caught her in a loose hug. Her eyes pleaded with him. He wanted to ignore them but couldn't.

"I'll see you tomorrow."

He leaned down and covered her mouth in a brief but

solid kiss. He held her from him by her arms before releasing her completely.

Denver shoved his legs into his pants and put on his shirt, before slipping his boot on. He didn't expect her to stand and watch. Once he was done, he waited. She reached for a robe on the back of the door and moved so he could get by. He reached for her hand and captured it taking her with him as they traveled to the front.

He glanced into a room they passed. He assumed it was the music room she'd bragged about. He'd missed it when they passed earlier. His mind had been on one thing and one thing only. He considered retracing his steps to take a peek, but decided to save it for another time…maybe.

He scooped up his hat as he passed the couch and went straight for the door. He turned before reaching for the knob. With his hat in hand, he circled his arms snuggly around her waist, bringing her mouth into position for his possession. He released his uncertainty and used all his energy to communicate his feelings.

Yes, he was falling in love with her. How could she not know? Next to his ranch and the people who depended on him, she'd taken his heart. Denver didn't know when exactly it happened, but it had. He would be hard pressed to walk away.

He understood her hesitation. He was home. Hers was in New Orleans. Home was all she knew. It was safe. It was where her family lived, where she knew things best. Yes, they needed time. Was she worth this ride? Yes.

He took his time and gave her all the passion he could muster. Trish held him tight. Her fists were full of his shirt. He felt her tremble, heard her sniffle.

"We're good." He whispered into her hair.

She bobbed her head up and down.

"Okay. I'll see you in the morning."

She showed no sign of letting go of him or his shirt. Again, he had to set her away. He reached for the door. He didn't dare look back. He couldn't. He rushed out of her building and to his truck before he changed his mind.

His drive was long. Once in his quarters, he went straight to the shower. He turned the water pressure to sharp and the water indicator to cold. He hated the thought of washing away her scent but he needed to cool down, for more than one reason.

He walked straight to his bed, pulled back the covers and fell in. All he could think about was her silky skin and how quickly she had melted in his arms, how she had yielded to his stroke and how her voice had shrieked his name. The cool shower didn't do a damn thing for him.

Even before the alarm sounded, he sat up on the side of the bed with an erection as hard as a log. "Damn!" He sat for a few moments longer before entering the bathroom and repeating the ritual of an ice cold shower as he'd done last night. After he dressed, he went to the kitchen. He was too early for the coffee; the timer had yet to do its job.

He wandered into his office. His hand paused after turning on the lamp above a large gold envelope. He picked it up and looked at the writing on the label. Quickly, he ripped it open. His eyes scanned the cover letter. He slapped it down on his desk and slumped down into his chair.

Once he regained his senses, he picked up the phone, ignoring the time, and dialed Ankit's number.

"Ankit, I wouldn't have called had it not been important."

"This better be damned good, Baldwin."

"Trust me, it is. I'm heading to your place."

"Now? This can't wait until a decent hour?"

"This is a decent hour, man. See you in a few."

He dropped the phone into its receiver, snatched up the contents of the envelope and headed for the door.

Coffee still wasn't ready. He'd just have to live without any for now. He marched to his truck and jumped in, dropping the papers in the passenger seat.

He reached for the keys, which he always left in the ignition. They weren't there. "Damn!" He shoved the door open.

Last night he'd taken the keys out and didn't realize they were in his hand until he was in his quarters.

He'd dropped them on the side table. His wallet was still in the glove compartment. He only took it out when he wasn't on the ranch. Denver hustled to his room, grabbed his keys, and hurried back.

This time, before he got to his truck, he spotted CR.

"I have to leave now. I'll explain when I return. Take care of the startup for me this morning, please."

"No problem. See you when you return."

"Thanks."

He got in the truck and took off. He reached for his phone and let out yet another explicit growl. He wanted to leave a message for his mother...for Trish. She might be gone when he returned. No time to fret over it now. He pushed the accelerator, turning sharply onto the paved street from his gravel road.

He pulled into Ankit's circular drive and was and ready to press the doorbell when it flung open.

"Don't you dare ring that bell. I did all I could to not arouse my wife. Imagine three little curly headed kids bolting down those stairs. My wife would have my hide. Never mind you and your 'I-can't-wait' ranchman's ass. You get to go home afterwards."

Denver watched his long-time friend and lawyer in amusement. While Ankit went on to the blue-collar side of life, marrying his college sweetheart, having three of the most adorable kids Denver had ever seen, he couldn't help but wonder what would have become of him if he had followed his own heart and left this damn ranch and Texas.

Just last night he'd proclaimed it as his beloved. In fact, it was a hard and sometimes unforgiving place. With all its flaws, there was no other place in the world like it. He had to admit that he loved his home and ranching was all he'd ever known. He was where he was supposed to be.

"You get to see them all the time. It wouldn't be so bad to see my God kids, now would it?"

"Keep moving…and keep it quiet."

He shoved Denver forward.

"Okay. Sorry."

Denver waltzed down to the den and into Ankit's office. Ankit followed seconds later with two steaming cups of coffee.

"Bless you, my brother."

"Humph. Let's get to it. What's so dang important this early in the morning?"

It took a minute for Ankit to scan the cover sheet and his eyes widened. "Oh…shit!"

"My sentiments, exactly."

CHAPTER 21

After Denver left, Trish was a complete mess. What could have been a perfect evening, she'd ruined by opening her big mouth. The soul-searing kiss before he left should have reassured her, but she worried about what Denver thought of her. Would he be glad to be done with her once she got in all her hours? She'd spent hours beating herself up.

She promised to make it up to him if he gave her a second chance today. She hurried through her morning tasks, not adding more lotion to her legs or conditioner to her hair. She grabbed her backpack and practically sprinted to her car.

Last night, she forgot to tell him that she didn't have class, study group or on-duty call today. She was as free as a bird. She would stay the entire day. She turned the curve nearly on two wheels. She wanted to get to the ranch earlier than usual.

Her heart rammed in her ears as she kicked up dust on the unpaved road. She slowed and eased through the gate, heading for her usual parking spot.

Her spirit plummeted when she saw that Denver's truck was missing. With trembling fingers, she turned off the ignition and bolted from the car. Hope rose as she thought he might have parked someplace different. She stomped the path and headed to for the tack shed first. Her heart sped as she walked in. Nothing.

She headed for the first grange and immediately went to the first bay. Winter's head snapped up when he heard her footsteps. She was happy to see the animal but disappointed not to find Denver. His ATV was in the shed and his horse was in his stall. Dejected, she walked over and petted the stallion before moving to his front. The easy-keeper's body was as stellar as the man who rode him. He was lean and bulked in all the right places.

"Where is your master, Mr. Winters? He seems to be missing in action."

She hugged his neck the way she'd always done and the way he seemed to like best. On a mission, she patted Winter's back and continued her search for Denver. She went to several more barns before hearing CR in the back. She moved with purpose, hoping her search would end at the back of the barn.

"Good morning," she blurted.

"Morning, little lady. We got a lot to do today. We can use your help with the paddock. We got some work to finish up there. It'll be the new stud farm."

Denver had been preparing a portion of a field specifically for breeding horses and raising foals. He'd told her about it the first evening at her apartment, the day he found out another bidder had contested his offer.

She tried not to look disappointed. She was here to earn her hours. If that's how she did it today, so be it.

"Okay, I'm ready when you are."

"Then, let's get you a belt."

CR reached for the smallest one he could find, and handed it to Trish. She strapped it on and the hide slid down her hips. The tools they would use to shore up the paddock probably weighed more than she did.

"Here." CR held out his hand for the belt. "Let's see if we can shorten it."

He used a knife long enough to gut a man from head to toe to shorten and then prong new holes to secure the belt in place. When she tried it again, she rewarded his work with a fat grin.

"Aw, alright, let's get to work. The sun will be high directly."

"Wait." She moved past him and huffed her way back to the tack shed. She walked to the locker where Denver had gotten her a hat. She picked the same one she'd use before and hurried back.

She rode on the back of a wagon with three other hands. Trish didn't come right out and ask about Denver's whereabouts. Instead, she sulked as she followed CR's instructions. Her saving grace was the beautiful prairies and breathtaking fields of wild flowers.

Her disappointment at not seeing him lasted a good two hours until she overheard CR tell Glen that an emergency came up, requiring him to leave before dawn. After hearing that, she worried. Had something happened with the auction? Was he going to lose the herd? She understood how important it was to him.

The sun rode her like a second skin. Sweat soon soaked her T-shirt beneath her cotton shirt. She drank plenty of water, per CR instructions. What he didn't understand was that once water went in, it had to come out.

It was fine for the men to go relieve themselves in the bushes, but was CR really expecting her to do the same.

She huffed and puffed over the thought until she had no other choice. She looked behind her several times before going in a shaded bush. She was appalled. She would let Denver know that this was not what she signed up for. If he didn't like it, so be it.

"It's about time for us to bring you in, Trish. Here's your chance to escape."

She hadn't told CR either she could stay the entire day. Leaving would get her out of the scorching heat but the paddock still needed work. More hands would lighten the load, even if her load was about half of that of the men.

"I'm good, CR. I can stay until the end of the day."

He lifted his hat and scratched the sideburn over his ear. He looked at her closely and shook his head.

"You mean you'll stay out here instead of going home."

"Yep, I'll stay."

"All right then! Parker will bring out some lunch in a minute. You want me to tell him to bring you anything in particular."

She didn't truly understand his question at first. But finally she got it. CR was making special accommodations for her. She assumed, in his own way, he wanted to take care of her.

And after lunch, the sun found her at every turn. She used the bandana CR gave her to wipe the sweat from her face; her shirt sleeves were now too soiled to use on her face.

She heard a horse snort in the distance and knew it wasn't the horses tied to the hack. They'd been grazing not far away. Everyone turned and just as she caught a glimpse of Denver in the distance, her heart leaped in her chest.

Winter trotted with the elegance of a trained ballerina.

His head bobbed up and down. The man on his back sat tall and regal. Denver was too far away to see his eyes but she felt him watching her. She focused on the spot just beneath that hat. She knew with certainty that his eyes were directly on her.

She'd long since removed the tool belt. It had proven to be a pain in the butt. And when she saw him approaching, all sensibility left her. Trish dropped the tool in her gloved hand and began to walk at first but then took off in a full sprint. She didn't stop to think that the men behind her might wonder what the hell she was doing. She didn't care. Her mind was on one thing, one person.

Her hat blew off and she saw Winter stop and Denver dismount. She sprinted even faster.

CHAPTER 22

When he spotted her car still parked at the barn, he frowned. He went from one building to the next looking for her. Denver knew CR would be working on the paddock. He didn't think the ranchmen would have her out in the damn sun all day long. His heart raced when he found one empty shed after another.

Denver went to the corral where Lightning spent his days. She'd been spoiling the rotten stallion and he no longer listened to what Denver had to say. Checking there, he still didn't find her.

He checked the house. Maybe she was keeping his mother company. He raced up the stairs, across the porch, and through the back door.

"Mom?"

"In here, Den."

Her voice trailed from the room connected to the kitchen. He walked in and let his eyes adjust to the different light. Trish was nowhere in sight. His mother's voice garnered his attention.

"Hi, baby. Want something to drink."

"Hey, Mom. Not right now. I have something to do first. I'll be back. I have some great news."

"Oh, okay. I sent--"

He didn't hear the rest. He was in motion. He backed Winter out of his stall after tugging at the saddle to make sure it was in place. With his boot in one of the stirrups, he threw his leg over and in the same flow, slapped Winter's belly. With the reins loose in Denver's hands, the animal took off. He galloped the entire distance from the house to the edge of the paddock.

He slowed when he saw the group huddled. The instant they turned, he spotted her.

"Good Lord, what the hell is CR thinking. Surely he hasn't had her out here all day." No one was around to hear him.

Heat furred up his neck and his temple throbbed the moment he saw her walk and then sprint toward him. His whole body buzzed. "Whoa." Winter stopped and Denver dismounted. He couldn't see anything, anyone else, only her. He took a few steps and then waited.

The closer she got, the harder his heart pumped. He couldn't tell what was wrong but something definitely was not right. The look in her eyes scared him. He opened his arms and she leaped right into them. He turned several times when she landed against him to keep her from knocking them both over.

She held him tight. He did the same. Her breath was ragged and her body hot, even her hair.

When he stopped turning, he kept her snug against him, her feet dangling.

"Hey, babe. Why in the devil are you out here?"

He didn't recognize his own voice. He couldn't break the choke hold she had around his neck. Trish held on for dear life.

"Are you okay?"

"Yes." She sounded completely out of breath.

He sat her on her feet and she finally released him enough so he that could get far enough away to see her face. Her skin was flushed but her smile was perfect. It took his breath away.

"Why are you out here, Trish?"

Her eyes danced. He touched the side of her face and her gloved hand landed on top of his.

"I'm helping fortify the paddock."

His anger returned. He looked past her, looking for CR. The man must have known Denver was searching for him because he turned his back.

"Don't be mad at CR. I asked to be out here."

"Why?" He barked. "Do you know how hot it is? Grown ass men don't survive this heat. CR knows better."

He frowned, forgetting that the woman before him wasn't the focus of his disdain. Her hand on his face traveled to his chin. She squeezed it.

"Please, Denver, don't reprimand CR for my part in this. It was my decision. I wanted to come. Please."

"Get your hat, were going back."

"But, they're not..."

"You're going in. We can talk about this later."

She stared up at him like she might contest him. Her mouth opened, then closed and then opened again. No words came out. She turned on her heel and went to get her hat. He was two steps behind her. Once she retrieved it, she started for the group.

"Where are you going?"

"To get my belt."

"They will bring it back with them. Can you stay with Winter for a minute?"

Denver didn't wait for her response. He continued until he was at the center of the group. Their questioning looks told him that they did not understood what had just occurred with Trish. He didn't care. He didn't owe them an explanation and he wasn't about to give one.

He directed his attention to CR.

"We need to talk before the end of the day. We have a lot to discuss. How long before this will be ready?" He pointed to the remaining planks.

In a so many words, he told the old man that he would wait until the rest of the men weren't around to chew his ass out. But he also needed to know that they hadn't wasted time out here, catering to Trish. They still had a lot to do to be ready.

"I'll be back a little after four," CR replied.

Denver nodded, turned and walked away. He took Winter's reins from Trish's hand, mounted his horse and then reached down and lifted her behind him on the saddle. Locking her arms around his waist, he slapped the reins.

"Hhaaattt"

He urged the animal forward while making sure he didn't drop his precious load. They didn't slow until they neared the barn.

"Whoa."

They'd ridden back in complete silence. He handed her down before he dismounted. Tossing the rein around an outpost, Denver's hand snaked down her arm. He seized her fingers as he pulled her in the direction of the house. The refreshingly cool air met them and he walked straight to the refrigerator and retrieved two bottles of water. He handed her one and popped the lid on the other. They still hadn't exchanged a word. He pulled her through the house this time. He only glanced his mother's way when they passed her in the den.

"Denver?" She called. "Trish? What's going on? I thought…"

They didn't stop until he stepped through his office door.

They moved completely through the room until he turned and propped his rear on the front of his desk. Finally, he released her hand and crossed his arms in front of him.

Trish glared at him. Her eyes narrowed. She was mad but he didn't care. He was the one with liability, especially, if she had a damn heatstroke from being in the sun all morning. How would he explain that something had happened to her? She wasn't completely faultless. She had a loaded tongue and attitude to match. He knew it wouldn't take long.

"I wore my hat. I drank water. We took breaks, Denver."

"You shouldn't have been out there. Who cleaned the bays?"

She looked away then crossed her arms and looked back at him. "I planned to do them when I returned."

"When?"

"I knew I'd be here the entire day. I forgot to tell you last night." She managed a small smile. It vanished when he didn't smile back. "I wanted to spend the day here. I thought maybe you would take me back to your pasture."

He didn't twitch or acknowledge her reply. Instead, he rose to his full height. Her eyes followed his; her head tilted back. He moved past her but not before she caught his wrist. He turned around.

He wanted crush her in his arms, but what would that do? At this rate there was no way to make her to understand what happened today? From now on, he planned to give her specific instructions. She was not going to like it, but it was for her protection. And his.

"You should not have been out in the field."

"But how is that different from when I was with you, Denver?"

"We weren't out there digging or setting fifty-pound posts, Trish."

He glared down at her. She didn't flinch and he didn't expect her to. What the hell was he going to do with her? They stood at odds for a moment before he walked away. Again, her palm settled on him, this time on his stomach. It stopped him in his tracks. Her small hands burned straight through his shirt, shooting heat straight up his spine. It was bad enough that she stirred him with a simple glance. She had all of his power. Touching him made him lose all perspective, even in the seriousness of this recent transgression.

Covering her hand, he did exactly what he'd wanted to since she'd raced toward him in the field. He pulled her in and covered her mouth. Denver intended one firm peck but her sweetness tripped him up. He couldn't stop. He rather enjoyed how she melted in arms.

He lifted his head at the knock on the door; luckily, he'd locked it behind them.

"Denver? Everything okay, dear?"

He sighed and releasing Trish before heading for the door. He turned the lock and pulled the door open. Instead of looking at him, his mother peeked around his shoulder. Once she saw Trish, she glanced up and smiled. He wouldn't let her keep it.

"Trish here was out in the field all morning. If something would have happened to her, we could have been in big trouble."

He glanced at her and bolted from the room, leaving

Trish and his mother to look at his back.

Damn! Now everybody was in his business. He had to deal with questioning glances from his men and his mother now.

Of course this would raise a few eyebrows, especially from his mother. Even so, he was relieved to not have to hide his feelings any more.

He guided Winter back into his bay and gave him water before he brushed him down.

"What do you think, old guy? Will this woman be the end of me or what?"

His thoughts returned to the previous night when she went on her rant about Texas. What did it mean for them? If she planned to return to New Orleans, this would be useless for him. He didn't want to invest himself in a temporary relationship.

Would enjoying her body be enough for him? He'd purposely avoided relationships because it was as much an investment as his work on the ranch. His heart was already committed. How could he make his heart cooperate if it was better to let her go? He continued to brush Winter, heavy in thought.

Winters started moving around.

"Settle down, man."

He had to remember not to take his frustrations out on his animal. Winter had always been good to him. Denver swung around on hearing her soft voice.

He hadn't heard her footsteps. Winters obviously had.

"I'm sorry, Denver. I wasn't trying to cause problems today. I really do need these hours to finish my class."

With the brush suspended in the air, Denver turned. "Do you think I would terminate our agreement because of what happened today?"

She didn't answer. He set the brush down and pulled

her into a kiss. He slipped his tongue into her mouth, rediscovering the places that made her moan. She circled her arms around his waist and held on tight.

He didn't lift his head until they were both breathless. He paused before he started again. This time they clung together, still in Winter's bay, enjoying the awareness of their bodies pressed together.

"I just want to make sure you stay safe. Is that okay?"

"Yes."

"So, what tale did you tell my mother about what we were doing in my office?"

"I told her the truth."

"Which truth was that?" He lifted his left eyebrow.

"That you'd taken advantage of me."

"Humph. That's a tale and I know it."

"Don't be so sure."

"Come on, we have bays to muck."

"Are you helping?"

"Doesn't look like I have a choice, now does it?"

They worked on opposite sides of the barn. She moved quicker than he did and he thought for sure she was short-changing the job, until he looked into her bays.

"How do you do that?"

"Mr. Baldwin, I work smarter, not harder."

She grinned from one ear to the other. Their interlude was interrupted again. This time it was Ankit.

"Denver!"

Ankit's voice grew louder as he yelled Denver's name from outside. Her smart mouth would have to wait for his response. Trish followed closely as he left the barn.

"Hey, there you…" Ankit stopped mid-sentence, his attention drawn to Trish. "Well, who do we have here?"

"You're married with three curly-head kids, remember?"

"Yeah, but a beauty like this could make a man forget."

Trish moved around him with her ungloved hand held out.

"Hi, I'm Trish."

"Well hello, Trish."

CHAPTER 23

Ankit Bertolli was as handsome as he was smooth.
What he lacked in build, he clearly made up for in looks.
His dark curly hair and dark almond skin made you look
twice. He was almost as tall as Denver, but not quite.

"It's a pleasure to meet you, Ankit," she greeted the
man she'd heard about.

"So, Den, my brotha, where have you been hiding this
one?"

Ankit continued to hold her hand. Denver snatched it
from him and frowned. From the way they acted, she
guessed they were friends as well business associates.

"Trish is working here for class hours at the Vet
Clinic."

"Is that a fact?"

Denver's revelation seemed to spark even more
interest from Ankit, but it pissed her off. So, she was just
a damn ranch-hand. Ankit eyes glistened as he appraised
her, but his charm fell short. She stormed off, not looking
back at either of them.

She went back to the bays she'd yet to finish. She

jerked the rake across the hay, using all of her energy on the task. It kept her focus on the work and not her anger. The more she stewed, the madder she got.

Behind closed doors, she was his most precious. Publically she the damn stable mucker. And that damn, smirking Ankit. Who did he think he was?

She jerked the rake again before tossing it to the ground. She kicked the straw.

"What are you so worked up about?"

His voice caught her off guard, like she'd been caught knocking over his mother's favorite vase. She refused to let him play with her. She'd done her eight hours. It was time to go her merry way. She rushed pass him.

"I'm done. Your bays are spotless, Mr. Baldwin, master."

"Trish?"

He rushed behind her but she kept moving. He would kiss her and think it would okay? Not tonight.

Trish ignored his repeated calls. Just as her hands touched the handle to her car, he circled her waist.

"Trish, what's eating you?"

"You're eating me, Denver. Trish is just the damn worker!"

"Didn't say 'just' and had you stuck around you wouldn't be so mad, baby. Ankit knows about you. He was pulling your strings, both of our strings."

She searched his face for truth. She expected to find amusement, but didn't. She took a long breath. The back and forth with him was not sitting well with her. She stepped back to put space between them. She glanced away trying to hold her emotions in check.

He reached for her and she moved back even further. As much as she yearned for his touch, she didn't want it right now. He closed the space between them but didn't try to touch her. He bent his head low enough she could feel his breath on her face. She closed her eyes in response.

"Baby, look at me."

His command didn't reach that place that it normally did. He touched her cheek. Trish's eyes popped open and glared at him.

"I'm sorry. Please, forgive me. I know it's been a long day."

She moved away from his touch. Yes, it had been a long day. Perhaps she'd gotten too much sun. She fought the tears stinging the back of her eyes. She pressed her lips together to keep her composure.

"Yes, I'm tired. I'm leaving. Is that okay?"

"Yes," he said in barely a whisper.

Without another word, she moved to her car. She saw Mrs. Baldwin watching them but refused to make direct eye contact with the woman. She didn't want his mother interfering. Trish slipped behind the wheel, turned the key and sped off. She refused to even look in the review mirror for fear she would turn back.

She kicked rocks as she went to the side entrance to her residence. She drank two bottles of water before peeling away her dirty, sweaty clothes. She stepped into the shower and for the first ten minutes, just stood beneath the electrifying spray. Finally, she lathered her hair with her favorite shampoo, followed it with conditioner.

Ready to slip into her pajamas, she saw a small glossy card on top of her dresser drawers. She picked it up turned it over. She'd already told her friend she would not attend the summer-end party. She'd thought she would be spending the night with Denver. But now...

Instead of reaching for her favorite PJs, she slipped

into a pair of snug low-rider jeans and a red top. She reached for her heeled sandals. Because her hair was still wet, she pulled it up into a bun and applied a light coat of foundation, some mascara, and a deep red lipstick. She tucked her small wallet in one of her back pockets and her cell phone in the other. Grabbing her key, she left the apartment and extinguished the lights.

Trish headed straight to the Student Recreation Center. When she walked in, Chris pulled her by the arm.

"I thought you weren't coming?"

"I changed my mind. This place is packed."

She scanned the room. The Greeks had coordinated this event to raise funds for the American Heart Association. The music lasted until midnight. Her energy had quit more than two hours before. She was exhausted.

"I changed my mind again," she told Chris. She headed back to the car and put her aching body in it and drove back to her apartment. By the time her head hit her pillow, she was gone.

Her chiming phone woke her. She looked at her alarm clock and then groped for her phone.

"Hi Mom."

"Oh, child, you sound terrible."

Not as terrible as I feel. She sat up in her bed. After talking to her mother, Trish turned her phone completely off.

Today was a good day to complete her final publication.

Technically, she was only short two hours of completing her requirement. If only she'd stay at the ranch a couple of extra hours, she would be done.

"Wait!" She pushed away from her laptop. She had her hours. The day she'd gone back to check on Lightning would constitute hours completed. Would Denver sign off on them? If she had to, she'd ask CR.

Trish tapped her fingers on her pencil, contemplating her options. *Suck it up or work at Evans Library every night of the week next semester,* she concluded. She huffed at the thought. Nothing would replace the missing pieces of her heart. Yes, she'd fallen in love with Denver Baldwin. Why else was she behaving so irrationally?

"Ugh, study, Trish. Enough of your daydreaming."

She decided to take her studying to the outdoor park just outside her building. She found a shaded bench and pulled out her laptop. The fresh air did wonders. Ideas appeared from the blue sky and before long, the pages she needed were full.

"Can we start over?"

Her fingers paused as she looked up. In one hand, Denver held his well-worn hat. In the other, a small bouquet of wild flowers. She looked from the flowers to him a few times before accepting the bunch.

Trish took a small whiff of the flowers and patted the empty space next to her. He sat, but not too close. He turned toward her. His eyes were red, and the lids were puffy. She caved to her urge and palmed the side of his face. She could tell he was exercising restraint. For that, she had to admire him.

"I don't want to make excuses for how you felt, but I do want to tell you I'm sorry. You mean so much more to me than you think."

He glanced away for a moment and then shifted and turned to her completely.

"I'm going to just come right out and tell you how I feel."

She sat silently. His arm hugged the back of the bench as he considered his words.

"Trish, I'm in love with you. I do love you. I want a

chance to figure out how to make this work. Will you do that for me, please?"

CHAPTER 24

Denver sat on pins and needles and waited for Trish's answer. According to his mother, it wasn't the most macho thing to do, but given all they'd learn about this woman, it was the right thing to do if there was any hope of convincing her to stay in Texas.

He believed that might be both of their hang ups; having to choose, having to give something up. He didn't want to make her choose. He just hoped love would help them choose together. To get things started, he had to make the first move. It was only right.

He expected debate from her, a challenge. What was important to her? She still had to make a lot of decisions in a year's time. He'd hate to think he let her slip from his grasp.

Trish did what she'd managed to do since he'd known her. She shocked him. She flew into his arms. He had to catch her and her wayward laptop at the same time.

"Oh my god, I've been going crazy, Denver. School has consumed me, but I don't want a job that becomes my life. It's important to have someone, someone I love.

It's important they love me back."

She kissed him briefly and rattled on. "I want this. I want you. I love you, Denver."

Relief washed over him. He kissed her but didn't linger. He hadn't expected her answer so easily. She was strong willed. He admired her for that. He promised to slow things down. Right now, finishing her residency was her number one priority. He needed to get that herd to the ranch. That was his top priority.

He'd told his mother how he felt about her. She already knew, she said. He told the men as well. Everyone seemed elated. They really liked her.

"We work as a team, right?"

"You make me happy."

"You make me happy."

She kissed his chin, then his cheek, then both of his eye lids and finally slipped down to his mouth. Her lips parted and she flicked her tongue in his mouth. It was he who broke the kiss.

"I have good news."

"What's that?"

"I got everything cleared with the herd."

"Great!"

She pumped a fist. It felt great to have someone special to share good news with. She seemed to get him. She was okay with him being a rancher.

She worked hard. Hell, he'd complained about her trying to pull her weight.

"We learned today that my challenger is a knacker. Do you know what that is?"

She frowned. "No."

"It's someone who buys horses at auctions for the purpose of slaughtering them. He's been fined in for not declaring his intentions at the start of the auction in previous cases."

"He was planning to take a healthy herd to a slaughter house?"

"Yes. The auctioneer gave very specific instructions. His bid would have been invalid if he'd won it."

They spent the remainder of the afternoon talking and stealing kisses. Sprawled out on her sofa, Trish worked on her publication again. He slept. A delicious aroma from the kitchen startled him awake.

"I stand to gain fifty pounds messing with you, sweet lady."

"I'm sure we can find a way to work it off."

He dropped his head back and roared at her suggestion.

After their tasty meal, he cleaned the kitchen while she finished her paper.

He slipped into her music room and sat down behind the keyboard. When he started playing, Trish appeared with an astonished look on her face.

"Looks like the Brooks clan isn't the only one musically blessed." He finished a couple of runs and looked up. "Some of us are better than others." He grinned.

"No, you're doing great. This is a pleasant surprise. Where did you learn to play?"

"I took lessons as a kid. My mother plays at church."

"Wow, Mr. Baldwin. Looks like someone has been hiding talents."

"That ends today, my love."

She picked up her bass and hit the drum sequence on the keyboard. She joined him in a succession of song snippets. Placing her bass back on the rack she moved onto his lap. What started out as play, ended in play that landed most of her clothes on the floor.

She straddled him on the bench and he moved his arms beneath her thighs. After few moments of hip rolling, he stood so they would not snap her piano bench in two.

"Hold on, baby."

Denver stopped several times on their way to the bedroom and covered her mouth with hard kisses. Trish responded willingly each time. He continued the assault even after they entered her bedroom. Her being naked, with the exception of her panties, gave him the access he wanted. He moved his fingers down her back and savored her satiny skin with his rough palms.

Once at the edge of the bed, and he placed her on the cool comforter and held her legs up. He kissed the insides of them as Trish wiggled her way to the center of the bed. He drew his lips down her body. Her scent filled his nostrils as he pressed his tongue against the fabric covering her moist opening. He groaned, willing his desire to slow while he worked to bring her pleasure.

Denver pressed his lip around her still covered bud. Her hips instantly lifted. He alternated lightly pinching and then licking her.

Trish shuddered when his mouth completely covered her. His tongue slipped beneath the fabric, pushing it aside and inside of her. She rolled her hips meeting each suckle. When she peaked, he moved above her, pulling her panties completely down her legs.

Once rid of her pesky fabric, Denver filled her completely. His thrusts began hard and fast and didn't wane until they both fell over the edge.

Once he regained strength, he led Trish to the bathroom. Together, they washed each other. He'd had every intention of leaving her to her writing after they'd finished. But once they left the shower, their flame reignited. Both ended up back in her bed. This time, he took his time loving her. He caressed and kissed every inch of her body. She returned the favor, sending him on a sensuous journey. When he finally entered her, they moved with a precision that, by far, was their best lovemaking ever.

Like before, Denver didn't want to leave her but he had early morning chores.

"What time will you come today, babe?"

"After I make my final posting at Evans Library. About midmorning."

He hugged her close. "Okay, I'll see you soon, my love."

"See you soon."

"I Love you." He released her and dropped his hat on top of his head.

"I love you. Be safe."

"That I can do, but only for you."

****

By the time daybreak arrived, he was ready to see Trish again. He watched a game on a sports network channel but didn't pay attention to a single play. His mother prepared Sunday dinner as she'd always done. They rarely had company but now that Trish would be over, she went overboard.

"You're not feeding an army, Mom."

Traditionally, he would finish his chores by sunrise, watch a football or whatever available game on at the time; often times, the game watch him, and in the evening, he fed the animals and put out fresh water.

After a night of sweet loving, they would cuddle up and watch television. In the weeks after Trish became a usual insertion into their lives, she arrived at the ranch by midmorning.

In that time, she had delivered three of four new foals. She'd also taken a short break to go home before she had to be back and ready for in the fall semester of her final year.

He had yet to go home with her as he'd promised but they made plans for late November.

He grew nervous in the week prior to their pending trip. He'd talked to her parents often but not to any of her brothers. From what she had told him, they were overly protective.

All three were married and had children but Trish was the princess. He teased her one night as they made love.

She lay face down while he straddled her from behind. "I bet your brothers would break my neck if they saw me on top of you this way, wouldn't they?"

He lightly pinched her bottom, forcing her to growl his name. With all the jesting, he pretended to be afraid. But by the end of their interlude, he confessed that he would protect her from any man, including her brothers.

The new herd had adjusted well and his entire crew was once again fully engaged. When the day finally arrived to drive to New Orleans, he left his overseer specific orders.

As they pulled into the city, he felt an instant kinship. Every place they stopped, people spoke to them. Men grabbed his hand and gave it a hardy shake.

Once they arrived at her parents' house, he realized the magnitude of her family's wealth. He knew Trish didn't love him because of money. He had his own wealth. Seeing her here made him wonder how she'd adjusted to Texas living so easily.

"We're good?" She leaned over and kissed him. It was their saying every time they approached a challenge.

"We're good, baby. I got you."

"Okay, let's go meet the parents."

"I'm ready." It was a lie but he had to tell himself he was ready anyway. He would do anything for Trish. It started here and today.

CHAPTER 25

Trish rolled her window down once they'd reached the Garden District and ducked her head through the window. She inhaled the air, reacquainting herself with the scent. She knew it well, like the back of her hand. She'd squirmed in her seat the moment they crossed the causeway and took the 610 bypass. She kept looking between the familiar surroundings and Denver.

"Home, Den. This is my home."

She smiled broadly, hoping he felt the same excitement. They'd made these plans months ago because he needed time to make arrangements at the ranch.

This weekend was Bayou Classic season. If she had to cut off one of her legs and leave it as ransom with her professor, she was coming to Bayou Classic.

She nearly bolted from her seat the moment the gate opened and Denver pulled their rented SUV into the circular drive. She didn't wait until the car was in park before she unsnapped the seatbelt. Lord forbid, she would rot away if she had to wait until he walked around the car to open her door. She leaped forward when her mother exited the house.

"Mommy!" she shrieked.

Trish wrapped her arms around her mother tight and squeezed extra hard. Her mother's hugs were exactly the same, full of love, comfort and very addicting. Trish had not realized how special they were until she moved to Texas.

"My baby. Look at you. My god, I'm so glad you're here."

"I missed you, too, Mom."

They hugged a while longer until her mother's arms loosened around her. Diane pulled away and looked up.

"And who is this handsome young man?"

Trish knew full well she was grinning like a cat. She held her hand out to Denver and he slowly approached. His eyes centered on her and then moved to her mother.

"Mommy, this is Denver Baldwin. Den, Mom in the flesh."

"Come here, son. It's good to finally meet you in person. My, you're handsome."

Denver shyly entered her mom's embrace. He pecked her cheek before they parted.

"It's a pleasure, Mrs. Brooks. Thank you for your hospitality."

"Nonsense. We're happy to have you. Come on in, you two. Let's get something cool to drink."

Trish entered the house and paused. She swiped her hand across the banner of the stairwell.

"You guys go on. I want to go upstairs really quick."

She didn't wait for their approval. Instead, she ran up the stairs like a ten-year-old, burst through the door of her room. She immediately jumped into her bed. She rolled around on it a few times, enjoying her memory-foam mattress. Sitting up, she looked around as if she was seeing it for the first time. She caught her image in the tall mirror and waved.

"Home." She sang.

"Trish?" Her father called from the bottom of the stairs. She bolted down the stairs like a little kid and when she reached the second to last step, she leaped into her father's arms.

"Daddy!"

She inhaled his woodsy cologne and closed her arms and eyes tight.

"Hey baby. Welcome home."

He placed her on her feet and looked down into her face. His smile was warm, reassuring. That was why she loved him so. He'd been the best dad a girl could have. Tears rose to the surface but she took a big breath and smiled instead of releasing them.

"You know you're being rude, leaving your guest down here while you're upstairs in that room of yours. I know that's where you were, right?"

She hung her head. "Yes, sir. But only for a minute. I really miss home."

"I bet you do. Come on. Let's go put Denver at ease. I swear he looks like he's ready to bolt."

He chuckled and placed his arm around her shoulder.

"You're not being mean to him, are you Daddy?"

"Of course not. I actually like him. And it would seem that he's been taking care of my little girl. You look great, sweetheart."

"Thank you, Daddy. I do think you're bias though. This hair and these nails? I really need some TLC."

She pulled at the ponytail flipped over her shoulder and held out her hands. She'd taken to doing her own since time for pampering was rare. She couldn't wait to get to the salon. She'd notified Brandi before she left

Texas. They had appointments tomorrow.

"You look fine to me, little princess. Besides, I'll leave the torturing to your brothers. You know those three."

"Daddy, please talk to them. I don't want them practicing on Denver. He's really not the type."

"They'll be fine," he said as they entered the kitchen.

She caught a whiff of the gumbo on the stove and her stomach growled. They'd only stopped once to gas up. She hadn't wanted to waste time getting home. She looked at Denver who seemed to be waiting on her. She pulled from her dad's embrace and walked straight into his. She gave him a reassuring squeeze. She could feel the tension in body. She recognized that look; the look that said something was bothering him. She looked at him but she spoke directly to her mother.

"It smells wonderful in here, Mommy."

"Just wanted to make sure I had your favorites. And, of course, we wanted to make sure Denver didn't miss Texas too much."

He smiled. Her comment seemed to put him at ease. His hold on her back eased.

The four of them sat at the kitchen counter, ate gumbo and talked. Denver told them about his ranch and his plans to expand. Her dad nodded as Denver talked and offered to give him advice should he want it.

. "Thank you, Mr. Brooks. I'll certainly take you up on your offer."

They shook hands. "You bet."

"Well, I know you guys had a long ride. So, I'll show Denver to his room to freshen up and relax for a little while."

"Thanks, I'll do the kitchen while…"

"No, I got that. You can go get settled in as well. The gang will be over in a couple of hours, okay?" Her mom touched her face softly.

"I got the bags." Denver stood.

Trish propped her elbows on the counter, resting her head in her hand. Her father waited until Denver and her mom had left the room before he spoke.

"How are you doing, sweetheart."

"Good. I have until summer, and then I should be pretty much done."

"Pretty much?"

"I have to decide where I want to practice."

There was a short silence. She hadn't talked to her parents about where she would end up. At one point, she'd worried that Denver would pressure her but he hadn't said a single word. She felt torn. She loved home. It was where her family lived.

But since meeting Denver, she couldn't imagine her life without him. It was almost a given that leaving the ranch was not an option. He would kiss her tenderly and tell her not to worry. She would know when it was time for her decision.

"Have you narrowed your choices?"

"I have, but the jury is still out."

"I see. Does this decision have anything to do with Denver, if I may ask?"

She nodded. "It has a part. But I don't know Daddy. We're still new. I love him. I love the kind of man he is and he treats me very well."

"Like my princess?"

"Yes, sir."

He nodded again and reached for her hand. He raised it to his lips and planted a fatherly kiss on her knuckles. She rewarded him with a smile.

"Do what will make you happy, honey. I've taught all of my children to have a mind of their own. Most importantly, I've taught you all to always love one another and family, yes?"

"Yes, Daddy, you have. I'm so grateful for such loving and supportive parents."

"You make it easy. So, follow your heart. But be smart about it, you hear me?"

"Yes, sir."

She moved around the counter and hugged him then walked up to her room. Denver had deposited her luggage by the door. She was not sure which room he occupied but decided she would find out later. She stepped into the shower and then climbed into bed after pulling a T-shirt over her head. The soft tap on her door stirred her. Her mother peered in.

"Hi."

"Hi, you must have been exhausted."

"Yes, but Denver should have been too. He did all the driving."

"Yeah, I think he just walked out to the garden. Your brothers and their families will be here soon."

Trish grinned. All of her brothers were married and had children. The last time she saw them was Easter. She could only imagine how much the kids had grown since then. She kicked her feet over the side of the bed and stood.

"I'll be down in a minute."

"Okay, dear. Don't be long."

Trish got ready quickly and stopped in the kitchen and swiped a meatball from the crock pot. Moving to the patio door, she watched Denver from behind. His hand brushed across several of her mother's rose bushes. He squatted then looked back as if he knew she was watching. She walked across the lawn. He stood when she got near.

Without words, he captured her mouth. His moan was audible. He feasted for a long moment and she allowed it. She imagined her mother watching from the kitchen window and that was okay. He didn't try to grope her or anything that might be disrespectful. When he pulled away, she instantly felt the lost. The last couple of days had been so busy preparing for this trip, that they'd not made love all week. How she wished she could have him right now.

"Rested." He devoured her with his eyes.

"I love you."

"I know. I love you."

"How about I give you a tour?"

"Lead the way."

And she did. They walked pass the expanded garden with the huge gazebo in the center, down to the lake and ended up at the spot where her brothers had brought their girlfriends--now wives--when they wanted to make out away from prying eyes.

"What's this place?"

"It's formally known as the shaded tree."

Denver looked up at the massive oak draped with green and gray moss. When he looked back at her she asked, "So what do you think?"

"It definitely provides shade."

"No, you don't get it yet, but you will."

She shoved her hands beneath his T-shirt and moved her fingers across his skin until they moved up his back. She pressed herself against the bulge she expected to be there, and it was. She kissed her way up his neck until she reached his bottom lip. There, he met her at the middle of this dance, pressing her hips into him. He broke away from their kiss.

"We're at your parents. Your father will snap me in

two."

"There's a reason why this is called the shaded tree, Den."

"Ah, I see."

He lifted a brow and then picked up where they'd left off. His hands cupped her behind and Trish lifted her legs and wrapped them around his waist. He held her firmly against his rock-hard erection. His jersey shorts clung to his hips. She tried her best to work them down.

She'd been so lost in the heat of their exchange that she did not hear Trae calling her name. Denver did and immediately pulled away. He lowered her to the ground.

"Shoot!" she spat, breathless.

She'd never interrupted any of them when they'd been on their own escapades. She looked up at Denver and shook her head. Straightening her clothes, they walked away from their hiding place. A few steps more and she saw Traekin coming up the path. She dropped Denver's hand and reached to hug her brother.

"Hey, sweet-pea. What are you doing out here?"

She pulled away. "As if you didn't know."

"I'm telling Momma."

"You better not." She punched him.

"Trae, this is Denver. Babe, this is my brother, Traekin."

"Nice to meet you, man." They exchanged a handshake.

"Come, the gang is waiting for you."

When they got to the garden, Travis and Michael were deep in conversation. She leaped forward with a yelp as she greeted Michael first. She saved the last hug for her favorite brother in the whole wide world. Everyone knew and accepted it, probably because he was the oldest.

"Come here, pumpkin."

He swung her around and she held tight. He landed a loud kiss to her cheek.

"I've missed you."

She gazed into his face with delight. "I've missed you."

She turned to make introductions. "This is Denver Baldwin." She reached for his hand. "These are my brothers Michael and Travis."

"Denver," Michael and Travis said in unison with a nod.

Travis turned to her. "The kids are waiting to see their TeeTee. Why don't you go on in while we have a little chat with my man, Denver?"

Trish looked from her brothers to Denver, and then back to Travis, shaking her head. "No. Play nice, please."

"We will. It's good. We gotcha."

She looked into Denver's eyes. He nodded. She started to leave but turned back. "Don't be out too long. Mom has dinner waiting."

All three of her brother nodded and held up their hands. She took one last look at Denver and headed into the house. She peeked out of the window but was distracted yet again, this time by her oldest nephew Christopher.

"TeeTee! Where have you been?"

CHAPTER 26

Denver pulled up to his full height the moment Travis stepped closer. Dude was as big as two linebackers twined together. He stood his ground and refused to coward down. They locked eyes. Had he met Travis in a dark alley, alone, Denver would have gone the other way.

But this was Trish's brother, her protector probably all of her life. Now she was his, which meant time out for old dude. Travis couldn't be much older than he was, still, if he had to out run him, he could. Denver waited for the first move. It wasn't his to make. He had nothing to prove.

"So, man, I don't understand what my little sister sees in you. Why are you here?"

Denver tilted his head at Travis in defiance without a word. He wasn't about to respond to that. He waited for more and didn't have to wait long. Travis took another step forward, so Denver shifted his position, just in case he had to defend himself. He couldn't imagine that Travis would pick a fight with everyone else just yards away in the house.

He thought about it for a moment. The operative word was 'in the house.' He'd wrestled with bulls before but he wasn't about to do that here.

"Obviously he was interested in that shaded tree." Trae added.

Denver shot him a side glance but watched the biggest one still standing in Denver's space. He pressed his lips together, trying to control his temper. If he'd had sisters, he'd be on defense as well. He just wanted to keep his head, to be cool. He thought about Trish. What would it do to them if he fought her brothers?

"What were you doing with my little sister in the damn bushes?" Travis hounded him.

It was his turn. He took a step forward.

"Man, what I do with your sister, my woman, is my business. Not yours."

Travis towered over him and there was no place to go but back. But the other two had moved in as well, he noticed. He wasn't going back down. He might get his ass kicked, but it wasn't like it hadn't happened before.

He closed his hands into tight fists, contemplating who he would punch first because somebody was going to get a lick if he was going down. All three were big dudes. Had he met them on his territory, one on one, he figured he would best each of them, especially the big one. He narrowed his gaze.

"You know we can kick your ass right now?" Michael sneered.

Denver glanced his way. Yes, Michael was the smallest of the bunch. He would get the first lick, mainly because he opened his damn big mouth.

"Yeah, you might."

Denver looked back at Travis who had dropped his head forward. Travis stepped back and lifted his head, wearing a big-ass grin. The other two standing on either side grabbed him in a tight hug. All three laughed. Denver eventually joined in. Travis gave him a bear hug.

"Man, we were just messing with you. You stood your ground. You would have gotten messed up pretty bad, but man, anybody willing to take our ass-whipping for my little sister is alright with me."

He held out his hand. Denver accepted it. Then Denver noticed a brand on his right forearm. Damn! This dude was a frat. He initiated the ritual hand shake that confused them all. Michael stepped in next and exchanged the ritual, followed by Trae.

"Damn, man! Speak."

Denver smiled before he stated his credentials.

"Aw, hell. Trish didn't tell us this. You're alright." Michael slapped him on his back and grabbed his shoulders, pushing him towards the house.

"Come on, let's get some grub. Welcome to the Brooks' house."

Relief washed over Denver as Michael led him into the house.

They could hear the chatter before the door opened, but when Denver walked in the room quieted. He met Trish's worried eyes. She physically slumped when he smiled at her. Holding a beautiful little girl by the hand, she walked up to him.

"Everyone, this is Denver. I'll let everyone introduce themselves because there are too many. Don't worry," she said to Denver, "you're not going to remember all the names."

She was right. There were names he would never remember. He tried to recall the kids' name because he loved children. But when he called Trevon, Chris, they were all ready to correct him.

"I'm Chris, Uncle Denver."

The endearment shocked him from the little guy who was the spitting image of his father. Denver smiled, touching the top of Chris' head.

"You're Chris. And you are Trevon."

The kids cheered. He could get used to this. He realized that he was not only the center of attention for the kids, but when he glanced up, Trish's mother, Diane, was watching him as well. She winked at him as he talked to the children.

Denver ate so much he couldn't move. He'd heard about the New Orleans food and hospitality. Sure enough, the Brooks family lived up to the reputation. After dinner, going to the basement for a jam session was a ritual that blew him away. Trish hadn't lied. Her family, her entire family, kids included, participated in more than an hour's worth of music extravaganza.

When everyone left, he stood behind Trish, arms circling her waist.

"Can I walk you to your room?"

"How about the shaded tree?"

"I already just about got my ass kicked because of you and your shameful tree."

"Does that mean you're scared?"

"No. I want to make sure I make it back to Texas with all of my body parts."

"Yea, you're scared."

She turned in his embrace and kissed him lightly.

"I can find my own way, thank you. Remember I'm headed out early to the spa in the morning. You're sure you will be okay?"

"Of course. If I could survive the likes of your giant-ass brothers, then I can make it."

"I hope they weren't too bad."

"Trust me, they tried. And why didn't you tell me they were my frats?"

"You boys have a way of wanting to find things out yourselves. But trust me, that's not why they like you."

"Then why?"

She draped her hands over his shoulders. "You're a good man, and I'm crazy in love with you."

"Humph. That's not what you said a few days ago."

"Let's walk to the tree and I'll show you just how much."

Trish moved his hands up the sides of her mini sundress. As she drew his hands higher, he realized that she didn't have on panties. He instantly stirred.

"You have my attention."

"Let's go and see what magic is under that tree."

She led the way, quietly closing the door behind them.

CHAPTER 27

Trish sidestepped the paved walkway and took a path she knew well. She and her high school boyfriend, Greg, used to take it whenever they snuck off from the group. They moved to the heavy foliage but never went very far. Except one night when they decided to go all the way. She wanted to make sure no one heard them.

This was how she'd discovered the shaded tree. At the time, Michael was under it, fully in the throws with Denise. They weren't married at the time. And of course, she and Greg didn't do as planned because Michael caught them rustling in the bushes. He promised to skin her hide but he could never act on it, for fear she would tell on him.

"I'm a grown-ass man, Trish, he'd said at the time.

"I'm still telling."

When she and Denver reached their destination, she slipped the straps from her shoulders and moved her dress to bare her breasts and hips. It was dark, but she could feel his breath on her face.

"Oh, baby, I need you. Right now, Den."

He lifted her off of her feet. Her legs circled him as he guided his erection to her opening. And when the tip entered, she gasped.

"Promise me you will be quiet."

When she didn't answer, he repeated, "Promise, Trish."

"Yes," she answered drugged by him, wanting more of him.

With her thighs over his arms, she held on as he pumped in and out of her. He moved her up and down with his arms, some long, slow strokes and then a short burst of quick ones. She could feel her orgasm but didn't want it to end yet. She had no control. She held him tighter as the fire burst through her in elation.

She squeezed her muscles around him and he pulled away from her mouth, clamping his lips against her shoulder. He grunted as he lowered her, adjusting his own weight to avoid tumbling over. They clung together until their breathing returned to normal.

"This tree is magical."

"Told you so."

The following day everyone huddled beneath open-side tents, enjoying the delicious aroma from the grills, and live music filled the air around them. Trish stood in a group of her girlfriends when Greg, her high school boyfriend, walked up and wrapped his arms around her.

"Hey, darling. I'd hoped to see you here."

"Greg," Trish tried to push him away, but he held her tighter. She saw Denver out of the corner of her eye and tried even more to move from Greg's grasp. Trae and Michael trailed behind Denver.

"Ah, Greg, this is my boyfriend, Denver." She reached for Denver's hand, but still Greg didn't release her.

"Hey man, what's up." Greg smirked.

Michael and Trae walked around them and pulled Greg away. "How about we do a little talking, Greg?"

"Sure, I've been meaning to talk to you, Mike."

"Okay, let's do it."

She turned and looked up at Denver when the three walked away, he stepped back and returned to the chair he'd vacated earlier. He was distant the rest of the weekend. His attitude hadn't improved, even after they'd packed up the car for their trip back to Texas.

Denver wasn't feeling Greg's over-friendly gestures. He didn't buy, "that's just the way we do it here in Nawlins, bae," when she tried to explain his actions. In fact, Denver was still a little salty about the whole thing. He wouldn't show his displeasure while around her family, but he hadn't touched her since they left her parent's house.

"Would you like me to help drive."

"I got it." He glanced out of the side mirror. "I thought you had some studying to do."

Code-word, shut up and let me have my peace. She decided to let him stew most of the ride back. When she couldn't hold her bladder any longer, she asked him to make a stop. And when he pulled into her parking lot of her apartment complex, she didn't say anything. She'd thought that they would go back to the ranch. He needed to return the car in the morning anyway.

He brought her bags in and sat them by the laundry room. He pulled her close, kissed her and he was almost out the door when she stopped him.

"Den, are you going to stay mad at me?"

"I'm not mad, Trish."

"What's wrong?"

"Baby, I'm exhausted. We both have long days tomorrow."

"All of what you said is true. But your behavior says something totally different."

Silence. She stepped back and pulled the door open for him. He turned and walked past her.

"Be careful, I love you."

"I love you. I'll call you tomorrow."

"Okay."

She closed the door. She'd peeled away every stitch of clothing by time she made it to the shower. She climbed into bed and pulled the covers over her head. She was too blue to do any studying. She'd just drifted off when her phone chimed. She lifted it to her ear without looking at the display. She was supposed to call home to let her family know she'd made it but forgot.

"Open the door, please."

She dropped the phone without replying. She took her time pulling back the locks. For some reason they clicked extra loud. When she pulled the door open he was leaning against the jam. He stretched to his full height and looked down at her with weary eyes.

Seeing him so rundown broke her heart. Trish reached for him, pulling until they were fully behind a closed door. He moved like a rag doll.

"I'm sorry."

She waited.

He reached into his pocket and pulled out a box. Denver held it loosely between his fingers. He cupped her face with his other hand.

"Sorry, I got a little high strung."

She wanted to say really? Instead she kept her mouth shut, mostly because she wanted to know what was in that box.

"I guess I'd taken possession before I'd been officially given the permission."

He lifted the box again. She wondered what he was rattling on about. She was equally concerned about the contents of the box. He had yet to tell her.

"I don't want any man, touching what's mine. I'm clear about that, Trish. And you brushing it off really ticked me the hell off."

All the pauses made her antsy but she tried hard to not blurt out her thoughts. Denver could be deep and profound at times. He liked taking his time. This was one of them.

"But after thinking about it, I had no say. This fool thought he was within his rights." He held up his hand. "Don't say anything, Trish, please."

Clamping her lips shut, she just watched him.

"He thought he was within his rights, having known you before. But had you been my wife, he would have never gotten the idea that it was okay."

He held up the box again and placed it in her hand. They shook. Her entire body shook after hearing words like mine and wife.

"I already talked to your father, asked him for his blessings. My intent was to propose to you while we were with your family, but, you see, my love, I let my rage blind me to the opportunity to make this proposal special. Because, had I done this earlier, the evening would have turned out differently. For that, I'm sorry."

She stood with the box in one hand and the other covering her mouth to keep her sobs at bay. He bent on one knee and reached for her hand.

"Trish, would you please make my life richer by becoming my wife? I promise I will do whatever I can to make you happy. And I know that may mean leaving Baldwin Ranch behind."

CHAPTER 28

Yes, he had been out of sorts, unusual for him and his normal, unruffled personality. Perhaps, because of the unfamiliar surroundings, with strangers. He'd had a grand plan, one that went straight to hell with his over-reaction. But he was determined to make amends.

His worn body dropped to one knee, waiting on her response. Her tears said a lot. Still, he needed to hear the words from her lips. He hadn't expected to gain her father's permission so easily, but Alvin had shared the conversation he'd had with Trish about her torment in deciding where she would be in a year's time.

Alvin Brooks told him that he wanted Trish to be happy. He gave his instant approval. Denver didn't take his agreement lightly. He'd watched Trish and her Dad's special interaction. He had big shoes to fill.

"Please, darling, put me out of my misery," he begged. "Yes."

She met his lips as he stood. He took the box from her hand and placed the triangle-cut diamond on her delicate left finger. He closed the loop around her once more, savoring her warmth.

"I promised your father we would face-time him when it was official. It's late tonight but we'll do it in the morning. Is that okay?"

"Yes." Her voice quivered.

"We're good?"

"Better than good."

He chuckled before he kissed her fully. "Your man is roasted."

"Let's get you in the shower and then to bed."

"Are we cleaning and then sleeping?"

"I thought your tail was exhausted?"

He grinned and allowed her to lead him to the bathroom. She didn't join him but he took his time, letting the warm spray bring him back to life. She peeked into the bathroom and he beckoned her in, but she left, leaving him to finish on his own. Once done, he climbed into bed behind her but made no attempt to make love. They had cause to celebrate. They snuggled instead.

Just before his alarm chimed, he rose above her, pressing against her legs. Already bare, there were no formalities required.

"Good morning, my love," he whispered into her ear.

She parted her legs, bringing them over the back of his. His entry was quick and steady; his strokes were long and deep. She was already moist and ready. When she groaned into his mouth, he moved his hands to her buttocks and moderated his strokes to slow and easy.

"Yes, love me, Den. I need more."

Offering her what she wanted, he moved even deeper until his world spun out of control. He'd not wanted it that way, to lose control so fast because he hadn't been sure he'd done his job in getting Trish to the same destination.

Her limp body beneath him once he returned from his eclipse said she had. He chastised himself, promising to do better, determined to ensure she got what she needed each time.

Totally satisfied, he rested on his elbows and knees until he could pull away. He gently draped his limbs across her.

"This is what I'm looking forward to the most." He kissed her brow.

"I'm looking forward to breakfast in bed." She countered.

"Baby, you've just been served."

"Very funny. You have to take the car back this morning?"

"It can wait. I have a few things to take care of."

"Anything I can help you with?"

"You already did. What time is your next session?"

She groaned and buried her face in his chest. "I don't want to think about school. I enjoyed my freedom while at home."

He knew Trish was at countdown. In a few weeks, she would have a short vacation. She had to cover the hospital the week following Christmas but at least they had that holiday off together.

"I have early morning session today."

"Just think, you don't have any mucking chores."

"You know what, you're right." She laughed. "I really didn't mind."

"I don't know anybody, myself included, who doesn't mind that damn chore."

Denver knew he was right. He'd like to think that because it gave her a chance to be at the ranch, she didn't mind and did what she thought made him happy.

"In that case, I'll let CR know you'll come by once you

finished your day to clean stalls."

"Dear Sir, you may tell our friend whatever you like. But please believe, when I get there, the only stall I'm mucking is on this body." She kissed him hard. "Come on, Mister. You have things to do. And, this girl right here needs some time to prepare herself for the world today."

"I know it's still early, but first let's call your parents."

"Not looking like this, we won't."

"Then I suggest you hightail it to make yourself presentable. You have ten minutes."

"Wait, it's too early."

"Your dad goes to work at six in morning."

"Oh, he does."

"And, your mom…"

"Is up with him every morning…" She paused

"Ten minutes," he warned.

Trish's mother, Diane, was almost as emotional as Trish. The first question she asked was how long did she have to plan a wedding? The second question was when would she get to meet Beatrice in person?

When Denver reached the ranch, the light of day had just pulled over the horizon. He showered and put on a fresh shirt and denims. Strolling with extra oomph in his step, he stopped at his usual place first, the coffee pot. He was startled to hear his mother's voice behind him.

"How did it go, Den?"

He walked over and planted a kiss on her cheek before hugging her briefly.

"Good morning, Mom. It went better than I thought. You officially have a daughter-in-law to-be."

"Thank God! Congratulations son. She's a good girl."

"I know. Thanks, Mom. I have some stuff to do this morning. You think you can hook me up with a special dinner tonight?"

"I know exactly what I'm going to fix."

"Thanks, Mom. You're the best."

He waltzed into his office and picked up the phone.

CHAPTER 29

Trish extended her left arm and wiggled her fingers. To her delight, the solitaire diamond winked at her. She paused as the implications of what it all meant sank in. Although Denver said that he would go wherever she wanted to, the truth was that the most logical thing to do was to remain in Texas. He'd spent his entire life here, had put all of his sweat and tears into building a successful brand. He was making the hard work his father had sacrificed a legacy to continue.

Lost in thoughts of her future, she didn't hear Butch walk up behind her.

"Morning, Trish. What brings you out so early?"

She'd just walked down the alley that housed all the different kinds of habits in the local mercantile. She'd been to this merchant a dozen times and had not run into Butch. This was the first place she'd met him, and she'd purposely not run into him over the last seven months. This time of day was when most ranchers were at the peak of their work hours, which explained why the warehouse was practically empty.

For her it was the best time of day to pick up equipment and supplies she used. She was already at the opening when he spotted her. There was no place to duck, especially since he saw her before she saw him. She turned slowly and tried to smile.

"Morning, Butch. Funny catching you here this time of day."

He removed his hat. His light eyes were headlined by dark bushy brows. He nodded the way he always did, placing his hat against his chest.

"Ain't seen you around much. Thought you'd given up that foolish notion of being a lady vet and hightailed it back to the city. How you been?"

This is exactly why she couldn't stand this man. He always found the means to rub her the wrong way. She wanted to smack that shit-eating grin off of his face. She censored her anger to a light hint of aggravation. This time she was certain her face had a smile on it because she pulled her lips up as far as she could.

"It's really good seeing you, Butch. Now if you don't mind, I have a chore to complete."

She held up her list and tried to sidestep him. Butch moved the same direction, blocking her passage. Grinning really hard down at her, he stepped closer.

"Been waiting a long time, little lady, for you to hold up your end of the bargain. You promised me a dinner date."

"Sorry, I've extremely busy. You know, that foolish notion as you called it, I'm finishing my residency."

"You still at the hospital?"

"Yes. This is my final year."

"Well, ain't that a lick. You gon' be one of them animal people. Heck, perhaps, you should come on by my place so we can test out your schooling, and all."

"Sorry, Butch, that's not going to happen."

"Why not? It's not like there's plenty of places here to test the waters."

"Trust me, there is."

"Well, still. I think we could become real partners, if you know what I mean."

He reached for her arm, grasping it loosely. When she attempted to pull it free, he grip tightened. She frowned up at the cowboy and the voice behind her made her hair stand on end.

"Butch, unless you want to lose that arm, you better remove your damn hand. Right now."

She saw the transition on Butch's face. Had his eyes been a pistol, Denver would be dead in his tracks. Instead of letting go, he gripped her wrist even tighter. Trish stood between them. She'd been forgotten in the conversation, or should she say, in their stare-down.

Denver moved behind her. Her back now touched his chest and his arms circled her waist. For the first time since knowing him, the energy radiating from him was frightening. She glanced up into his dark face. She instantly knew there was a problem between him and Butch. And although his eyes spoke of danger, the reassuring squeeze from the arm around her soothed the anxiety she didn't quite understand.

His eyes touched her briefly, and then went straight to Butch. The thought of fists crossing--with her in the middle-- unnerved her. But the rumbling in Denver's chest added concern to the mix.

"I'm not going to tell you again."

And in that instant, Butch released her arm and stepped back. Placing his hat on his head, he tilted it in her direction.

"See you around, Trish."

Trish dared not utter a single word. Instead she glanced at the hard lines in Denver's face. She hadn't said anything in the whole exchange between them and almost didn't say anything now for fear those thorns would be turned on her. Still curious about what had just happened, she turned in his arms.

"What was that about?"

"You had a list to get to, right?"

Ignoring her, Denver moved away, leading her by the arm. He held out his other hand for the list. When she didn't quickly comply, he stopped and stared into her face.

"Butch is not someone you should deal with. Not now. Not ever," he said through clenched teeth.

"Why? I can take care of myself, Denver."

He didn't say a word before turning. A heaviness settled between them. She didn't know how or why, but indifference crept between them. Finally he said, "Fine."

He stalked away. There was no embrace or kiss or goodbye. She watched his rigid back until he crossed another alley in the huge warehouse. She looked both directions each man had taken. Huffing, she journeyed back to where she'd been heading before that all started.

When she was done with her list and it was packed in the back of the hospital's hauling truck, she slammed the door hard and headed back to the clinic. Her team, for the rest of the shift, evaluated a herd with colic. The supplies she'd picked up were meant to treat the animals. They suspected that maybe the horses had eaten moldy hay or something else they shouldn't have.

The animals arrived from a nearby ranch where the owner complained that the horses showed signs of extreme bloating. They had rolled, and in some cases, laid down. It wasn't a good sign.

She thought about Denver's animals. They hadn't suffered any major ailment since she stepped foot on the ranch. The hands tended to them extremely well. The foals she'd delivered were doing great.

Carefully, her mask in place, she measured a sedative for the one horse in the group diagnosed with tapeworms. Her gloved hand gently patted the horse's back. He'd lost so much weight that she could see his bones.

"Don't worry, big guy. You will feel better in no time," she cooed in the animal's ear.

Thoughts of Denver lingered, but she couldn't slow down to call or to drown in self-pity. She didn't understand how she continued to misbehave when it came to a difference of opinions between them.

She didn't give a rat's ass about Butch. Didn't he know had he not interfered, she would have put Butch in his place? She pulled off her glove and looked down at her ring finger once again. She'd been on her own since she arrived in Texas. After breaking free from her father and brothers telling her what to do, she was about to enter another relationship where she had to listen to a man.

She was on a different mindset. Was this worth the ride? She'd been ready to make a fresh start, on her own, before he waltzed into her heart.

CHAPTER 30

Every time he and Trish took two steps forward, it didn't take long before they were forced to take three steps back. He'd realized early that she was strong-willed and stubborn. He didn't have the heart to change her. However, he found himself taking more steps back to keep the peace than he cared to. He'd not had to deal with a woman who was hell bent on following her own mind. She hadn't challenged his manhood, she just challenged everything else.

Admittedly, they'd had far more good times than challenges. He didn't need her to be submissive but things--and people like Butch--were unbendable. He loved her. He had promised her father to protect her.

And the one person he'd damn sure protect her from was Butch Monroe, even if it killed him.

Butch had already ruined someone he'd cared about. Breaking his neck back then would have been a service to mankind, but it wasn't meant to be. Denver's action at the time wouldn't have stopped Maria from driving head-on, into an eighteen-wheeler. She would not have recovered and Butch had been the cause.

While rape and an unplanned pregnancy wasn't the end of the world, Maria had chosen death.

It broke his and her family's hearts and took years to recover from. It was the reason he'd originally wanted to leave Texas. His father's falling health pulled him back. He took his responsibility to heart and drowned out the pain of remember Maria or seeing the likes of Butch Monroe.

He shook himself physically. He couldn't spend his time or energy thinking about Butch. As for his fiancé, he would call her as soon as he got a break. He had to tell her to stay away from Butch. He hated thinking about what might have happened had he not come along. He'd gone to the dry goods store to pick up last-minute supplies.

When got back to the ranch and unloaded everything, he went straight to his office to print the documents Ankit had sent him earlier. He made a second copy and placed them both in a pouch.

Things were coming along nicely. He smiled, thoughts of Butch dismissed. He concentrated on his arriving visitors.

Denver had partnered with another rancher in a futurity agreement. The incentive was designed to promote a particular breed of horse. In the last batch he'd acquired, he made out with forty or more Hackney. He intended to use them for backbreaking. The distinctive high-stepping, light-harness horse would bring a premium from show-horse buyers across the country. The Dexter's ranch would bring several Quarter stallions to the ranch for backbreaking with his mares.

CR and a dozen other men roped off an area to corral a set of broodmares on one end of the paddock. The selected Hackneys would be on the other end. The partner and a few of Dexter's ranch-hands were expected to arrive in a couple of hours. Denver gave his last-minute instructions just before Juanita Dexter and her men arrived.

She stepped down from the black F-150 looking like a runway model. Her long thick wavy curls danced in the wind. Her fitted denim shirt with sleeves rolled up to the elbow and the tail tucked into snug worn jeans, and she wore hugged nipped-toed, snakeskin boots. Lean, tall, and beautiful, her forty-plus years would put any twenty-something to shame.

Removing delicate fingers from her work gloves, she extended them to Denver. A smile as bright as a flawless diamond twinkled at him.

"Denver, so great to see you again."

He accepted her hand. It felt as soft as silk. She almost met him at eye level. He admired her flawless face covered with a hint of makeup.

"Juanita, welcome to Baldwin. Can I get you and your men some refreshments?"

"I'm anxious to see what you have. Why don't we do that afterwards?"

"Sure. That works for me."

With a side glance, he watched how Juanita eyed him. He chose to ignore it. He put CR between them, letting him explain the details they had in mind for the stallions and mares. Every now and again, she would glance around CR.

They were just about finished with the pairing selection. Denver leaned against the fence with one foot propped up. Juanita moved and stood next to him, their shoulders almost touching. She tilted her head as she spoke.

"You know, Denver, we would make a powerhouse. Baldwin and Dexter's ranches together? Not to mention we would make some awfully beautiful children."

Her comment caught him completely off guard. He was ready to step away when Trish waltzed over. He heard her speak to the others and her gait slowed when both he and Juanita turned around. What he saw in her eyes stole his heart. He instantly moved and met her halfway. He leaned down and captured her lips, not giving her a chance to speak.

"Hi, baby."

She glanced up, her eyes searching his. He smiled. She looked past him, and directly at Juanita. Clumsily, he turned, reaching for her hand.

"Babe, this is Juanita Dexter, from the Dexter Ranch on South Bend. Juanita, this is my fiancée, Trisha Brooks."

Juanita lifted an eyebrow as she pushed from the fence and held out a hand to Trish. He felt a shift of energy from Trish.

"It's a pleasure to meet you, Trisha." She batted her eyes at him before she continued. "Denver and I are going to make great partners, aren't we?"

He squeezed Trish's hand, looking at her and not making the mistake of glancing Juanita's way.

"She's right. We have one of the best chances of cornering the market with this pedigree."

He pointed to the stallions from Dexter's ranch. He glanced at Juanita, who seemed to enjoy this awkward situation. While she seemed delighted, Trish looked fit to be tied.

Trish moved toward a stallion, lifting her hand to the black forelock. She whispered something in its ear that caused him to bob his head up and down. She passed her hand down his stripe, holding her hand in front of its nostril to let him become familiar with her scent. She patted his neck before turning back to them.

"This is a great animal. Aren't you boy?"

She gave him another strong pat.

"Trish, you seemed to be really good with horses."

Juanita walked around her and touched the horse from the other side. They seemed to watch each other. The seconds drew into eternity to Denver. He, too, moved forward.

"Trish is our resident equine vet," he offered as if to break the static in the air.

Trish gave him a disapproving glance before she stepped away.

"Is that right? Perhaps, I'll have you come by and check my herd."

Trish headed back to Lightning. She didn't pause but glanced back at Denver.

"Sure. Your partner knows how to reach me."

Denver groaned inwardly. He watched her stick a foot in a stirrup. As her rump hit the saddle, she slapped the spurs into Lightning's side and he took off. Trish lowered her upper body close to his neck. That made it easy for them to gallop away at high speed. They kicked up dust as woman and horse disappeared.

CR strolled up next to him, looking in the same direction.

"Oh, boy." CR looked at Denver and then in the direction Trish and Lightning had gone.

"Yep," Denver muttered under his breath. He then turned back to Juanita and put on his best cowboy smile.

It took a little more than two hours to finalize the visit. He and Juanita signed both sets of documents. One he gave to her. The other he would give back to Ankit to file. His friend should have been there. It would have saved Denver from witnessing the encounter between Trish and Juanita.

He opened her truck door as she climbed in. She gave him a saucy smile. With a wink, she placed her hand on his.

"I mean it, Denver. Change your mind, let me know."

"Trust me, Juanita, I have someone who makes me happy."

"If you say so."

"I do. We'll talk again soon."

"Sure thing."

He waited until her truck and the empty trailer disappeared up the road then strolled through the kitchen door. He walked into the midst of a laughing fit between Trish and his mother. They covered their mouths, turned their heads and continued to snicker.

"What are you two up to?"

He looked from one to the other. Trish's smile faded when he looked at her. She placed the kitchen towel down on the countertop.

"I guess I'll head out."

"Head out where? I thought we were going to have dinner?"

"We've already had dinner. Yours is in the oven."

His mother dropped her towel on top of Trish's and headed for the den. She briefly hugged Trish.

"I'll talk to you tomorrow, sweetie."

It was supposed to be a celebration dinner, the three of them. Denver hadn't expected the business with Juanita to take so long, but it was something that couldn't be rushed. He blamed Ankit. Had he been here, he could have taken care of things.

"Wait Trish, we need to talk."

He tried to pull her close. She backed away.

CHAPTER 31

As Denver reached for her Trish escaped his hand. She didn't want his stale glances. He'd given Juanita Dexter all of his attention. He'd coerced her here by making a big deal about celebrating over a special dinner. She'd rushed only to arrive and find him rubbing shoulders with another ranch owner. Had she known she needed to dress the part, hell, she would have dressed better.

She had to admit, she was inexperienced. Lately, she'd been lucky to garner a man's attention. She wore faded denims, top and bottoms, secondhand boots, no makeup, and her hair was generally pulled back into a ponytail. The only living creatures interested in her of late were the horses and Professor Jones's eleven-year-old mutt, Jasper.

She was a hot mess, both physically and emotionally. When had she let herself go? Back in New Orleans, she wouldn't dare leave the house without makeup or a stylish designer outfit. She visited the salon every week and shopped for a new outfit every week as well. None of that worked here. No one cared. Besides, she'd ruined more clothes and shoes than she cared to admit. So she conformed to her environment and now look at her.

Trish caught a glimpse of her reflection in the mirror and cringed. What did Denver see in her? While she enjoyed his love making, she was still learning from him. She had a smart mouth and attitude to frame it all. Compared to the stunning and refined Juanita Dexter, she was a turd.

Juanita was gorgeous, tall, had flawless skin and perfect hair. She was obviously a professional man-stealer. The way the woman gazed into Denver's face, Trish wanted to snatch her hair out. Needless to say, her inexperience put her at a disadvantage. She would be prepared next time.

When he didn't join them for dinner, disappointment rather than anger infused her. Trish understood that in his business there were no standard hours. Some days his work began before daybreak and didn't end until long after sunset. If she didn't understand anything else, she knew from watching her father and brothers that business sometimes got in the way of family. Drawing a balance took effort.

Once Denver's new venture got under way, she prayed things would return to normalcy. He'd brought in more than thirty additional men. This new venture was good for business. Everyone worked to learn their part for now.

"Babe, we really need to talk, especially about today."

"Go talk to your new partner."

She'd almost made it to the door before he caught her. He chuckled as he pulled her close.

"So, is that why you're so salty with me right now?"

"No. I don't care if you make goo-goo eyes at that old woman. She's two days older than dirt," she huffed.

Denver grabbed her by the middle, squeezing her. His head fell back and she felt his laughter bubble through her. When he caught his breath, he placed his forehead against hers.

"Say what? She's not that old."

"You would know, wouldn't you? Don't mind me if you lie in a crypt with that Drac-Juanic-ular. Don't expect me to care. Get off of me, man. I don't have time for you." She pushed against his chest.

"I will always have time for you."

"You didn't today. You were too busy courting that cradle-robber."

"Ms. Dexter is not that old."

"See you called her Ms. I saw all that dam gray hair at her temple. Old biddy."

Her comment made him laugh even harder. He held her tighter and placed his mouth at the base of her neck. He rocked her for a few seconds before he raised his head.

"I love you, Trish." His face grew serious. "I love you because you are my life. I don't have heart for anyone else."

She watched his dancing eyes, trying to find the truth in them. She could feel all the anxiety from earlier simmer to the top again. He frowned.

"I don't want Juanita or anyone else." He pecked her lips. "No one has been able to make my body feel this way."

He closed his lips on hers. She felt his rise, demanding every fiber of her body to respond. She slid her hands up his back and pressed firmly, forgetting Juanita for the time being. He didn't stop until they were panting for air.

"Come on. I still need to talk to you."

She followed him willingly. After that kiss, she would

go anywhere he asked her to. They moved to his office for what she thought would be a steamy interlude. Instead, he pulled her down next to him on the small couch.

"About today, at the mercantile…"

She tried to pull away, but his firm hold drew her closer.

"Wait, darling, please. You have to hear me out before you get upset. I promise you, I would never tell you what to do, which is why I'm asking. Please stay clear of Butch Monroe."

"Den…"

"Just hear me out. You'll understand."

Trish sat, numbed by what he told her. Hearing about Butch made her happy she'd not accepted any of his many requests. After a while he had stopped pursuing her and put his sights elsewhere.

"I'm sorry, honey. Promise me you'll stay clear of him. I don't want to go to Texas prison because of Butch."

She nodded after burying her face into his shirt. "I really do have to head back. I don't have six-thirty mucking duty; however, I do have an early hospital shift."

"I'll walk you to your car."

He stood and threw his arm across her shoulders. Once at her car, he took his time blessing her with a soulful kiss. She didn't want to let go. They'd only made out a few times in his quarters when his mother wasn't home. Trish just wasn't comfortable with the idea otherwise. The few times they enjoyed his bed, Beatrice had been on one of her overnight trips. Of course, she didn't count the dozen or so times they'd ridden out to the pasture together.

She could never look at the brook near the small closet of bushes the same. They'd had many afternoon escapades. He laid her so good that it was hours before either of them could move. They slept naked in the shade, undisturbed as flowing water sang them to sleep. Had it not been dark, that's exactly where she would have asked him to take her.

She snuggled close and when he opened her driver side door, she didn't want to get in. Denver's growling stomach protested. She stood on her toes and kissed him briefly.

"I love you, Denver."

"I love you, my love. Drive carefully. Let me know when you make it home."

"I will."

He stepped back as she started the car.

CHAPTER 32

Denver stood in the moonlight until he could no longer see Trish's car lights. He returned to the kitchen, devoured his supper, and after a short shower, went to bed. Moments before he drifted off, his phone rang. He answered.

"Hey, babe, what took you so long?"

There was a silence and then a click. He glanced at the phone but didn't recognize the number. He considered calling the number back, but a call from Trish interrupted his intention.

"Hi, baby, you make it okay?"

"Yes. You sound beat."

"I am beat but I could still lay down some loving on you." A smile eased across his face with the simple thought.

"Frankly, I think you're all talk, Denver Baldwin."

Trish's sultry voice tapped a nerve that went straight to his rise. He rolled on his back. The sheets grazed him as if it was her gentle touch. Without letting his mind go there, he quickly sat up.

"It's easy to talk smack when you're nearly across the other end of the county."

"Yep, that I can. So what are you going to do about it?"

"Tonight, my love, I'm going to let you talk your way into some stuff."

"Promise?"

"You'll have to wait and see."

"Well, I accept your challenge for now. Get some rest tonight, and I'll see you tomorrow afternoon."

"Sweet dreams. I love you."

"I love you more. Good night."

She disconnected before he could rebut her claim. Trisha Brooks didn't know it yet but he'd walk through hell for her. She'd gotten into his blood and there would be nothing on this earth to keep her from him.

When he woke up the next morning, she was still in his system. He pressed the one key that connected to her number even though it was four in the morning. She answered on the first ring.

"Good morning crazy man."

"I'm only crazy for you. Time to get up."

"For you, not for me. I've got at least another hour. What do you want, man? You've already stolen my dreams."

Denver chuckled. He loved this girl for so many reasons. He looked in the mirror. The grin on his face said a lot of things. He was the happiest he'd ever been.

"I have a dilemma."

"Oh," she replied.

"Yeah, see, I'm missing you this morning."

There was a short pause before she responded. The sweetness of her words would stay with him the rest of the day.

"It won't be long, Den, in a little while you won't have to wake up without me next to you, right?"

He closed his eyes, savoring her words. She was right. He'd hoped to decide on a wedding date last night. He didn't want a long engagement. If he had his way, he would marry her tomorrow. Of course, that wouldn't happen.

Both mothers would have a fit. He didn't want a huge wedding but knew he might not have a say. For him it didn't take much. For her and their mothers, it might be a different story.

"You're right, my love. To be honest, I can't wait for that day." He paused briefly. "Listen, I just needed to hear your voice this morning. Try and go back to sleep. I'll see you later today."

"Okay, I love you."

"Love you, honey."

He dropped the phone into his pocket and continued on with his routine for the day. He had one more meeting with Juanita. This time it would be at Ankit's office. Filling his canteen, he waltzed down to the barn and saddled up Winter. Halfway down the path, to the south end, he met CR and two other hands.

"Hey, boss man, congratulations."

CR held out his hand and moved his horse close enough to grab Denver by the arm.

"Thanks CR. This was your doing."

"I must say, it'll be nice to have another woman around this place."

"Just remember, she belongs to me."

"Uh, yeah. Got that. But you can't stop us from looking at that pretty face."

"Looking is all you will be doing. Now, get to work. I'm not paying you to sit around gabbing about my intended."

He moved on and when it was time to go to Ankit's office, he might as well been dressing up for a wedding. He wore trim-legged denims that snuggly hugged his high polished boots and a neatly iron striped shirt tucked inside. His belt hoops were adorned by the ornate belt his father had given him for graduation.

He moisturized his freshly shaved face and smoothed his sideburns with his index fingers. Satisfied with his appearance, Denver grabbed his gray Stetson and headed for his truck.

"Damn, boy. What you all dolled up for?" Ankit cracked when he waltzed into his conference room.

He intentionally arrived early to make sure they talked before the others arrived. Without responding to his snide remark, Denver slapped the signed documents on the table and slipped into the nearest chair. He wasn't messing with Ankit's shenanigans today.

"Alright, let's see what you've undone." Ankit reached for the folder.

"There are a few changes, but nothing either of us would object to."

"Okay, let's take a look."

They huddled over the papers, discussing the pen and ink changes to the document. It didn't take long for Ankit to clean up the contract and print new ones that all parties would sign. When Ankit went to his office to retrieve the printed copies, Denver took a quick moment to text Trish. The message essentially asked her to be ready in a couple of hours. He would pick her up.

He stood when Juanita, her lawyer, and one of her ranch hands entered the conference room. He shook her hand and pulled back her chair.

"My. You clean up well, Mr. Baldwin."

He watched Juanita appraising his body. He hadn't dressed for her. He planned to take his wife-to-be someplace where they could be alone with no interruptions.

If Juanita wanted to admire his looks, so be it. The only approving eyes he was interested in were Trish's.

"It's great to see you again, Juanita. As always, you look stunning." Denver nodded towards her before he glanced at Ankit, who gave him a sideways smile.

They talked through the changes of their agreement, made the day before. When all the papers were signed and notarized, Juanita stood. All the men at the table stood, too.

"Gentlemen, it's great doing business with you. Now I think this calls for a celebration. How about you all join me for a drink?"

Although she spoke to everyone in the room, her attention centered on Denver. She held his hand much longer than she should have. He pulled away, more swiftly than he intended.

"While your offer sounds enticing, I have another engagement. But please feel free, Ankit, to join them if you wish."

He knew his friend liked socializing, especially if it might bring more business to his firm.

Juanita's next words surprised them all. "Celebrating your engagement, I take it."

Denver looked at the shock in Ankit's face. He'd not had the chance to tell him the news yet. They'd gotten straight down to business, trying to finish up their part before the others arrived. Looking at Juanita, he nodded.

"We have some early planning to complete."

"Don't forget what I said yesterday. My offer still stands."

Although she didn't say what the offer was, everyone in the room seemed to know what she meant. Their gazes all followed her.

"Have a good evening, Juanita. Take care."

When she and her colleagues left, he turned to Ankit and lifted his shoulders.

"Look, man, I wanted to tell you myself."

"What? Your oldest and most loyal friend is the last to know that you've placed a ring on a girl's finger you met six months ago."

"Not exactly."

"By the way, have you guys discussed a pre-nup?"

"Her family is loaded. If there was one to be signed, it just might come from her."

"Loaded, huh?"

"Loaded."

Denver's phone rang. He looked at the number and frowned. It was the same number from last night.

"Baldwin."

He could hear the breathing on the open line but nothing else. He clicked the end button.

"Wrong number?"

"Don't know. It's the second call."

They talked for a few minutes longer before he left and headed to Trish's apartment. When he got to her door, his hands tingled and his heart pumped hard in his chest. He was surprised he could hear her pull back the locks, his body was booming out loud. And when she finally opened the door, he reached for her and crushed his mouth against hers, not giving her time to greet him with words. He pulled her closer and a groan escaped his lips.

The door was still ajar. With little effort, he stepped into the foyer and kicked the door shut with his boot. Still intent on swallowing his woman whole, he held her with all of his strength.

Denver lifted her, mouths still locked, in hopes of feeling her entire body against him. He squeezed even tighter. She grew limp and molded herself against him. She tasted so sweet, her response was so intoxicating, he nearly lost his footing.

And when he finally drew away, it was just for long enough to catch a breath before he started again. He had to get his fill or go crazy. She dominated his every thought all day. After leaving Ankit's office, he couldn't get to her quickly enough.

CHAPTER 33

Trish reached for anything that would make the room stop spinning. His glorious, mind-altering kiss sent her senses to the galaxy and back. She had this to look forward to each night and day?

When Denver finally released her, she gazed at his face. Something was different. She couldn't tell what just yet, but something definitely had changed.

He touched his lips to ear. His warm breath sent shivers down her spine. "I've missed you."

Reluctantly, she pulled away to look at him. His eyes seared her soul.

"I've missed you. Are you okay?"

Trish ran her fingers down his jaw and cupped his chin.

"Everything is good. Ready?"

"Yes."

He helped her into the truck. She grabbed his hand before he backed away.

"Den, you would tell me if something was wrong, right?"

Denver touched the side of her face and leaned in, placing a kiss on her cheek.

"Yes, darling. We're good, I promise."

She watched him climb into the driver's side with a wide smile in place. He reached over and covered her hand. Maneuvering the truck, he headed to Bryan, TX. When they reached Café Capri, she was the one who wore a broad smile. This was her favorite place to eat.

She ordered her usual, Cajun Tortellini. It was the closest thing she got to Cajun that actually resembled her native food. Denver ordered Tortellini Alla Capri, a creamy sauce pasta with ample amounts of surimi crab and mushrooms. She scooped a fork full of her dish and offered it to Denver. He accepted her offer.

"So, tell me about today," she said.

They'd mostly talked about her day on the way. They'd also talked about driving to New Orleans, this time to take Beatrice to meet her mother. The two had been in constant conversation since learning about the engagement. They'd decided that the wedding would be in New Orleans.

"We signed the final documents today at Ankit's office."

"Oh. Guess you saw Martisha and her cronies."

He laughed, drawing attention to them, snuggled in the corner of the quaint restaurant. He shook his head several times before shoving a forkful of pasta into his mouth.

"Well?" She pressed him for an answer.

"Yes, Ms. Dexter was there, and no I still don't want that woman, Trish. We're business partners."

"You don't want her, Den, but she has the hots for you."

"You're making things up. Why don't you like her?"

"I don't know anything about her to like or dislike her."

"Well, she's the last of your worries."

"I see."

He placed his fork down, sat back in his chair and stared. After that kiss this afternoon, she knew in her heart he was telling the truth. She decided not to focus any more energy on Juanita or her own inexperience.

They finished their meal and were headed back when Denver's phone rang. He seemed hesitant to answer but eventually did. He looked down at the phone before he pressed the talk icon.

"Who is this?" He blared into the device.

Trish turned and watched Denver across the dark space. When he spoke again, it was softer.

"I don't know anyone by that name, man. I'm sorry. How did you get this number?"

She waited patiently. After a short minute of silence, Trish assumed the caller tried to answer Denver's question. He finally spoke again.

"Yes, I was in New Orleans, but…"

Again silence. Trish's ears perked upon hearing New Orleans. She shifted in her seat.

"No. I can't recall anything like that. I'm driving right now; perhaps you can call back tomorrow. But I'm not sure how much I can help you."

He nodded several times and said, "Talk to you tomorrow."

"Who was that?'

"I don't know. Someone named Joshua Lambert. He says he saw me in New Orleans during the Classics. He wanted to know if I knew some of his people."

"Well, do you?"

"No babe. Can't say that I do."

She knew someone by that name but it couldn't be Michael's Josh. It didn't make sense. Still the caller must have worried Denver. He remained distracted, even as he left her at her front door.

"I'll see you at the ranch tomorrow?"

"Yes, right after my finals."

They were about to go on Christmas break. As an upper classman, she didn't have to pull hours at the hospital but she'd volunteered. She planned to stay in Texas anyway to spend time with Denver.

"Okay, call me when you're heading out."

"Den?"

He turned and waited reluctantly. When she didn't say more, he stepped back and hugged her.

"I'm sorry, baby. I love you."

"I know. You want to talk about it?"

"Not tonight, sweetheart. Get some rest and do well tomorrow."

She accepted his brief peck and then closed the door. She leaned against the frame as she looked down at her ring finger and sighed. This man was hers and she could hardly believe it.

Of late, he had a lot on his plate. She wished she could erase some of his worries, especially the ones from tonight.

She remembered the days her mother filled in when her Dad had to relocate overseas to protect business assets. And the time when Katrina hit New Orleans, her mother stepped in while her dad and brothers took care of the front. Her mother handled everything else. Not to mention the time Travis traveled into the oncoming hurricane to find his wife, Autumn.

Her mother was the glue that kept their family from falling apart. Trish prayed she would have that kind of discernment when her time came to be Denver's rock. She got the feeling he could really use her help.

Right now, first things came first. She had to finish up before she would be free to concentrate her soon-to-be husband. He'd been very stern in his behest that she remained focus on finishing first.

When the phone rang, she had the phone in her hand on the first ring.

"Just wanted to spend a few minutes with you darling, before I laid my head on this pillow."

"I wish I was there."

"Humph," he responded. "You just don't know how much I wish it, too."

They talked and then she prepared for bed. Trish took her books to bed for one last review.

What she found the next morning was paper stuck to her face, arm and leg. Some had even found their way to the floor.

"Good, Lord, I sure hope some of this stuff hopped from these pages to my brain."

She chuckled out loud.

The finals were mere margin of study material she'd consumed. She felt confident after her finals and called Denver before heading to the ranch.

"You ace your finals, right?"

"I believe I did."

"Good. How far out are you, baby? I'm missing you."

"I'm about ten minutes away."

Trish found Denver unloading square bundles of hay. The bales had to weigh fifty pounds or more, yet he tossed them like they were ice cubes. And, although he was sweaty and funky as all get out, she greeted him as if he'd just taken a fresh shower. "Hey, you." She leaped into his arms.

"I'm all sweaty." He dropped everything and welcomed her into his embrace.

"I don't care." She tasted the salt on his sweaty lips. His shirtless chest soaked her cotton shirt but she didn't shy away from the intimate exchange.

"I'm almost done. Did you bring a change of clothes?"

"I think I still have some on the side-hanger in the mud room. Do you need help here?"

"No, but I'll have to go out to the west gate. Thought you might want to take a ride with me."

"Yes. I'll get Lightning ready."

Along the ride, they stopped several times. She enjoyed picking wildflowers and tucking them away in her side bag.

"Babe, who was the caller from last night? You seemed a bit distracted by it?"

They squatted on a rock just off the trail. The sun was descending above them. She sat close, her arm locked beneath his.

"Some guy who asked if we knew members of his family. When he called today, Mom didn't know any of them either. We think perhaps they were relatives of Dad. We don't know much about his family. For some reason, Dad never really talked about them."

"So where did you see this guy in New Orleans?"

"During all the ruckus with your boyfriend."

"He's not my boyfriend. He hasn't been a friend for more than eight years."

"I don't think he knew that."

Oh, boy. She hoped they would not replay the events from the tailgate. She didn't want to relive that humiliation again. "Are you forgetting that I'm pledged to you?"

She held up her ring finger. He placed a kiss in the

center of her palm.

"No, baby, I haven't forgotten." He sighed before continuing. "I told him we would meet him when we go back in a couple of weeks."

"Speaking of home…" She cheered. "You think we can leave a day earlier."

"I don't see why not. I will have more than enough coverage. I'll let Mom know."

And as if Beatrice had heard them, Denver's phone rang.

"Hey Mom, we were…" He turned to Trish. "Okay, Mom, we're on our way right now."

Denver stood quickly, reached for Trish, and moved towards their stallions.

CHAPTER 34

Denver pulled Trish as fast as her legs would go to keep up with him. He helped her mount Lightning before leaping up onto Winter. He spun the horse around and slapped it with his reins.

"Hhaaattt!"

The horse's hoofs noisily stomped the ground. Tabdak tabdak! Tabdak tabdak!

He prayed to God that Trish kept up with him. He occasionally looked behind him. She was right there on his tail. When they neared the paddock, he slowed.

"Whoa."

He leaped from the animal and took off to the half-opened gate.

"What's wrong?"

CR met him in a rush.

"Several of the broodmares are casted."

The ranch-hand huffed as he tried to keep up with Denver's long strides. He didn't need this now. It was near time to breed the tribe set aside months ago. He'd picked the best of the lot and had hoped mating would begin.

"Exactly how many is several?" He barked, not breaking his pace until he was near the horses lying on their sides.

It was six; he counted as he glanced across one section of the paddock. A knot the size of a basketball hit him in the gut. The back of his eyes stung, competing with the bile rising in his mouth.

"Damn!" He threw his hat to the ground and covered his face with his hands. His callused fingers continued down to the base of his neck. Trish whisked past him. How could he have forgotten her? He caught her around the waist before she went closer.

"No, babe. Don't. They might be infectious."

"Den, please. I know what I'm doing."

He looked at her and studied her face. He didn't want anything to happen to her. The horses could have picked up something that could spread. They had all seemed healthy but out in the fields, they could have contracted anything.

"It's okay."

He hesitated but eventually released her. She removed the bandana from her neck and covered her nose and mouth, securing the corners behind her head. He watched as she slowly approached the first mare. She spoke softly at her.

"There, girl. What's going on with you, ladies? These guys are trying to boss you around?" she cooed, moving so that the animal could see her.

She bent and checked the horse's barrel. Her hand gently moved from the mare's fore down to the midsection. She continued to speak softly as one hand gently patted the animal even after her examination moved down to its dock.

He and the men stood watching, mesmerized by how calm the animal rested. Denver moved closer and kneeled next to her. He watched her watch the horse's eyes as her hands roamed certain parts of its body.

"There you go, lady. It'll be okay."

"What is it?"

She finally looked his way. "Has this area been sprayed with pesticides that you can remember?"

He shook his head, desperately trying to think if they'd had any parts of these fields sprayed.

"No."

"What about the hay? We may want to check the bales to make sure there is no bacteria in them."

"There is hay we use for the barn and there's a different roughage used for feeding. Both are stored in different places. We only get what we need so that everything is used within a set timeframe."

"From the feel of this mare's belly, she's a little blotted. Just a little colic, aren't we?"

She rubbed the horse's blaze. She checked all six mares, all with same symptoms. Trish ordered the hands to help the animals to their feet and sent them to be stalled.

"How long? We…"

"Just a few days, babe. I think I have something in my bag that will help. After a few days, they should be okay."

Trish touched his face and reached up to kiss him. Her touch alone was reassuring. He pulled her close.

"Thanks, darling."

"It will be fine. Don't worry."

The six stalls were all in the same barn so their progress would be easy to monitor. Trish added a sedative to their water. When she went to shower and change, Denver went to his office to make a few calls.

****

His mother handed him a cup of coffee across the kitchen bar. Trish sat with a cup tilted up her mouth. "We're leaving early to meet your parents. I'm excited," Beatrice said. "I feel like I know them already. And we've been making good progress on this wedding, you know? So what time are we heading out?"

Trish's eyes moved to his as her cup came down to a saucer. She was waiting to see if he'd changed his mind. He hadn't. If the mares were doing okay as promised, there was no need to delay their trip.

"Yes, for now, we're leaving in a few days."

He kept his gaze on Trish. She smiled and his world again felt at peace. He trusted her judgment. He'd made several calls to shift a few work schedules so that the ranch had twenty-four hour coverage, just in case.

"Good, I have some packing to do. I'll leave you two love birds alone while I get my list together."

He shook his head. When his mother was out of earshot he mumbled, "We may have to ride on top of the truck if she has her way. I know this woman. She's planning to haul everything but the kitchen sink. It wouldn't surprise me if she had two cows already butchered and in the deep freezer, ready to go."

"Shame on you, Denver Baldwin. I'll talk to her, okay?"

"Won't do you any good. I'm just saying…"

"So, what do you think of a Mardi Gras wedding?"

He had no idea what that meant so he waited for more details. He really didn't care, as long as they got married. He'd hoped they didn't wait long.

"Will that be too soon?"

He placed his cup down and took the stool next to her. Cupping her hands, he kissed her forehead.

"I want to marry you tomorrow. If I thought I could get away with it, I would."

"Yeah, my mom would have both of our hides."

"So, Mardi Gras…"

"February. Not a lot of time, I know, but my mother knows I've always wanted a Mardi Gras wedding." She paused, turning his hand over. "I haven't given her an exact date. I know we needed to finalize one. I did tell both of them, maybe not next year but the following."

He pulled her from her stool. "I don't want to wait, Trish. I want us to start our lives together as soon as you will allow it."

Trish glanced away. His tugging brought her attention back to him.

"School is the only obstacle I'll submit to. Everything else does not fit in the equation. Please, babe."

"So this February?"

"Do I have to wait that long?"

"I want a wedding with my family and friends, in my hometown."

"Then, February it is. Will that give you and your family time to prepare?"

"Yes. Oh, wait, what about your family? Your friends are here? I want them to share in our celebration."

"My family is small. There's no one left on my father's side that I know of."

He hesitated. The phone call from Joshua Lambert made him think there might be family they didn't know anything about. The last thing they needed was unexpected family. He'd do anything to protect the start of their union and to also protect his mother.

"I have my mother's sister, Aunt Grace and her husband Thomas. They don't have kids so pretty much that's it. And, for the hands, we can have a reception here when we get back."

His suggestion seemed to make her happy.

"So, February it is. That makes me extremely happy, Den."

"That's what I'm here for." He kissed her firmly. "So, now what's my reward for this good deed?"

She pushed away and slapped his hand.

"You've already gotten your reward, mister."

"Come on, girl. In two days, I'm not going to be able to get any of this honey. What am I supposed to do?"

"I'm sure you'll figure it out. Right now, we need to look over these plans so when we get home, we can talk all this over with our parents."

She pulled out her journal and opened it. He groaned. He didn't care one bit about the wedding details. She could do whatever she wanted. His only concern was the wedding night, after they were behind closed doors.

"Maybe you'll give me a little under the magic tree, you think?"

"What I think--" She shoved the planner closer to him. "--I think we have work to do."

****

It was like pulling teeth to get his mother to leave behind half the stuff she'd packed for the trip.

"Mom, we don't need all of this."

"I just want to show the Brooks a bit of hospitality, you know."

"Really, it's not necessary." Trish came to his defense. Once on the road, she talked the entire way. That made the trip relatively quick. When they pulled through the gates and turned into the circular drive, his mother's reaction was similar to his the first time he visited Trish's home.

"Oh, my. This is absolutely beautiful."

Alvin moved to the passenger door and opened both front and back doors. He swept Trish up in his arms and hugged her before helping his mother from the car.

"Beatrice, so wonderful to finally meet you in person. Welcome to New Orleans."

Diane followed the same order as her husband. When she got to his mom, they both squealed with delight.

"AWWWW, girl, it's so good to be able to hug this neck."

His mother towered over Diane, but they rocked and rocked for the longest.

"Beatrice, welcome to our home. Remember this is home for you too."

"Oh, child, I thought it was hot in Texas, I think ya'll got us beat."

They all laughed and went inside. The Brooks' had prepared for their arrival. They were fed like royalty and given room assignments. Denver had the same room as last time. And like clockwork, he heard the knock at his door before Trish peeked in.

"Are you okay?"

"Yes, baby. Thanks for checking."

"How about a dip in the pool?"

"How about a little honey under the magic tree."

"I'll see what I can arrange. Meet you down in a few." She pulled away from the door but quickly stuck her head back in. "Den, I have every intention of making you pay."

"For what, may I ask?"

She held up red thongs between two fingers and then tossed them into the room before closing the door. He seized them and held the dainty fabric to his nose.

"Oh, damn."

His arousal grew despite his weariness. He slipped into his swim trunks and a T-shirt and with the panties balled in his hand, he sauntered down the stairs.

CHAPTER 35

Trish tiptoed through the basement walkout patio door and headed for the pool just beyond the gazebo. Instead of diving into the deep end of the pool, she walked into the shallow part and swam across. In broad daylight, at her parents' house no less, she was as bold and brazen as she'd ever been. She'd been itching for him for the last few days. With all the commotion at the ranch and getting ready for this trip, they'd missed the love making she was desperate for right now.

She didn't have to wait long. Denver played the part, dressed for a dip in the pool. He didn't know it, but her parents and his mother had left the house two minutes before she went to his room. She waited in hot anticipation.

Denver bobbed up and down in the water, she guessed to adjust his body to the temperature. When he was in arm's reach, she pulled him to her by the shoulders until she was able to wrap both arms and legs around him.

"What are you up to, soon-to-be Mrs. Baldwin?"

"A little fun in the sun? You game?"

"You trying to become a widow before we're even married, little lady?"

"What are you worried about. I'm yours."

"Until I place that other ring on your finger, Alvin Brooks has the right to shoot my head completely off." He tried to push her away.

She put in as much effort as he did. She nibbled his chin and went for his lips." Baby, we're in your parent's house. I don't want to be disrespectful."

Trish tried again a couple times before she let go. Could she blame her temper on scorching sun or the flare of anger? When Denver caught her waist, she pushed against him. "Let go of me."

"Trish, stop it. What's gotten in to Trisha Brooks?"

He held her tight. Both tread waters to stay on top.

"Nothing. This was a bad idea."

"Damn right it was. You are not yet my wife, Trish. To make out in your family's pool would be a bit disrespectful on my part."

"Oh, but you can take me in the bushes?"

"Trish?"

She knew it wasn't fair to throw their make-out in the bushes in his face. But all was fair in love at all times. Tears gathered behind her wet, sticky lashes. She tried to fight them but they refused to stay in place. One by one they fell down her cheeks. Denver caught them with his lips. His soothing words only made it worse.

"I love you baby. I would never do anything to put you in jeopardy. Never. Understand me. You are my life, Trish, and I swear to you, I'll protect you with everything I have."

She wrapped her arms around his neck and held tight. Relaxing in his grip, she allowed him to pull her to the shallow end of the pool. He sat on the steps with her between his legs. Yes, she felt his arousal and knew he'd chosen her honor over the passion they could have shared.

"I'm sorry, Den."

"There's no need to be, my love. We have time. For this entire trip, we will refrain--"

She didn't let him finish. She covered his lips in a kiss, so tender, so sweet, it said everything that needed to be said.

She would behave. He was right. Her parents would be disappointed had they caught them. She cherished them but, more importantly, it changed the way she looked at Denver.

She swam to the center of the pool and waited. They enjoy the refreshing swim and then a quiet supper with their parents. The crew had yet to come over because everyone was busy getting ready for the holiday pageants and cantatas. They lounged in the family room watching 'This Christmas."

Her mom sat a tray on the coffee table with two servings of warm bread pudding and mugs of hot tea.

"Thanks, Mommy. Are you ladies still knee-deep in wedding stuff?"

"Sweetie, we're done. We just need you to do your part. Everything else is worked out."

"Wow, you two work fast," Denver said.

"This is my last official wedding. We've been planning this one for a long time, haven't we, sweetie?"

"Yes, ma'am, we have."

Denver phone rang. He dug in his pocket to retrieve it, looking at the device before answering.

He held it up. "Please excuse me for a minute."

Trish stretched her neck, hoping to hear his end of the

conversation. She prayed nothing was wrong at the ranch. Then she remembered the call from Joshua. A call from either would be upsetting. She tried to be in tune to him, missing parts of her mother's conversation.

"Something we should be concerned about, dear?"

She quickly turned back to her mother.

"Ah, before we left a few of the horses weren't doing well. By the time we left they seemed to be better. I'm just hoping it has stayed that way."

"Well, not to worry. Denver seems to know how to take care of his business."

"I know, Mom."

She looked at his profile as he stood by the window, looking out into the dark.

CHAPTER 36

"Joshua."

"Yes, sir. I hate to bother you again, but you said you would be in the city during the holiday."

"We arrived earlier today. I'm still not sure how I can help you."

"I talked to my mom in California. It would be best if we talked face to face if you don't mind."

Denver sighed heavily as he glared out into the darkness. He glanced at Trish. She was looking straight at him. He turned away before responding to Joshua.

"How about we do it early morning, tomorrow? Is there someplace we can meet?"

He dared not invite the man to his future in-law's house. So, when Joshua agreed to text him the address, he locked it into his phone. He slid back down on the sofa and stretched his arm behind Trish and pulled her close.

"Everything okay?"

He sucked in a very long breath and released it. He could feel eyes on him but he focused on the television screen.

"It was Joshua. I told him I would meet him in the morning, early." He glanced at her. "I hope you don't have any plans. I don't think this will take long but I want to make sure I don't interrupt any of your plans."

"No, we have the pageant tomorrow evening but that's it. I might go to the salon."

Trish pulled at a handful of her hair. He took it from her fingers and brought the lock to his nose. He loved the way she smelled but not nearly as much as he loved the feel of her body beneath his. Forgetting their agreement to no hanky-panky, his thoughts shifted.

"He asked me to meet him at Jackson Square."

"Do you want me to go with you?"

"No. It might be best if I did this alone."

"Do you really think this might be some long-lost relatives you guys know nothing about?"

"I don't think so, but we'll see tomorrow."

****

The moment he set eyes on Joshua, he knew something was terribly wrong. Luckily, he'd been sitting when the man walked to his table with his hand extended. For a moment he couldn't move. He understood clearly why Joshua thought they were related.

He stood and found his voice.

"Joshua?"

"Yes, I'm Joshua. Thank you for agreeing to meet with me."

"Please, take a seat. Have you had breakfast?"

The man could have been his twin had they been the same age, but Denver couldn't tell just how old he was. He decided to go all in.

"No. I could hardly sleep after talking to you last night."

"Well, why don't we get some coffee and maybe a little

to eat while we talk."

"Sure."

Denver held up his arm to get the waiter's attention. They both ordered and asked for coffee, black, and freshly squeezed orange juice.

After the man took their orders and brought fresh coffee, they sat in silence, looking at each other.

"Do you mind me asking how old you are, Joshua?"

"Twenty-seven."

Oh boy. Denver felt uneasiness move from his stomach straight up his back. He tried to calm his raging nerves. He needed as much information as possible before he jumped to conclusions.

"Are you from New Orleans?" He figured he would have to pull any information out of him.

"Yes, sir, I was born here. But I grew up in California with my parents. My dad was in the military."

A certain calm returned, but not much. There was still an unquestionable resemblance between him and the man seated across from him. Perhaps they were relatives from his father's side.

When their breakfast arrived, the young man opened up a little. Still none of the people he mentioned as relatives sounded familiar.

"My mother's name is Kimberly Lambert. Her maiden name was Nelson. She has one sister, Lisa, who lives in Houston."

His nerves surfaced again. Naming more people, even ones residing in Texas, didn't jog any recognition. When Joshua told him his mother had been adopted, he could understand their eagerness to connect with people who might be related.

"I still don't understand how you got my number, Joshua."

"I work for Mr. Michael Brooks. You were with him and his family. I explained we might be related. At first, he wouldn't give it to me but I've known his family since I was a little kid. Once I explained the situation, he gave me your number."

"And exactly what is this situation, Joshua?"

Denver didn't like the direction this conversation was heading. He was prepared to walk and leave the breakfast tab with the man. He'd talked to all of Trish's brothers and not once had Michael told him someone was looking for him.

"My mother and her sister are looking for their birth parents."

Denver frowned and sat back in his seat. He watched Joshua. He had no clue how his mother looking for her parents had anything to do with him. Then an alarm as loud as the cathedral bell went off in his head. He leaned forward and propped his arms on the table.

"Do you have picture of your mother?"

"Sure."

He pulled out his phone and swiped his fingers across its face.

"Here. This is at our last family reunion. My mom and Aunt Robin are in the center. They were both adopted by different families. They found each other about twenty years ago. Since then, they've had a family reunion every year."

Denver nervously cupped the phone and glared at the two happy faces, hugging each other. His fingers shook. The faces mirrored his own mother's. How could that be?

He handed the phone to Joshua but couldn't look at him for fear Joshua would realize that Denver knew exactly who these women were. His heart knew. But his mind still couldn't.

His parents had told him that the babies they had were still-born. Was it a lie? Did they give the babies away because they didn't want them? Had his parent's brief split been the cause? And if so, why would they lie to him?

There were more questions than answers and the more they bombarded him, the more agitated he became.

Denver glanced across the table at Joshua. He tried not to appear mad. At the same time, he wondered Joshua wanted from him. He'd lived thirty plus years without this knowledge, so why now. Now, when he was just getting what he wanted out of his life. His mother had a lot to explain.

"Look, Joshua, I'm not sure what you want from me, man."

"My mother and aunt have been searching for years for their parents. They had no real clues until the day I saw you."

"I fail to see what that has to do with me." He leaned forward on the table. How could he know this guy's true motives? Even if he was his nephew, so what?

"Mom found out that her birth mother's name is Beatrice White."

All the air caught in his lungs suddenly escaped. He groped for breathe. His lids dropped to offset the pounding in his head. His eyes flew open as he heard Joshua's voice.

"Mr. Baldwin?"

He saw concern in Joshua's face. He held up a hand to show that he was fine. He didn't know how to respond to Joshua's revelation. Nor could he keep this information to himself until they returned to Texas.

And, then there was Trish.

The last thing he wanted was to spoil her family's

holiday.

They talked more before he paid the bill and shook Joshua's hand. Denver pulled him into shoulder hug. The longer they talked, the more convinced he was that they were related.

"I'll call you later today. In the meantime, don't say anything to your parents, not until I've had a chance to talk to mom."

"Yes, sir."

When he got out of the car and entered the side door to the house, he searched for Trish. He tapped on her bedroom door and got no answer. He went down to the basement. Last, he moved to the family's den. His mother and Diane were looking through a family photo album.

Both women turned his directions with huge grins on their faces.

"Hey Denver, your mom and I were just looking through pictures of your darling, Trish."

"Aw, that's nice. I won't disturb you."

His mother's expression changed. He could never hide anything from her. From the look on her face, she knew something was wrong. He backed out of the room but didn't get far.

"Den, what's wrong?"

"Nothing, Mom. I was just looking for Trish."

"She's at the beauty shop with some of her girlfriends. With that gang, it's no telling when she will be back."

"Okay, I go up…"

"Hold it. Look at me Denver Baldwin."

Like most children, young or grown, he knew when his mother called his full name, he was in trouble. And as if the miracle he'd prayed for happened, Trish waltzed into the room.

"Hey babe. Don't tell me my mom is showing you

those awful pictures of me?"

Relief raced through him. He took the liberty of pulling her into a strong embrace.

"Hi baby, I need to talk to you. Now, please."

Trish traced her fingers across his forehead.

"Okay, let's go."

CHAPTER 37

Trish led Denver by the hand to the basement. The look on his face meant something significant had happened. Something didn't go well.

With as much calm as she could muster, she moved them to the oversized couch and waited.

"I think Joshua is my nephew, the son of one of my sisters."

"Wait. Didn't you tell me your sisters were still-born?

"I thought so, too. At least that's what I was told."

Not wanting to jump to conclusions, she waited for the explanation. And gauging from his expression, the news was not going to be good.

"Both of my parents told me the babies didn't make it."

"Have you talked to your mom yet?"

"No, I needed to talk this out with you first. I don't know how to break this news. I love her, Trish. I would never disrespect her or think less of her if she made a mistake. She's always been a good mother to me."

"I know, babe. I see it in everything she does."

"So how do I do this? I thought about holding it until we go home, but I'm not sure I can."

"You have a close bond with her, Den. You need to be honest. Just give her the facts. Allow her to tell you her story. Whatever she tells you, it will be what she honestly believes is best for you both."

He kissed her, his hand cupped her face. She saw the uncertainty in his eyes. "Do you want me to go with you?"

"No, I think I have to do this alone. I don't want to put her in any more of an awkward position than I need to."

He waited a few seconds before standing and heading up the stairs. He turned before climbing the steps until she smiled.

Trish tried staying busy while she waited. She made four batches of cookies for her sister-in-law's dance studio. Reggie sponsored a citywide Christmas cantata and every year it grew.

She did a walk-by of different rooms in the house, not knowing where Beatrice and her son might be. As she pulled the last batch of cookies from the oven and set them in the bay window over the kitchen sink. She spotted them under the gazebo. Her curiosity got the best of her. She walked out the patio door and heard Beatrice's low sobs.

Trish moved toward them. As she neared, Denver looked up and locked eyes with her. He needed help. She moved to the other side of Beatrice and wrapped her arm around the part of her body he hadn't managed to embrace. She laid her head on her back to offer comfort.

Just hearing Beatrice broke her heart. It was hot but they were covered by the topper. When Trish pulled away, her intention was to return to the house for some water and a cool towel. But Beatrice straightened as well. Her face was completely flushed and her eyes as red as beets.

She reached for Trish and Trish willing accepted her embrace. She didn't know what to say. She said the only thing she could.

"I love you, Mom Bea."

They'd originally agreed that Trish would call her Bea, but Trish didn't feel right calling her by her first name.

"I'm going inside to get you some water. Actually, you should move into house. It's cool in the basement. No one is down there."

She nodded and Denver helped Beatrice to her feet. They walked to the door of the basement. The cool air welcomed them. Trish held one hand. Denver still had his arm around his mom's waist.

"I won't be long."

She looked at Denver. His eyes and mouth drooped downward. She touched him before moving to the fridge near the bar. She pulled out two bottles of water. She also took a bar towel and passed it under a stream of cold water. Placing everything on a tray, she walked back and set it next to Denver.

Trish handed him the towels first and poured water into glasses. After Beatrice wiped her face, Trish retrieved the towel and exchanged it for a cool glass of water. She also handed a glass to Denver. Both finished their entire glass.

She got up to leave but her future mother-in-law placed her hand on her arm.

"Stay sweetie. I want you nearby." Her voice cracked.

"Yes, ma'am. Can I get you anything else?"

"No, just sit with us. We're about to call my grandson."

Just hearing the words from her lips made Trish weepy. She couldn't imagine learning that the babies you thought you lost were actually alive and had started families of their own.

Denver dialed the number and Joshua answered on the first ring.

"This is Denver; I have someone who wants to talk to you."

He handed the phone to his mom. Her hands shook as she took the phone and placed it to her ear.

"Joshua, this is your grandmother, Beatrice."

She listened as the young man talked and out of nowhere, the tears began to fall again. Trish scooted closer to offer her comfort.

By the end of their twenty-minute conversation, she, Beatrice, and Denver were all wrapped up again. They sat in silence a long while before Beatrice broke free from the huddle.

"I'm going to go get cleaned up. I promised Diane, I'd help her make pastries."

Trish started to tell her that she'd done all of the cookies but decided it wouldn't change her mind. When she slowly climbed the stairs, Denver went to help her. She shooed him away.

"Stay with Trish. I'll see you guys in a little while."

"Yes ma'am," he answered and moved back to the couch.

Denver pulled her onto his lap and buried his head in the fold of her shoulder. He held her so tight she could barely breathe. She didn't complain or move. It was what he needed at that moment. It was the least she could do for him.

When he eased up, she cupped his face with both hands. He looked lost, hurt, and relieved at the same time. She wouldn't press him for answers. She figured he would talk in due time.

"I know you didn't hear our earlier conversation but from her reaction when I told her, she had no idea her babies were still alive."

"What happened?"

"She doesn't know. The hospital staff told her the babies were dead. She says she was out of it for several days. When they asked if she wanted to see the babies, she said no. My father paid the hospital for the babies' burial. It was just too hard for them to deal with."

"I'm so sorry, Den. Will she get to talk to or see them soon?"

"Joshua told me they've been looking for her for years."

"Will he come over?"

"He will come by the studio. I hope you don't mind."

"Of course not."

The afternoon air was thick with energy. Trish went to help her mom and Beatrice finish the goodies for the evening cantata. The packed boxes were placed at the side door.

Diane hugged her first and then showered special attention on Beatrice. To see them together, one would have thought they'd know each other all their lives. Arm in arm, they left the kitchen.

"Come on, my sister; let's go get all dolled up. As cute as you are, you might attract some eyes your way."

"Child, ain't nobody looking at this old girl." Beatrice laughed and patted her mother's hand.

Trish was sitting at the high bar, staring out of the window, when Denver came up behind her.

"Did you save your man at least one cookie?"

She turned. "Of course not. I know what a sweet

tooth you have, so…" She moved to the covered dish, opened the lid. "I put these aside just for you."

She handed it to him.

"That's my girl."

He rewarded her with one of his best kisses. She also handed him a beer when he took a seat beside her.

****

The studio was packed. Her brother, Michael, and wife, Denise, had picked up the goodies and had dropped them off at the studio. Trish smiled, remembering the days when she and her friends were forced to serve.

As they made their way further into the facility, she felt Denver squeeze her hand. She glanced up at him but his attention was on the far right of the room. Her eyes followed his. It was as if she was seeing double. He moved in that direction and she followed.

CHAPTER 38

Denver scanned the room for Joshua. His heart rammed against his chest and his body temperature escalated. Normally, that was his reaction to Trish but for a different reason. Clinging to her hand, she was bound to feel the energy racing through him right now. They seemed to have that connection.

And sure enough, she glanced up at him. He tried not to look down into her face. Instead, he squeezed her hand even tighter to signal he wasn't himself. He was thankful that his mom was paired up with Trish's mom, Diane. She seemed to be doing better than he was.

The moment he locked eyes with Joshua, a whole different sensation raced through him. For so long, he thought it was just him, his mother, and Aunt Grace. Becoming a part of Trish's family made him realize how much he'd missed having siblings or nieces and nephews. And here it was, instantly, in a matter of a day, he had what he was missing all along.

He kept hold of Trish's hand as Joshua neared. He needed her support to keep himself together. He wrapped his arm around Joshua's shoulder with a firm grip. Emotions he'd not expected surfaced and it took him a minute to pull away.

By looking at his nephew's face, he could tell Joshua experienced a similar turmoil. When Denver found his voice, he pulled Trish forward.

"Josh, this is my fiancée, Trisha Brooks. Baby, this is my nephew, Joshua Lambert."

He felt comfortable calling his new-founded relative by his relationship. Joshua didn't seem to mind.

"Hello, Joshua." She hugged his neck.

He smiled nervously. "Ms. Brooks..."

"Trish. Please call me, Trish."

"Trish. Thank you. I remember seeing you a few times at our office holiday parties. It's great to see you again."

"Same here. I missed the office party this year. Michael had it so early in the season."

"Yes, ma'am."

Out of the corner of Denver's eye, he saw his mother approach. Her eyes were already teary. She clung to Diane's arm as they neared. He reached for her and pulled her close.

"Josh, this is your maternal grandmother, Beatrice Baldwin."

Joshua wasted no time wrapping his arms around her. He picked her up from the floor and squeezing her tightly.

"Mo Chagren, Maw-Maw, don't cry."

Denver didn't understand what Josh had said, but it sounded endearing. Their embrace was so heartfelt that both he and Trish joined the union.

Joshua continued to hold on when his mother pulled away. She held his face with both hands, kissing each of his cheeks.

"You're such a handsome, young man. You look like my Den, here." Her voice was still filled with emotion and tears streamed down her face.

"I'm so happy to finally meet you, Maw-maw. I called mom. She can't wait to meet you as well."

Beatrice shook her head. "Me too, sweetheart. We've got a lot of catching up to do."

She placed another kiss on his cheek.

Denver noticed the attention they were getting from passersby. Some had knowing smiles and nods. The gestures warmed his heart. The holidays had a way of bringing out the best in people.

When they finally found seats, his mother sat between him and Josh, her hand folded in his. They'd found seats far in the corner where they could comfortably converse.

Instead of riding back to the house with them, Beatrice rode with Josh. Josh waited until they were again tucked away by themselves to start showing them pictures of his... their family.

Denver's sisters were spitting images of their mom. She swiped tears every time he pulled up a different image.

Josh's phone rang and he answered it immediately. "Yes, ma'am, hold on."

He handed the phone to his grandmother.

Denver didn't think she had tears left, but somehow, she found more. Finally, Denver decided to join Trish and her family. The siblings had gathered downstairs, along with all the kids.

"Hey, Uncle Den."

He smiled at Christopher and gave him a fist bump, then a hug.

"My man, Chris, you're getting taller by the minute. What? You're six feet tall now?"

Chris giggled. "No sir, I'm only ten."

"Well, you're going to be tall like your Pops."

"Yes sir!" He jumped up and down, his hand tapping Denver's shoulder.

Denver glanced around. The kids were huddled to one side of the room and the siblings were nestled together on the huge, circular couch. He moved next to Trish and pulled her onto his lap. She smiled at him before returning her attention to Denise, who seemed to have the floor.

Christmas Day seemed a blur. They enjoyed a noisy, but very enjoyable breakfast at Trish's parents' house, and then dinner at Travis's. In between, he and his mother spent time visiting Josh and his father's relatives. They exchanged gifts, and to Denver's his surprise, Josh had gotten him a crest to attach to his saddle.

"You'll have to visit soon, Josh. And, we'll make sure and connect with Robin when we get back to Texas."

In fact, he'd already discussed passing through Houston on their way home. The goodbyes in New Orleans were hard for everyone. Trish and his mom both had a tough time relinquishing the hugs they shared with Diane.

"Go on, now. You will make me cry. Go on. Be safe. We will see you guys in a few weeks," Diane fussed.

The Brooks' were going to make the haul to see them in Texas. The next time they all traveled back to New Orleans, it would be Mardi Gras season for their well-planned nuptials.

The stop in Houston ended with an overnight stay. The reunion between mother and daughter warranted more than a couple of hours.

****

Denver was so ready to get home, he could hardly

stand it. He was anxious to get back to the ranch to check on his herd, but more than anything he was ready to make love to Trish.

He was on a short fuse right about now. Even if he wanted to, he couldn't sneak her to his room and get his fill. So, he held onto his control a little longer. God helped them once they hit the county line. He had every intention of dropping his mother off at home, literally, and saving the trip to Trish's apartment for last.

True to his plan, he left his mother at the front entrance to the den and sped like lightning to Trish's. They couldn't get in the door fully before he started pulling at her clothes. Slamming the door with his foot, they raced down the short hallway to her bedroom.

"Open for me, darling," he groaned into her mouth.

Fully loaded, he pushed passed the moisture that welcomed him like he was king. He was.

CHAPTER 39

Trish screamed. Denver caught the wail in his mouth. She arched to meet him in a single thrust that had her skin peeling from her flesh. She dug her short nails into his back, encouraging him to give her more.

They hung half on, and half off of her bed, but neither complained. Denver continued long, deep strokes. He didn't stop, even when she had no more strength to hold on. She'd already left him with a back-bending orgasm that shook her entire body.

As she made her way down from the ride, he found his and collapsed on top of her. She welcomed his weight.

"Welcome home, darling."

She grinned and turned her face into his neck. He tried to lift up, but she held him. Trish didn't know when she drifted off to sleep nor did she feel him lift her into the center of the comforter. The throw at the foot of the bed covered her. Turning in the dark room, she could only make out the clock on the night stand.

She rolled off the bed and padded to the bathroom. His head was beneath the water when she slipped into the shower with him. He welcomed her with a kiss.

"I love you, Den."

He kissed her once more. Her freshly done perm was of no concern. She dipped her head under the water to hold the kiss he attempted to break. He turned his back to the spray and moved her against the tiled wall.

"You're hair is wet."

"You've got me wet in other places. What are you going to do about it?"

"Hold on."

She did as instructed, locking her arms around his neck. Leaving the shower with her slippery legs around him, they made it as far as the vanity top. They eyed one another as he entered her slowly. She dropped her upper body back, hands flat on the vanity top to support her weight. Denver's mouth traveled down and suckled her nipples as she moved.

Just when she was near her peak, he withdrew, picked her up and moved to the bed. He turned her on to her stomach, lifted her hips high enough to reenter her from behind. He used one hand to keep himself up above her, and the other, he used to massage the bud at her core. He stroked her inside and out.

Denver's lips and tongue set her body on fire. It wasn't enough that he filled her fully. He tortured her with his delicious, intoxicating kisses. The sensation was so intense, she could barely breathe. His hand rose, cupping her breasts, one at a time. He caressed them so good, she lost her upstroke.

She'd tried her best to keep up, to meet him at the end of each thrust. She trembled in his grasp, totally losing the rhythm. Luckily, Denver had control of it all. He held her in place, adding pressure with his hand, fueling her fire as he moved her from earth to the galaxy. She fell hard.

He pulled her up, still connected and rested with his legs beneath him, with her in his lap. He wrapped his arms around her and dropped his head to the crook of her shoulder.

Trish was sure that by now, her hair was a matted mess. She didn't care. She rested against him, enjoying their connection. When he finally lifted her and moved from the bed, he extended a hand. They went back to the bathroom. The water was still running.

The lukewarm spray turned cold as they finished cleansing one another. When they were done, they crawled into bed and drifted back to sleep.

Once again, she didn't feel him move but he had. The note on the pillow made her smile. 'I love you.'

She picked up her phone and touched the number to activate a call.

"Good morning, my love." She rolled over in the bed.

"Good morning, babe. What time do you go in?"

"In a couple of hours."

"Okay. Call me when you get a chance."

"I will."

"I'll be thinking about you."

"I will be thinking about you. Den?"

"Yes, babe."

"Thank you."

"You're welcome. Tell me what you're thanking me for."

"Laying a sister down, real good."

She met his laughter with a grin. She loved the way it sounded, how it vibrated through her when he was near.

"Soon, love, you're going to be chasing me away."

"I doubt it."

"We'll just have to see about that."

"Yep, we will."

"Have a good day, honey. I love you."

"I love you, Den."

****

The days following their trip to New Orleans flew by. She cleaned her apartment until it sparkled in anticipation of her parents' visit. She stocked her refrigerator but knew her mother would be carting the entire meat, seafood, and farmer's market in the bed of her father's truck. She and Mom Bea were so alike. Their age difference was the only thing that separated them when it came to characteristics.

She was driving Denver crazy with her special preparations but knew what her parents expected. They would sleep in her bed, which meant she would take the couch. Which also meant no loving for them until the coast was clear.

The day they arrived she had a clinical scheduled, the very last of the semester, and then a shift at the clinic. She could have switched with another resident but that would have meant she would have to make it up later.

Since her parents were scheduled to arrive late afternoon, she had one of her teammates at the apartment to greet them when they arrived.

As soon as her shift was done, Trish raced. She'd brought a change of clothing and showered at school before heading home. She even dabbed on a hint of makeup. Her mother would die if she showed up looking like a lab rat. She talked to Denver the entire drive.

"They love you, no matter what. I do, too."

She pulled into the second assigned spot. Her dad's truck was parked in the first. Patting her hair and puckering her lips before she got out, Trish grabbed her purse and headed to the door.

She could smell a delicious aroma even before she

reached her apartment. She'd bet the other tenants were salivating like she was. Turning the key and pushing the door open, she saw her dad first, lounging on the sofa.

"Daddy!"

"Hey pumpkin. I've missed you."

"Me, too."

She met her mom as she turned the corner. "I'm so glad you're here, Mommy."

"Honey, I didn't think we were ever going to get through Texas. Oh, my gosh. I almost forgot about this drive."

"Where's my son-in-law," her dad asked.

"He's coming over a little later."

"Have you been eating, Trish? You look a little thin, baby."

"Mommy, please. It's just that I'm not eating like I do at home, but yes, I'm eating, thank you."

She didn't tell her mother that her morning meal consisted of a breakfast bar and that she rarely had time for lunch, unless, of course, she was at the ranch. She did manage to eat a decent supper each evening, a meal she generally shared with Denver.

"It smells wonderful in here," she attempted to change the subject.

She got a sidelong glance from her mother. Trish kissed her cheek and went to the kitchen to discover what smelled so great.

"I talked to Bea. She told me that her girls and their families were coming to the wedding."

She turned worried eyes on her mother. She'd not wanted to burden her more than she had to. Deciding to marry so quickly and being given the wedding she'd always dreamed of had to be taxing on her mother and Bea. Now that her mother-in-law had found the children she thought were dead, Bea's time was now divided. Maybe they should wait until next year to get married.

She glanced away, tears filled her eyes. She didn't want her mother to see them but it was too late.

"Trisha, look at me."

She obeyed. She always did--well not quite. No sex before marriage had always been her advice. But Denver wasn't some random boy. He was her protector now, the man who loved her unconditionally. And the man she would soon pledge her entire life to.

"Yes, ma'am."

Her mom lifted her chin. The tears fell shamelessly. No matter her demand, they continued to flow freely. Damn. To quickly defuse the doubt she saw in her mother's eyes, she immediately explained.

"Mommy, we've always talked about my wedding day, since, I don't remember when. I just don't want to put too much on you and Dad."

"Girl, hush your mouth. Yes, we've been talking about the day you'd get married for a long time. Trust me, we have been preparing for this day. So, the wedding you want is the wedding you get, my darling. For the sake of God, it is the only wedding you'll have. Understand me."

Trish nodded. Folded into her mother's arms, she accepted her soothing hug.

"Baby, marriage is hard. Don't get me wrong, it's a beautiful thing, full of joy, some good loving and wonderful children who respect you. You respect them if you raise them right. But, there will be days when you'll reconsider your decision. And, with God's help, you'll pull through."

Trish looked at her mother through a teary haze. She'd always been a straight talking kind of woman, especially with her children. Everything she'd done had been for their good, as a family.

"I understand. Thank you, Mommy. For everything."

"You've always been our princess. In a short while you'll be a queen, Denver's queen."

"He makes me feel like one."

"Good, otherwise, I'd have to have his hide."

Her mother's comment made her laugh.

"I'm starved. Can we eat?"

"Aren't we going to wait for Denver?"

"Mommy, Denver could be in that field for hours before he's done."

Just as she bit into the first fork full of her mother's macaroni and cheese, her doorbell chimed.

"I'll get it." Her dad stood and opened the door without looking through the peek hole.

Trish, her mouth stuffed, raised her fork in salute.

"Come on in, son. We just started."

"Glad to see you guys made it okay."

He hugged her dad and greeted her mom with a similar hug. He finally made it to her, kissing her on the lips, even though she had food in her mouth.

"I see what your priorities are, little lady. I'm going to remember this."

Swallowing, she grinned at him. "I love you."

"Sure, you do."

They talked for a couple of hours before he said his good nights. She could tell he was dog-tired. When she walked him to his truck, they shared a passionate kiss.

"Please, be careful and get home safely."

"It's good to see your folks."

"Den? Call me when you make it in."

"I will, sweetheart. You worry too much."

"Yes. Good night."

She watched him pull away. When she returned to the

house, her mother was cleaning the kitchen. Taking the dish towel and a bowl from her hand, Trish moved to the counter.

"I've got this. Go on, rest. We're going to Baldwin Ranch tomorrow."

"Thank you, honey."

"No, thank you, Mommy. Supper was fabulous."

"Good night."

"Rest well."

Her dad had already gone to the bedroom. Trish put away the leftovers, and plopped down on the couch, her bed for the next few days. Waiting for Denver's call, she closed her eyes. She managed to fall asleep but she popped up sometime later like she'd been knocked down. She tried to get her bearings.

Looking around the room, she panted hard. She was home, her apartment. Why was she on the sofa? Then she remembered that her parents were visiting.

Denver. She hadn't heard back from him. Had she miss his call?

Trish fished for her phone. It was buried between the cushions. She looked at the device. There was no missed call. Shaky finger depressed the single number assigned to him. It rang several times and went to his voice mail. As if she'd summoned her mother, Trish saw the hall light switch on. Her mother came and handed her the phone.

"It's Bea, honey."

Trish's heart rammed hard against her chest. She thought it would pop out. She fumbled with the phone until she had a solid enough hold to bring it to her ear.

"What's wrong with Denver?"

She didn't bother with formalities or decorum. She stood as if that would get her the information she needed more quickly. Her mother started back to the bedroom and Trish followed, only she turned at the kitchen. She flipped on the light.

"Honey, don't worry, Denver is fine. The east barn caught on fire a few hours ago. He and some of the men went out to release the herd from there."

Trish covered her mouth to keep from weeping. She paced the space between the counter and stove, listening.

"I'm heading over--"

"No, Trish. Denver just asked me to call because he thought you might be worried since he hadn't called. He will call you in the morning."

Trish heard all that but wasn't really listening. She'd already made up her mind. She was going. She walked back to where her shoes were.

"Thanks for calling. I'll talk to you in a few."

She hung up and set the phone on the table next to the couch. She headed to the front door. Both her parents had dressed. She looked at them.

"Do you want me to drive?"

Her father was heading to the door. She hadn't expected them to be up at this hour or consider going out to the ranch.

"I'll drive, Dad."

They pulled away in her car, her foot heavy on the accelerator until she neared the unpaved road leading to the gate of Baldwin Ranch. She could smell the smoke even before she turned down the long road. She slowed and pulled in next to Denver's truck to park. She bolted from the car, racing up the path to the far end of tack shed.

Her heart had thundered the entire way there but when she saw the flames and the men attempting to put the fire out, she just about lost it. She didn't see Denver among them. She stopped. "Denver," she screamed.

He turned and she was in motion again, sprinting. She leaped into his arms and held on tight. She didn't realize she was sobbing until then.

CHAPTER 40

Denver saw Trish racing toward them. He dropped his hose, meeting her halfway before she was close to the flames threatening to spread.

"Baby, it's okay. Calm down. No one was in the barn. All of the horses are out."

She didn't hear him because she was sobbing uncontrollably.

"Trish."

She buried her face in his chest. His clothes were filled with smoke. He pulled her away quickly. She looked into his face through her tears and he covered her mouth. She pressed harder, holding him around his waist.

"Hey, we're good, right?"

Her parents were not far behind her. He saw them look toward the blaze and then at him. He shook his head.

"What can I do to help, Denver?" Alvin stopped inches away.

"At this point, we're just trying to keep the fire contained to the one building. I think the men have it under control."

He turned back to the flames before he looked down at Trish. She held him tight. He tried to comfort her by rubbing her back. She did not ease her grip.

"Come on. Let's head to the house."

"Are you sure? You can use all the help you can get." Alvin tried one more time with his offer of help.

"I think it will be fine. Most of these men are volunteer firemen, even though the fire truck hasn't made it here yet. I think they have it contained."

He pulled Trish with one arm and reached for her mother's arm with the other. They took the shortest route to the house's side door. Beatrice was watching for them and met them at the door.

"Oh, dear, I didn't expect you to come all the way out here and see this."

"Hey, Bea, girl. Sorry."

"Don't you worry. Denver has this taken care of. Please, come in. I was just putting together some drinks for the men. Can I get you something?"

Denver allowed the Brooks and Trish into the house before he followed.

"I'm going to go clean up in the mud room."

He didn't expect Trish to follow him but her hand grabbed a fist full of his shirt tail as she trailed behind him. Once in the mud room, he unbuttoned his shirt. Trish reached for a towel and dipped it under the faucet. She lifted it and wiped his face.

He took the towel from her hand, his eyes never leaving hers. She looked pretty shaken up. He didn't want to do or say anything that might upset her even more. He had no intention of telling her that someone purposely set his barn on fire. It had gone the perpetrator's way, they would have succeeded in torching all six of his outbuildings; had them completely in flames had Denver's timing not been just right.

When he pulled into the parking area and got out, he smelled the smoke right away. The boarding house was close by, so he was able to rouse his crew and they went into action right away.

They found a fuse that ran from the burning shed to all of the others. Severing it, they then doused the entire cord with water and kept the fire contained to one area.

They dug a trench around the building and filling it with water before they attacked the fire inside.

A few men herded the horses and brought most of the equipment from the back opening , while the others fought the flames igniting the fresh hay and straw they'd laid only days ago.

Trish stood close enough he could feel her tremble. She gazed at him as if waiting for him to confirm something she already knew. They had this connection of late that was more pronounced than when they first met.

"Tell me the truth," she finally said.

The towel was at the back of his neck as she eyed him. Denver sucked in a long breath and placed the towel on the rack, reaching for a T-shirt from the top shelf.

He took his time and she placed her hand on his chest as he pulled the shirt all the way down.

Denver covered her hand. "We'll talk, later."

"Den--"

"I promise we'll talk later. Right now, I need to help Mom get the men taken care of, baby."

He kissed her softly and pulled her close.

"I need your help right now, please," he begged.

She stared at him for the longest time, her forehead furrowed, eyes looking ready to tear up again. He rocked her briefly then moved away. Hand in hand, they went back to the kitchen.

The moms had already taken trays out for the men and were back for more. Trish picked up a tray and followed them out this time. Her dad prepared pitchers of water. Denver fell in place next to him.

"Thank you, Mr. Alvin."

"Glad I could be here to help."

By daylight, they were able to assess the damage. The county fire chief was on hand to write a report. The night foreman had already given his statement and when Denver sat with the man, a rancher himself, Trish was right there next to him. When they were finally alone, Trish's revelation socked him in the gut.

"I dreamt you were in danger. I've never done that before."

"I'm fine. Everything is fine. The building and contents can be replaced. I'm just thankful no one got hurt and none of the stock was lost."

"Who would do this, Denver? People could have been hurt."

"I don't know, babe, but I'm sure law enforcement will be looking for them."

****

Three days later, the men had completely gutted the structure and begun putting up new framing. The parents were in the den. Denver and Trish were curled up on the porch swing when he noticed dust kicking up along the road. Two vans, both white, moved at an alarming speed through the gates.

He sat forward, pushing Trish away as he stood and descended the steps.

He didn't know the intentions of the passengers in the vehicles or what their rush was. He moved quickly to where they would park along the fence.

He'd never had trouble at his ranch before the fire. After the reports were filed and went public, he'd gotten several visits from media outlets. He assumed it might be another television crew, looking for a story. The vehicles slowed and pulled in to an open spot next to his truck. By the time Denver reached the first van, a man as tall as a tree emerged from the driver's side.

"Can I help you?"

Denver approached the man cautiously. He was much taller. The man smiled and stuck out his hand.

"Jake Lambert."

Denver extended his hand as the name registered. It was too late to do anything but accept the tight bear hug the man enclosed him in. Denver only had a few seconds to recover before he was surrounded by two women. His sisters!

They hugged him so tight he could barely catch his breath. Between sobs and kisses to his cheek, he couldn't move an inch if he wanted.

"Look at him, Robin. I'm your sister, Kim."

"Let the boy breathe." Robin drew back and eyed him through a teary gaze.

Denver was so overwhelmed, he couldn't find his voice. He clutched both sisters' hands. Tears filled his own eyes. That was something he had not done since the death of their father.

"It's great to finally have you both here. Mom--"

He didn't get to finish before he felt his mother's trembling hand on his back. He turned and searched her face before moving aside. She touched each woman's face, before opening her arms to them. Both leaned into her embrace. The weeping sound of sorrow and joy filled the air. Every single person standing and watching the exchange had wet eyes and cheeks.

When they finally moved toward the house, Beatrice wouldn't let her girls go.

They sat on the couch, she in the middle. The three were all hugged up. He imagined that they would continue their conversation about what really happened at the hospital the day they were born.

Days after Josh's revelation, Ankit had joined the team of lawyers petitioning records from the hospital and the state. He met the same resistance that Kim and Robin's lawyers had met, even with the open records policies that were now enforceable. Record retention practices were different in those days. Cash payments were not recorded for transactions. The staff involved were now deceased.

The only saving grace for both sisters was the fact that their adoptive parents had retained the birth mother's name. Kim's adoptive parents were a military couple who couldn't have children. There were limited options for African American couples looking for adoption agencies.

In Robin's case, she'd been adopted but returned because she had hearing problems. She had been placed in foster care for a number of years. And, like Josh, seeing him with Trish's family in New Orleans, it was Robin who initiated the search after running into Lambert at the VA hospital in Houston.

He had dragged a little boy by the hand who'd dropped his toy and was crying because his father wouldn't stop long enough for him to retrieve it. Robin chased them down to return the dropped toy. Everything after that had led them to Baldwin Ranch.

Shortly after his new found family arrived, the house went from quiet to a roar equal to a fierce thunderstorm. Not only did they all talk fast, they all talked loud as well. It didn't seem to bother his mother one bit. He'd never seen her smile so much.

The house had five bedrooms, not including his quarters which comprised of his master bedroom and another room that rarely, if ever, got used. He moved to the quarters with the hands and gave his space to the Brooks and Trish. She helped him change the linens before kissing her sweetly.

"So, this is what you get to put up with?"

He looked down into her face. She wore a huge grin. He no longer saw the worry he'd seen for days. Even after their in-depth conversation about her dream, she followed him every place he went even though he'd assured her they couldn't do anything about what happened.

Well, not every place. He couldn't get her into his bed or on one of his field trips to the west meadow when he requested it.

"Yep, welcome to my world. You haven't even met my Uncle Ted and his crew. Just wait."

"I can only imagine. Now, you've put your crew and mine in one place. We'll likely be run out of the city."

"You just might be right, but it'll all be worth it."

"Hmmm…"

She tipped up on her toes and kissed his chin. "Sweet dreams."

"Get some rest, my love. I get the feeling we are going to need it."

And indeed, they did.

The Lamberts, Moores, and Rustins were a lot of company. What surprised him most was how solid a unit they became as a family in such a short time. By the end of the week, his brother-in-laws, Jake and Oscar, plus two of Robin's sons, pitched in and finished the frame and roof on the structure they had to rebuild.

Meals in the evening were the best. When it was time

for them all to leave, of course Beatrice took it the hardest.

"We promise to come back," Robin assured her. "It'll be hard to get rid us now, Mom." The endearment brought her to tears. "And we'll be at wedding next month."

"We wouldn't miss it for the world. We will be there early," Kim added. "Now that me and Jake are retired, we can come and go as we please."

Knowing that he, too, would have family there for their wedding brought Denver relief. He was ready to do it, even if there was no family there to share in the occasion. Since his family planned to attend, the excitement he was missing originally suddenly grew like the love that was growing for his siblings.

Trish's parents left a few days later and now they were back to their old routine.

It had been weeks since he'd made love to Trish and he intended to make up for all the lost time.

He reached her apartment while she was still at the clinic. Denver decided to surprise her with dinner. Well, hamburgers weren't exactly cooking but he would challenge anyone who thought his grilling skills didn't qualify as such.

She looked beat when she dragged in the front door.

"Hi, babe. It smells wonderful in here."

"Hurry up and shower so we can eat."

Trish took her sweet time. He'd put the burgers in the warmer and had just finished garnishing the salad with ripened tomatoes from CR's garden behind the tack shed. He put it all on the table and went in search of his bride.

When he reached the bedroom, she was curled up at the foot of the bed. So much for dinner, he thought. He sauntered back to the kitchen, placed their salads in the fridge and covered the burgers.

He then turned off the lights, went back to the bedroom and kicked off his boots. In one swift move, he picked up Trish's sleeping form and moved them both to the center of the bed.

She barely stirred when he picked her up. Pulling her close, he draped his arm and leg over her and closed his eyes. He had to be exhausted as well because he didn't remember drifting off. He stirred when Trish moved in his embrace.

"I fell asleep on you," she mumbled.

"That you did. You owe me for my gourmet meal I prepared for you."

"Really? Exactly, what did you prepare, Chef D.B?"

"My nationally renowned hamburger made from pure Texas beef and a salad every woman would die for?"

"That don't sound real gourmet to me, sir, but I'll gladly repay you for your overcooked Texas beef and wilted greens."

He squeezed her tight and tickled her neck with his after-five beard. She yelped and struggled to break loose.

"I'll show you overcooked."

He pinned her down on the bed, his legs straddling her, pinning her beneath him. With her wrists gripped in hands above her head, he leaned down until their lips were inches apart.

"Take it back or pay the price for your blasphemy."

Denver could feel her breath on his face. Her eyes bore into his. Her body beneath him reminded him that he'd not loved her in weeks.

Without hesitation, he covered her mouth and suckled her sweet lips like they were the best dessert he'd ever had.

CHAPTER 41

"I have no idea what you're talking about." She lowered her lids to escape his passion-filled gaze. The warmth of his body and his growing erection had her panting.

With all the tugging, they'd managed to move to one side of the bed. Still, he had her pinned down pretty good. Trish tried to shift beneath his weight but couldn't. She succumbed to the throb of his erection sending signals to the warm place between her legs. She fought to keep them closed, but lost. She opened, and Denver slipped right between them, pressing his way to her undoing.

"I've missed you, my love," he moaned, coaching her mouth open.

She'd refused his lure to their favorite necking spot. It was a test of sorts. One she hadn't shared with him yet. Trish knew she would be leaving in another week to go home for final preparations for their wedding.

Her mother had taken care of much of it and Trish had picked out her dress online from her favorite dress shop. It was similar to a dress she'd tried on last time she was there. They knew her dimensions and size, but she'd lost a little weight since she'd been home. So the final sizing and hemming was still on the 'to-do' list.

One of her other most pressing tasks was meeting with Father Landry. He would be officiating their ceremony and Trish

imagined one of the padre's questions would be about their intimate relationship. She wanted to be able to tell him the truth, that they were not having sex. Yes, it was a technicality, but without having to coach Denver when he arrived, he would be able to say the same thing.

It was important to her to take the sacraments at mass, having lived up to her part, even if it had only been recently. Turning her head, she was able to break his hold on her lips. He moved his attack to her neck and was heading down her body when she stopped him.

"Den?" Her hands braced against his shoulders.

"Yes, baby."

She pushed him away. He stared.

"Can we talk?"

A sinful grin creased his face. "We are talking."

"Really, Denver."

He frowned and lifted himself up, the passion still heavy between them. She couldn't ignore it. Sitting up, he pulled her with him.

"What's wrong?"

"Our wedding is three weeks away."

The look on his face spoke volumes. "Yes."

"Don't look at me that way. I haven't changed my mind."

"Good because I wouldn't want to lock you up in one of the sheds."

"You wouldn't dare." She tried to look tough. "But

really, on a serious note."

"Okay, I'm listening."

"We have to meet my bishop before he marries us."

He groaned and moved his feet to the floor. She grabbed his arm.

"Seriously, Denver. This is important."

By the end of the conversation, he agreed with her but wasn't at all happy about it. He stood and held out his hand to her.

"Does this mean we can't have the supper I slaved over?"

She grinned and took his hand.

****

When they were ready to leave Mom Bea had to go back into the house for a bag she'd left. Only God knew whether or not they would let her check the three bags Denver had already hauled into the back of his truck. Two of the bags were big enough to carry two grown men in.

"Whew, I can't leave this."

Her mother-in-law carried a brown leather train case in her arms. She hugged it like it held her life's possessions. When Denver delivered them to the small airport, Trish was certain the baggage checker would turn them and their luggage away. But her father had chartered a plane to bring them directly to Louis Armstrong International Airport. Otherwise, they would have had to go to Houston or Denver and then transfer to flights headed for New Orleans.

For the first time since they'd started this journey, Trish had a tough time leaving Denver behind. While his gentle kisses at her temple were soothing, they didn't keep her from clinging to him. He would come in a couple of weeks after taking care of Baldwin Ranch business. He and the crew had worked out coverage, especially since the barn fire.

Denver changed the subject each time she asked about the investigation into the fire.

She knew he worried about being away for so long. He'd be in New Orleans for a week until the wedding and then they would go away for a few days before returning to Texas.

Trish could only miss so many weeks away from the hospital herself. In fact, she'd just finished a sixteen-hour shift to make sure she didn't lose hours she needed to fulfill her requirements. Denver finally eased her away from him.

"I'll see you soon, my love. Take care of yourself for me."

"I love you so much."

His smile sent reassurance through her. He took his time kissing her and she savored his sweet, tender lips.

"I love you."

She clutched Mom Bea's hand the entire flight. And, as the days rolled into a week, she grew antsy to see him again.

The girls had arranged a bridal shower. What had she been thinking, planning a wedding in such a short timeframe?

Her phone rang and she answered it right away. She and Denver talked every day. She'd waited for his call today.

"Hi, Mister. I've missed you."

"Is that a fact? If you missed me so much, how about a little honey under your favorite, magic tree?"

"What am I going to do with you, Denver Baldwin? You know I'm weak right now. I just might give you whatever you want."

"Promise."

The doorbell rang before she could answer. She headed to the door with the phone still to her ear and moved the lock to open it.

"I just might take you down under that tree."

Trish stretched her eyes as wide as she could to make sure they weren't deceiving her.

"Promise?" He smiled the way he always did.

Denver dropped his phone as he looked down into her face. She screamed, jumping into his arms.

"Aw, that's my girl." He squeezed her tight, but not tight enough for Trish. "Missed me?" he cooed in her ear.

She couldn't respond. She hadn't expected him for another couple of days. Showing up early was the greatest gift she could hope for.

He offered her a sweet kiss that made her moan. She drowned in the warmth of Denver's his embrace. His lips tasted as sweet as pie. She wasn't ready to release him yet.

"So, are you two going to come in or go out?" They were so caught up in their reunion that neither heard her dad enter the foyer.

Trish's head fell onto his chest when he lifted his head.

Her dad stood close. Denver acknowledged him. She felt that low rumble in his chest she was so familiar with hearing when he talked.

"Hi sir, glad to see you again."

"Come in, son. Happy you made it safely. And you couldn't have gotten here soon enough. This little girl is driving everyone crazy."

Denver accepted her father's hand and shook it briefly. They both stepped inside and Alvin pushed the door close behind them.

"Thank you. I'm a few days early. I've been missing her."

"And I have been missing him," she completed the circle she'd made around his waist.

"Welcome. I'll let you guys get back to your reunion."

Her dad leaned down and kissed her forehead before patting Denver on the shoulder. He then headed to his office.

"Now, you were saying," Trish turned her face back to Denver.

"Come here, my love."

His strong arms fastened around her, opening the floodgates to that special place only he could reach. She lost her footing and melted into his body. She forgot they were standing in the foyer. Securing her by lifting her from the floor, Denver appeased her longing with extreme passion. His tongue danced in her mouth, still she couldn't get enough. She wanted more and needed more.

CHAPTER 42

Denver's head popped up at a second intrusion. This time it was her mother. She cleared her throat noisily. He lowered Trish to her feet, placing one last peck on her lips before acknowledging her mother.

He released Trish and reached to hug Diane.

Trish had made him hard as a rock. All the hay tossing, ditch digging, and the icy cold showers, hadn't taken away his desire for her.

He thought seeing her in the flesh would help him keep it all in prospective. But that shit wasn't working either. Damn the counseling session. Damn staying at her parents. He needed her in a bad way. He was willing to get a hotel room just to lay her down. He only needed a couple of hours to love her fully, deeply. Then all would be right in his world.

All those notions and ideas came to a head within moments of his arrival. He doubted he could get her alone for more than five minutes.

"Denver, son, you are here early."

"Yes, ma'am. I miss my love."

And no sooner had he gotten those words out, his mother waltzed down the stairs. Her descent quickened when she saw him.

He hadn't mentioned his plans to anyone, including his mother. She would have spoiled his surprise. He knew she would have told Trish of his early arrival. So he'd kept it to himself.

His sisters had arrived several days before and were heavy into the preparations for his big day. For this he was grateful. They would be there for their mother. Their bond was growing quickly. At first, he was concerned but they made it easy.

Being with and talking with them, he felt like he'd known them all his life. They'd talked every single day.

And like he'd imagined, it was the job of the older siblings to love and encourage him. Their goodbyes always ended with 'I love you so much.'

"Oh, my God! Den you made it." Beatrice instantly went to his arms and squeezed him tightly. He'd missed her as well.

"You're early, son. You should have told me."

"I wanted to surprise Trish."

"When did you leave? Is everything alright at home? Who's…?"

He held his finger to her lips. For now, he only cared about getting this wedding done so he could take his wife home. For good.

"Everything is fine."

He pulled Trish close again. He hadn't noticed until that moment but his bride had dark circles around her eyes. She hardly, if ever, wore makeup when they were in Texas. But the hot humid summers could be harsh on the skin and he'd noticed the expensive moisturizers and cleanser she used to care for, not just her face, but her hands and hair as well. He liked that. Trish's skin was flawless. And her eyes were clear. He looked closer and touched his finger to the side of her face.

"Everything okay, my love?"

She smiled, but it was missing that joy she always possessed. Her eyes danced as she looked up at him. He felt it in her touch. Something was wrong. How had he missed it earlier?

Perhaps his excitement helped him miss it. Now he was anxious to find out the root cause.

"We can talk later. Let's get you freshened up and fed. I know it's a long haul from home."

He held her as she tried to pull away. Yes, he'd heard her say home, but right now something else warranted his attention. He glanced up at their mothers before looking back into Trish's face. By looking at them, he could tell the women weren't nearly as aware that something was wrong. Yet he knew.

"Ah, we're gonna take a walk in the back for a few minutes."

He pulled Trish by the hand. Neither uttered a word until they were out of hearing distance from everyone. Taking a seat on the closest bench, he pulled her close, draping his arm around her shoulders. He kissed her cheek. "Tell me what's wrong, baby."

She glanced away but when she turned, her eyes were glassy with unshed tears. Seeing her this way broke his heart. Whatever it was, she'd kept it hidden during their daily talks. There was a list of things to do each time he talked to her.

She'd been extremely busy, more so than she'd been at home. Daily clinicals and student lectures had kept her extremely busy. When she got to the ranch, he'd made sure they had down time, even if it was just a long, quiet ride.

Here, no one ordered her to take it easy. He imagined she didn't have time for such pleasures since she still had a lot to do in order for the wedding to go as planned. Perhaps, they should have waited.

He looked at her. Trish laid her head on his shoulder without saying anything. He picked her up and moved her to his lap, cuddling her like a little girl.

"I'm here now, darling. I'll do whatever you need me to do." She nodded. "Have you been sleeping?" She nodded again. "You haven't changed your mind, have you?"

His question caused her to look into his face. Her answer was in her eyes. She didn't need words. He cupped her face and placed his forehead against hers. When she spoke, her voice was low and raspy. Her warm breath felt sensuous on his face.

"I'm enjoying my wedding experience, Den. It's just that I've been missing you. I don't want us to be apart again if we can help it."

He closed his eyes, feeling her energy. The prickly, thick sensation made his breath catch in his throat. "I'm cool with that. Right now, I want to know that you're okay."

"I am."

"Can I make love to you under that bewitching tree of yours?"

She burst into a laughing fit. He relaxed on hearing her. The energy changed and his heart was well again. He kissed her cheek.

"Not even if you kissed me senseless."

"Are you sure?" He kissed his way down past her neck.

"Stop it, you animal."

He stood, still holding her. "What if I drop you into the deep end of that pool?" He pointed his chin in the direction of the pool.

"You better not, Denver Baldwin. I wouldn't marry you if you did that."

"Really?"

"Not a chance."

"Well, I just might have to take this up with the authorities."

"What authorities?"

"Wouldn't you like to know?"

"I…"

"Trish, you have a call, bae." Her mother yelled from the door.

She groaned and headed back to the house. Denver twined his fingers with hers as they made their way back to the house. Before he opened the door, he kissed her again.

"I love you, Trish."

She smiled. "We'll see when you talk to Father Laundry in a few days. He's rough."

"I can handle it."

"I know. I love you, too."

When they entered the room, there were several people he didn't know waiting for them. They swarmed around him, reminding him of his first meeting with her brothers. These ladies he could take, in fact all of them at the same time.

"Well, is this your cowboy, cuz?"

A tall red head moved in front of him fist. Then they all circled him. What was wrong with this family? Would he have to prove himself to every one of them? He eyed each one as they passed in front of him. One eye brow lifted.

"Yep. What you think?" An eyebrow lifted.

Another passed him and winked. "I think I like him."

The smallest smiled up at him. "Hey cousin, we're Trish's first cousins from Bossier City."

"Hello, cousins from Bossier City. I'm Denver."

"We know this, smalls. Welcome to the family. I'm Tracy."

Each young lady introduced themselves. He had trouble remembering all the names of people he'd already met, not to mention own his new family.

"I see you met the crew." Trish walked up behind him. "Don't worry; this is only a fraction of the gang."

"You don't say," he replied and kissed her briefly. "If you don't mind, I'm will be upstairs."

"Love you," Trish called after him.

"Love you," all the ladies cooed in unison and giggled.

He shook his head. "Oh, boy."

****

In the days that followed, Denver was happy to find a quiet spot anywhere. They'd finished the appointment with Father Landry. He was two seconds from dragging Trish by the hand and heading to the courthouse. Their mothers would kill him but at least he'd die a happy man.

When Ankit arrived, they did wedding rehearsal and then lunch with the family. Afterwards, while groom and best man took time to get Ankit's tux fitted, they had a chance to talk.

"Good Lord, how many people are there in this family?" He asked.

"More names than I'll ever remember." Denver slapped Ankit's shoulders several times.

"You ready, brother?"

"I am. I love this woman. All of this, I'm doing for her. I'm just a simple cowboy. You know I don't care about none of this."

"Suck it up. Trust me it will save your life later."

"Man, I hear you."

"Your peeps seem to be doing good."

"This ready-made family is unbelievable but I'm loving it."

"Not to put a damper on your weekend, Den, but you have some business to take care of when you get back."

"Who?"

"Kevin Jones."

No, he didn't want to think about the barn fire now. He had a wedding to get through. Tonight, they would spend some party time with their frats, courtesy of his brother-in-laws. And then, he would go back to his hotel room and wait for the extravaganza the parents had planned.

He reached into his coat pocket and handed Ankit two boxes.

"I'll keep them safe."

"I know. Let's get a drink."

"Now, that's the get down; let's do it."

He wouldn't get to see Trish again until the early morning service. Following mass, they would parade from the cathedral to the hall. But just because he couldn't see her, didn't mean he couldn't talk to her.

"Let me make one last call."

"Man, you'll see that woman in the morning. Right now it's time to do some celebrating."

"You can say that. You'll lay next to a warm body tonight."

"Yeah, with three little busy bodies in between us. Trust, ain't nothing happening here, man."

He laughed.

"Hold on…" Denver held up his hand. "Hey baby,

just…"

"Hey, Denver. This is Brandi. Trish is in the bathroom. She's not feeling so hot."

Denver and Ankit were headed to the car. Denver looked at his friend and nearly went into a sprint.

"Brandi, I'm on my way."

He disconnected the phone and jerked opened the back-driver side door. He tossed his garment bag in and hopped behind the wheel.

"Something is wrong with Trish." He motioned for Ankit to hurry.

"What happened?"

"I don't know but I'm heading to her mother's house."

He literally turned the car on two wheels and sped towards the garden district.

He rushed to the house to meet resistance from the Brooks women first and then his own kin, his mother, and two sisters, Robin and Kim.

"Where do you think you're going?"

CHAPTER 43

Trish wobbled to her bed, the contents of her stomach now flushed down the toilet. She brushed hands away as she fell back onto her bed.

"I'm okay, stop it," she fussed. "I probably ate something that I shouldn't have."

"Girl, don't make me call your mother up here."

"Too late, I'm already here. What's wrong, sweetheart?"

Her mom moved between the parting group of women in Trish's room.

"I'm good, Mommy. Brandi is making fuss because I have an upset stomach."

Her mom sat on the bed next to her with her palm turned up. She placed it on Trish's forehead, at her temples then under her chin.

"Get me a face towel, please. Wet it with cold water," she ordered. One of her cousins went to do the bidding. Trish's mother turned to the group.

"Okay, ladies. Give us a minute, will you?"

Everyone except Brandi moved.

"You too, Brandi. She'll be okay."

Trish's mom folded the wet towel and gently pressed it against her face.

"There. Better?"

Trish nodded. "Yes, Ma'am. I just got a little queasy is all."

Her mom smiled. "Nervous."

Trish nodded. She didn't realize she would react this way. She'd been good all week, ready to get this weekend done with. She was ready to become Denver's wife. With all the people and all the activities, she was just overcome by it all.

"You'll be fine," Her mom started when there was a tap on the door.

It was Autumn, Travis's wife. She handed her mother a glass of water and turned to leave without saying a single word. All the men had been banned from the house, including her dad. So, the women had taken over the entire place.

"Sit up, sweetie."

Trish complied. "Slow." She complied again, taking small gulps of the water.

"It's normal to be nervous."

"But…"

"You have a worried groom downstairs. He rushed over because Brandi told him you were sick when he called."

Trish sat up, ready to leave the bed. Her mother's hand held her in place. Trish didn't realize he'd called. She worried about what he might think. She had to let him know she was okay.

"Mom…."

"His mother and sisters are downstairs guarding the door, of course. He'd threatened to break in if no one told him where you were and that you were okay."

She sighed. "Can I call him?"

"Now, that you can do."

Her mom handed her the cell phone she'd taken from Brandi's hand. Trish's fingers trembled as she held the phone to her ear.

"Hi, Den."

"Baby, are you okay?"

"Yes, I'm good. Don't worry."

"I want to see for myself."

She looked at her mother. "You're not supposed to see me until tomorrow. Really, I'm okay."

"Baby, take care of yourself for me, please."

"I will. I love you."

"I love you, too. I'll see you tomorrow?"

"You bet. Now I have to go and so should you, unless you want a butt kicking from a bunch of women."

"See you tomorrow, darling."

"See you tomorrow."

She clicked the phone off.

The rest of the evening was uneventful with the exception to food, dancing, and playing games. Instead of the scrumptious appetizers everyone else enjoyed, Trish's mother gave her chicken soup and saltine crackers. Trish was happy for the tasty meal. And instead of the champagne she'd intended to drink tonight, she had ginger ale like the kids did.

"Humph, this reminds me of the last Brooks wedding. I had to drink ginger ale back then as well."

Everyone laughed at her and she pouted.

"Well maybe a little later. We'll see how the tummy is feeling."

Her mom hugged her. And sure enough, as the night drew late, she and her maid of honor shared a toast while they huddled in her room.

"Girl, I can't believe you're getting married and moving to Texas. Texas! So far away from your best friend."

"I'm not that far. You can visit any time. It's not like I won't come home."

She leaned on her friend. They'd had all these great plans. Once she finished school, they were going to travel the world, go to all of the great places and meet all of the great men.

Well, she'd met one who'd turned her world upside down. She didn't care about meeting guys anymore. As far as traveling, she hoped that she and Denver would get to do that.

When her mother tapped on the door, the sun had begun to rise in the sky. She would have a light breakfast, a massage and then her makeup done before they headed to the cathedral. They'd packed her parade clothes to change into when the ceremony was over. Dennis had already placed them in her truck.

"Rise and shine."

Now as Trish slipped her arms into her dress, both her mom and Mom Bea were on either side of her, helping her get the contraption together. Tears of joy filled the room.

"Okay, Trish is the only person not allowed to cry." Brandi ordered. "We don't have time to do this face over."

When her dad finally came for her, she noticed something different about him. Tall and extremely handsome, he'd always carried a certain air. People always took notice of what he said, of what he did. He'd always been her knight. The guard was soon changing and they both knew it.

His smile was familiar, only it held a tinge of sadness today.

"My God, you look absolutely beautiful."

He bent and kissed her cheek.

"Thank you, Daddy."

"Ready?"

She took a long breath. "Yes."

He led her down the petal covered aisle.

Her nieces had covered the path and thoughts of the two made her smile. She moved at a comfortable pace, her eyes catching the smiles of family and friends along the way.

However, the very eyes she wanted to see most were still a good distance away. Why was her dad moving so slowly?

Finally, she saw him. His focus was clearly on her. It took her breath away. His eyes were intense, his stance rigid, with both hands cupped in front of him. He didn't move at the predetermined time. She'd passed the mark where he was supposed to make his way to meet them.

She trembled and felt her legs get wobbly. It must have been noticeable because she felt her father look down at her. She kept her eyes on Denver. And when he finally moved, she wanted to run.

They stopped at the appointed spot and didn't have to wait long for him. He eyed her through her veil. Father Landry asked the question that made her father lift her arm and place her hand in Denver's. She'd totally missed everything up to that. She'd not heard the priest or her dad's response. She did lean over to accept his kiss on her cheek.

"Hello gorgeous. I love you."

The tears started to flood. Denver turned to lead her the rest of the way and her feet wouldn't move at first.

He stopped and squeezed her fingers as she gazed up to him.

Finally, standing before the altar, they kneeled as Father Landry gave the prayer. "Let them come to me, and I will show them the way."

"Amen," everyone responded.

By the time Denver slipped the ring on her finger, she was trembling so much, she thought she would lose it. Denver held both of her hands tightly. She rewarded him with a tight smile. They repeated the ring ceremony vows and she placed the black band on his finger. They knelt for the last prayer after communion.

"May you have a blessed and long marriage. God be with you."

Everyone responded, "And with your spirit."

"Family and friends, it is my privilege to introduce you to Denver and Trisha Baldwin. You may now salute your bride."

This was the part she'd waited for. Denver pulled her close and kissed her like they'd never kissed before. It was so sweet, so tender; she had to look at him for a long moment before she allowed him to release her. He smiled and she did, too.

After they took pictures with the wedding party and family, and signed the marriage certificate, Denver pulled an envelope from his jacket pocket and handed it to Father Landry.

"This is for you, sir."

Trish changed into her parade gown. The sequined purple ball dress, with off the shoulder flaps, had a narrow waist and a wide tulle, hooped bottom. She exchanged her veil for an ornate crown and mask with satin gold ribbon tied behind her head.

Denver waited for her at the base of the float they

would ride. The preplanned parade route was the traditional Krewe du Vieux route at an early time since many of the local parades would start in a couple of hours. They would take one of the shortest routes to the reception hall.

"You are beautiful, Mrs. Baldwin."

Denver nibbled on her ear. She rewarded him with a kiss before he helped her onto the float as she hiked up her gown.

The wedding party was already on board. The three floats behind them held family and friends. A Limo with the parents took the lead through the crowded streets.

Trish had never grinned so much in her life. She tossed beads and doubloons out into the crowd as the music blasted. She saluted the crowd with kisses from Denver along the way.

"Is this what you envisioned your day to be like, darling?"

He placed his lips to her ear so that she could hear him. She turned in his embrace. His eyes sparkled with glee. She'd never felt so blessed until that very moment.

"I love you so much, Denver. I don't care if nothing else in this day goes as planned. It's everything I wanted and more. I'm so happy."

"That's all I care about, my love."

"You make me happy, Den."

"You make me happy."

"Hey, you two, throw some beads. You got all night to do that," Michael tossed beads at them.

They burst into laughter.

By the time they got close to their venue, she and Denver had all but forgotten about throwing beads. They'd locked arms and lips, tasting and testing their control. He wrapped his arms around her butt--at least he tried--and pulled her hard into him. He groaned into her mouth.

CHAPTER 44

Denver savored his wife's mouth like it was the best cobbler he'd ever eaten in his life. When he thought something had happened to her yesterday, he was ready to break through the guard that had been commissioned at her family's entrance. He texted her last night in the midst of his bachelor party. After she replied, he finally felt at ease, not that his mother wouldn't tell him if something was really wrong.

When he saw her come up that center aisle, it took everything in his heart to not crush her in his arms. He gave every ounce of himself. As the priest gave him the okay to kiss her, he tried to hold it together. It was hard, especially when he heard the weeping in the pews behind them. He knew one of them had to be his mother.

And even though, he didn't originally get the concept of a Mardi Gras wedding, this was the best. He would never forget this day.

The crowd cheered them on, celebrating their union. The minted doubloons they threw out had the Baldwin ranch crest and wedding date on them. Now that was a genius idea, he thought. He planned to bring some home for his crew.

Denver was so overwhelmed at one point that he simply couldn't contain his feelings. He pulled Trish in and kissed her deeply. The screaming crowd, the music, and the taunting of her family and friends were all lost on them.

"We're good?"

"We're so good."

They talked and greeted family at the hall. Trish hadn't touched her food at all.

"Are you feeling well, baby?"

"Yes, I'm okay."

"You haven't eaten anything, Trish."

"I know."

"Come on, let's sit for a minute."

They'd been moving from table to table. He caught his mother's attention, not on purpose, but she came over immediately. He didn't even have a chance to make a request of her because right behind her, his mother-in-law came with a plate in her hand. She smiled as if she knew the deal.

"Make her eat this, Denver."

"Yes, ma'am." They both nibbled from the plate.

The toasts were nonstop. Denver topped off their glasses. The last thing he needed was to be so wasted that he would not be able to enjoy his wedding night. After last night, he was surprised he wasn't hung over. He had to admit, he hadn't missed frat life at all.

Together they greeted more guests, cut cake, and completed the rituals of throwing the garter and bouquet. Now they danced.

"Are you enjoying your evening, husband?"

He'd already helped her and Brandi adjust her gown

and replace her shoes with ballet slippers.

"I'm having a blast."

He felt better since she'd eaten what was given her. She'd also eaten a small slice of cake.

"Sorry, Frat. It's my dance."

Travis came first, followed by her other two brothers. Each pinned a hundred-dollar bill to the sleeve of her dress. The number of people following their lead, including the women and children, left her with a dress nearly full of cash.

When her father finally returned her to him, she was grinning hard.

"Here you go, son. I believe this one belongs to you."

"Yes, sir. Thanks."

"So how much you got, mister."

"Your payment will come later."

"I have one more garment change. You'll be here when I get back?"

"There's no chance I leave here without you, Mrs. Baldwin."

"I'll be right back."

Trish returned wearing a provocative red gown that hugged her body. He whistled as she neared. He watched, admiring the way her hips swayed. He was sure she added the sway for his benefit. Denver opened his arms and she stepped into his embrace. He gave their guests an eye full, pulling her close and rotating against her. His hand behind her kept Trish in his grip.

"Are you trying not to make it out of this joint in this damn dress, Trish?"

Trish caught his bottom lip between her teeth.

"I have no idea what you're talking about Mr. Baldwin."

"Just remember. This is all mine to have my way

with."

"I'm ready."

"Not just yet, my darling. We have one last dance to complete."

"Lead the way."

Following Travis's specific instructions, he lifted his hand to the DJ, who made the announcement.

"Ladies and gentlemen, the bride and groom have requested you join them."

He cranked up the volume of Trombone Shorty's track, Hurricane. The crowd fell behind them with open parasols and white handkerchiefs.

"Hey! Hey! Hey!" The crowd chanted as they followed Denver and Trish's lead. They marched around the hall several times before the song changed to another city favorite. And by the time 'When the Saints go Marching In,' came on, he was ready to give the floor to the remaining dancers. Most had moved back to their seats by the middle of the second song.

"That's got to be more work than mucking stalls."

"I disagree." Trish rolled her eyes at him. She sat back in the chair, still panting. He handed her a champagne flute and held his up for his toast.

"Here's to a wonderful day. I love you."

"I love you more."

Trish started to kiss his cheek, but he turned, meeting her lips, savoring them before he pulled away. He upped his glass and emptied it.

"Here, here, my love."

Trish had to dance a few numbers with her girls. He sat back, enjoying the atmosphere. His mother sat next to him and took his hand.

"You look very happy, son."

"Mom, I never been so happy in my entire life. Thank

you for everything. And, I don't just mean this." He waved across the room. "I mean everything. You've always been a great mother to me."

"Oh, Den. You've always been respectful and helpful. You made my life worth living. And now you get to enjoy a life with a beautiful and caring young woman."

"Love you."

"Now, if you don't mind, I have grandbabies to go and spoil."

She patted the top of his hand and he watched her departure. He caught Trish's gaze as she headed his way. By the time she was next to him, her demeanor had changed. He pulled her into his lap.

"Well, Mrs. Baldwin, what's your story?"

"I'm done, Den."

"Done?"

"Yes. I'm ready to leave."

"All right, sweetheart. Let's say our goodbyes."

They started with the parents, then the siblings and finally the wedding party. Ankit had already taken care of his best man duties. When they reached the exit, a limo was waiting.

The short ride took longer than usual because of on-going Mardi Gras parades. He'd pulled Trish into his lap and her wayward hips pressed against his growing erection. His hands crawled up and down her back. He groaned with frustration because of her dress. It gave him absolutely no access, not even to her breast, which was peeking out from the hole near the high-neck.

"I thought I liked this dress. I'm beginning to change my mind," he whispered in her mouth.

She drew back and glared at him. "Why?" She frowned.

"It's too damn restrictive. I can't wait to take it off of

you."

"No worries, my love, it's comes off extremely easily."

"Hmmm, thank God for that."

They'd been so caught up in their interlude that they hadn't noticed that the limo had stopped. The driver had already moved around to the passenger's side, ready to open the door. He tapped lightly on the window to gain their attention. Denver would have to remember to have Ankit tip the man well for his discretion. He didn't have to give them a warning.

He pulled away from Trish's mouth. She protested. "I've got more for you. Let's get this evening started."

He pulled the key Ankit had given him from his pocket and unlocked the door. Trish waited as he pushed it completely opened. He lifted her into his arms, pressed his lips to hers and crossed the threshold. He stood there, pleasuring her mouth until he had his fill.

"You are my heart." He buried his face into her hair.

Lowering Trish to her feet, he closed the door. His mind was made up. The night was long and he planned to use every minute of it.

He kissed her slowly and sensuously. He didn't know which of them had moaned but it ignited the fire, setting the pace for his next move. Trish grew limp in his arms and he firmed his hold to keep them together. Lifting her again, he walked past the bar, set up with champagne and chocolate covered strawberries. There would be time for all of that. Business first. Get her out of that damn dress.

He unclamped one hook and the dress slid down her body. Beneath it, she wore a silk red tong that only covered the curly patch of hair in the front.

He admired her from behind before making his request. "Turn around for me, darling."

As she did, he reached for the clip holding her hair in

place. Her silky curls tumbled to her shoulders and draped them like a cloak. She was amazingly breathtaking. He had to repress his need to rush on.

Taking a long breath, he sucked air until he couldn't take in more. Slowly, he released it as his gazed traveled from her curvy legs and thighs, all the way to her full perky breasts, which he couldn't resist. Both hands circled them, adding more color to the nipples when he squeezed. His eyes continued their journey and stopped momentarily at her lips, which he couldn't resist either. He touched them lightly then pulled away.

And, finally, he gazed into her fully passionate eyes. He held there in silent appraisal.

"You're beautiful."

He kissed her nose and her chest rose, her eyes closed.

"I want to go slow, baby. You think you can help me with that?"

She lifted her eyelids and gazed back at him. Her breath caught. She leaned into his hands, still caressing her breasts.

"I don't know that I can."

Trish reached between his arms, forcing his hands away from her chest. She toyed with the ivory buttons on his shirt, opening the front. She reached beneath his T-shirt, her fingers grazing flesh, all the way up his chest. The unexpected move caused him to tremble.

"I can certainly try, Den. I'll do anything for you, my love."

She reached up and kissed his bottom lip. Her raspy reply stirred him even harder. He would have to do this alone. Trish was going to push until she got her way. It would be just like her to try and set the tone. He grabbed her wrist and gently pushed her away. He removed his shirt and then his pants as she watched.

CHAPTER 45

Trish was on fire, literally. The throbbing between her legs grew more and more intense. Who was he fooling? They might go slow some time during the night, but not right now. She needed him to fill her, to quench this hunger. And, she needed him now.

Yes, it was her fault they'd waited. Still, she was his. And he was hers to do whatever, whenever they wanted to do…anything. She yelped when he swooped her up in his muscular arms and placed her on the bed.

She dragged her fingers up his rippled, taunt stomach and chest. He gasped.

She snaked her way up the bed and he was with her with each move. His hand slipped up her hips and didn't stop until he cupped her face. His lips lowered until they almost touched hers. His eyes bore straight through her.

"You're going to make this hard for me, aren't you?"

"I need you so badly, Den. Please, baby, don't make me wait."

She opened her legs and wrapped them around his waist. With all of her strength, she tried to join them. But

Denver was much stronger and more in control than she was. Still she tried. When that didn't work, she stretched to kiss him and he pulled his head back.

"Relax, angel. I want to love you fully."

She heard his words but it was obvious he'd forgotten to make the agreement with the aching parts that made them one. His erection bobbed against her stomach. The mere thought of his silky hardness moving inside her made her tremble with need.

"Den?"

He sat up and she released him with no idea what he would do next. He leaned back on his knees and pulled her on top of him. With hands on her hips, he guided his fire stick inside. She thought her world had exploded into a million pieces.

Trish screamed so loud she was sure they heard her across the city. Denver held her tight until her muscle grabbed him with great intensity. He moved her hips slowly, greedy for more. She wiggled in his embrace, his erection touching places that made her hotter instead of providing relief.

He moaned, his hands trembled. She took the advantage and set the cadence. She plunged down on his every stroke. She was riding him like a woman gone mad. She'd lost control. Her finger dug into his shoulders as she seized her first orgasm in more than a month.

Denver held her tight, grunting his release. They both panted like they'd just completed a marathon. Their sweat-soaked bodies mimicked that thought. Forehead to forehead, they gasped to catch their breath.

"Now, can we slow this down?" He asked.

"Yes."

He lowered her to the bed, pulling her hands above her head. He released them and she allowed him to have his way, this time nice and slow.

He praised every inch of her body with his lips. They met this time with slow, deliberate thrusts that made her too weak to assist. She willingly enjoyed the ride.

After round three, they took a warm shower, donning the plush robes by the bathroom door.

Denver poured champagne and handed her a glass. She picked up a strawberry, and they cuddled on the couch.

"Here's to us and our new beginning."

"And what a wonderful beginning it is."

She offered him a bite of the strawberry. He barely left her any. At this point, she didn't care. She was all too happy to take what he left. She popped the last bite in her mouth and took a long swig of the sparkling wine.

****

It wasn't a part of the plan but they joined the family for church service mid-morning and followed them to the house afterwards. She was happy to stay under his arm. Wherever he went, so did she, including the bathroom. Denver didn't seem to mind at all.

Later that night, they went back to the hotel, made love again until the wee hours of the morning and again before the bellman came up for their luggage the next day.

When they boarded the plane headed to the Dominican, they talked quietly when they weren't napping. The long drive to their resort was well worth the ride. Their beachside bungalow set nestled along a white sand beach and soothing ocean waves.

Love making on their private beach was the best they'd had to date for her. Getting the sand, all of it, out of her hair was a totally different story. Denver tried to help only his hands riding her hips didn't help anything.

He kept finding himself between her legs.

"We go home tomorrow." Trish fumbled with the makeup case she placed in her suitcase. Their few days in paradise had come to a close.

Denver kissed her boldly. "Yes, sweetheart. It's going to be hard to leave this spectacular view."

They snuggled near at the open sliding door.

"Yes, but nothing compares to the meadows of Baldwin Ranch."

She turned in his embrace and looked up into his face. He lifted a brow. "What, no comment?"

"Nope. I already know home is God's country."

She tapped his chest and walked out to the patio.

****

When they pulled through the gate of the ranch, Trish's heart started racing. She sat forward. She saw people huddled everywhere. Some held signs, others held bundles of wildflowers. She pressed her hand to her mouth as tears gathered in her eyes.

"Oh, my God. What a wonderful homecoming."

"Yes, indeed it is."

Denver put the gear in park, got out and was greeted by a swarm of people.

"Hold you horses. Let me get the wife out of the truck."

They followed him to the passenger side door. When he pulled it open, the whole crowd cheered. He helped her down and she went through a reception line similar to the one on their wedding day. They all hugged her. Some pushed wildflowers into her hands. "Oh, my, these are lovely," was all she could say.

The celebration lasted well into the evening. It had been outside the entire time. Before CR and his family left, he hugged her extremely tight.

"I'm so glad you managed to fast-talk your way onto this ranch, little one. I was right about you from the beginning."

"I'm just glad you didn't turn me away. Thank you."

She kissed his cheek. He grinned up at Denver.

"Don't get any ideas."

"No sir, boss. See you bright and early. Is she mucking stalls?"

Denver looked from CR to her and burst out laughing. Trish dabbed him on the shoulder.

"No. Now good night to you. Your wife is waiting for you." Trish pointed and he grunted as he left.

"Are you ready to go inside, my sweet wife?"

"Yes, sir. I am."

Denver carried Trish through the door and headed straight to his quarters.

"Welcome to our home...at least for now."

He sat her down and she looked around the room.

"I think it could use a woman's touch."

"As long as you are between those sheets, I don't care what you do to the rest."

"Well, I think, first we need to test out these new sheets I had your mother put on the bed." She ran her hand down the sides of the bed.

"I'm more interested in seeing if we both fit in the shower. Want to try it out?" He stepped behind her and cupped her breast.

"Don't see why not."

CHAPTER 46

Denver already knew they would fit into his walk-in shower. It had double shower heads along one side of the granite walls and another two in the ceiling. It also had a built-in high-bench on the right side. He turned on all the shower heads, testing the water temperature before they entered.

He dipped his head beneath and Trish following his lead. He gently pressed her back to the wall and captured her mouth.

"I've been waiting a long time for this." He groaned into her mouth. "Hold on, baby."

Denver lifted her hips and slipped into her with ease. She held his slippery body as best as she could, meeting him at the top of every push. She bit his bottom lip and reached for the top one with same vigor. He filled her and somehow managed to hit all the right spots.

"Oh, you're so addicting, my love. I can't get enough of you."

He pumped even harder, his fingers gripped and squeezed her, digging deeper each time until he hit the spot that sent her sailing off the cliff. Lucky for her, he still had strength because she had none left.

When he lowered her to her feet, he pulled them beneath one of the overhead sprays. Groaning he drew away and reached for the shower gel.

After they were done, they took care in drying one another off before they slipped beneath the sheets.

They rested on their sides, Denver parked behind her with his arm securely round her waist.

"Sweet dreams, darling."

Trish squeezed his arm. "Sweet dreams. I love you."

The day had been long; the excitement of getting home and the celebration with their friends consumed them both. She quickly fell asleep and didn't stir when he slipped from the bed.

He eased out of the room, careful to close the door softly. He walked to the kitchen. The coffee pot had done its usual duty.

When he arrived at the tack shed, he went directly to his bike and checked it for gas. He boarded the vehicle and steered toward the west paddock. He checked the mares, fat with foals. They weren't quite ready to give birth. He was relieved that Trish would be on hand when the time came.

"Hey there, girl. Yes, she's back. Now you can quit giving the hands such a fit."

He patted the black mare they called Stacy on the rump. She'd been fit to be tied. When she and several of the others had taken sick, his wife had gone out each day to personally care for them. Well, he should say she'd spoiled them rotten. They weren't satisfied with normal treatment now.

She'd left specific instructions for their care. Of course, for the three weeks she'd been gone, the men complained that the horses were divas. He would tolerate it for now because they were bearing the fruit of their prosperity.

Stacy nudged him in the back when he was about to leave.

"I don't have time for you. Trish will be out later to see you."

She bobbed her head as if she understood. Once he finished his rounds, Denver headed back to the house. The smell of bacon hit him before he opened the door. When he entered, Trish's sweet humming met his ears. He smiled broadly.

"Good morning, baby."

He hugged her. The spatula she held lifted a fat flapjack that she placed on the platter with the others before she turned in his embrace.

"Good morning. You checked on the mares?"

"I did. You've created monsters."

"They can't be that bad."

"It's that bad."

"Well, I'll go see for myself when we're done with breakfast."

"Good morning," his mother greeted them behind a hidden yawn. "Whew, I've never overslept like this before."

Trish walked over and kissed her cheek. "Good morning. You didn't have to get up this morning."

His heart beamed. He couldn't be happier--until he thought about the sheriff's visit scheduled for this morning. Trish would be out of earshot because she had to be at the clinic. For that he was thankful.

"Good morning, Baldwin." The sheriff stuck out his hand when he arrived.

Denver accepted the firm grip and offered him and his

deputy a seat.

"Can I offer you a cup of coffee? My wife made a fresh batch of cookies."

"That's right. Congratulations. Good?"

"Thanks, Sheriff. Yes, we're good."

He pushed a cup of coffee his way. Ankit had already consumed a cup and three of the cookies.

"Man, you're going to be fat. Just watch what I tell you," Ankit had complained before the sheriff arrived.

"I'm not the one behind a desk all day, my man. She can cook whatever she wants."

They began with more small talk then got down to business. The sheriff cleared his throat.

"So, Baldwin, I have a deputy on his way to the Dexter Ranch to pick up Keith Jones."

"Why would Keith be on my ranch?"

"When I talked to Juanita, she didn't know anything about this incident. She promised to remain quiet until we picked him up."

"Is there anything else you can tell me?"

"Apparently, he left a bundle of wicks and a small gas can with his name on it in the field just past the juncture to your road. Do you remember seeing any vehicles along your property in the last couple of months?"

Denver couldn't remember anything. He'd been preoccupied with Trish. The night he came home from her apartment when he had seen lights from a truck but hadn't thought anything of it. He'd been dog tired and ready to plow down in his bed.

"We'll look around a little more if you don't mind and we will let you know what we find."

"Thanks. I'll be interested in learning why someone wanted to burn me out."

After the two law officers left, he and Ankit sat and

talked for a while longer.

"Do you think Juanita had something to do with this?" Denver stood looking out of his office window.

"Man, I don't know what to think. It would be crazy if she did. She stands to lose a ridiculous amount of money from this deal if it doesn't go well. Why would she chance that?"

"I don't know, brother, but someone is trying to mess with my money and my livelihood."

****

Weeks had passed since Denver had heard from the sheriff. Keith provided them with a sufficient alibi. He had no idea how his can had gotten to the field beside Denver's property. And yes, he'd purchase wicks from the country store several months before but had used them all on the Dexter Ranch.

They were back to square one. In the meantime, life on Baldwin Ranch was as smooth as life could be.

He enjoyed waking up next to Trish. She'd moved all of her belonging out of the apartment even though she had to pay rent through the end of spring.

"You have a meeting with Juanita today, right?" Trish looked over her shoulder at him.

All the transactions since signing the official documents had been done through the lawyers. Occasionally there was a teleconference, but he hadn't seen Juanita since the day in Ankit's office.

Denver looked at Trish to gauge her mood. She looked at him expectantly.

"Yes. We're meeting here." He frowned. "Are you going into the clinic today? I thought you were on the schedule."

She smiled and walked over to drape her arms around his shoulders. "I am on the schedule but I might have to stay to keep an eye on my man. That old biddy might be up to her witch spells."

He pulled from her embrace. "Now, Trish, you know better than to talk about people. Besides, I'm a married man, remember?"

"Oh, I remember. Let's hope the crypt-dweller does, too."

He dropped a kiss on her cheek. "I think that's the least of your worries."

"We'll see."

"While it's still safe, I think you better get going. Otherwise I'm going to have to help you out of these clothes."

"Unless you plan to miss your sister's birthday party, I suggest you keep it moving, my brother."

"Oh, so you take it there?"

"Yep, keep it moving."

He held his hands up in surrender. But as she passed, he tried his luck one last time and pulled her close to cover her mouth with his. His hands pressed her snuggly against his rising affection. She surrendered to his explorations. Denver shifted his stance, spreading his legs apart and moving his hips forward. She moaned so he gave her more.

CHAPTER 47

No matter how much she tried, Trish couldn't resist him. He didn't play fair. She would have to remember that later. He knew exactly what to do to seduce her. She pined for a taste of his loving.

"Have you changed your mind," he whispered in her ear.

She tried to find her voice. It didn't help that his hands were on reconnaissance and her body was the target. She pulled away, only to be lured back again. She found her voice.

"Yes... I mean no."

She pushed against his chest and gazed at him through blurry vision. His lips enticed her but she found strength.

"I've got to go, Den."

He pecked her lips and released her. His eyes still held the passion she'd come to know. All she had to do was give him the signal and they were on.

"Sure?"

"Yes, for now."

"I don't know. I might decide to keep my sugar once

you leave."

"I'll take my chances."

"Okay, I love you. Call me later."

"I will."

Trish took one last look and pushed through the door. He winked at her as he folded his arms across his chest.

Once she got to the clinic and slipped into her coat, she joined a group headed to the surgical clinic. Today, she was the lead surgeon removing a benign tumor. The procedure was relatively simple for her. She'd done dozens before.

"Great job." The head of the surgery department slapped her on the shoulder later.

"Thanks."

She took a few minutes to call Denver but her call went straight to voicemail.

"Hey, hon. Just had a few minutes. I'll call you back later. Love you."

She returned to the store room to replace some unused tools back in the cabinet. She noticed the list taped to the door and frowned. Many of the items on the list were the things required to pen a herd scheduled to arrive early in the next morning. She pulled the sheet down and walked over to the clerk.

"Hey Amber, who was assigned to fulfill this list?"

Amber glanced down at the schedule. "Um, Derek. But he called in sick today."

Trish glanced at her watch. Her next appointment wasn't for another two hours. So, she removed her coat and hung it on the hook, then reached for the van keys.

"I got it. I should be back in about a half hour."

"Okay."

She hummed during the ten-minute drive, parking directly in front of the back-loading door. She continued to hum as she made her way down the aisle. Her cart was nearly full and she was having a tough time shifting it.

"Let me help you with that."

Trish froze. Her gloved hands went slack on the handle bars of the cart. She took a calming breath and turned. Denver's words echoed in her ears as she mustered up a smile to hide her sudden concern.

"Hi, Butch. Do you live here?" She chuckled hoping the crack would ease her tension.

She looked to see if there were other people around.

"What? Are you looking for Denver? He's not here, I made sure of that."

She frowned. What the hell was he talking about? Exactly what did he mean? What did he do to Denver? Her heart rammed against her chest and heat raced to her face. She dropped her gaze to the floor before looking back up at him.

"What do you want, Butch? And what have you done to Denver?"

His cackle made her flesh crawl. His eyes looked hazy and darker than the usual light colored chestnut. His sneer intensified her caution. She looked around again for someone, anyone to come to her rescue.

Butch moved closer and Trish dropped her hand from the cart and stepped back.

"The last time we were you here, your friend wasn't so nice."

"My husband, Butch."

"Yeah, I heard about that. That's too bad. You missed out on all of this." He grabbed her wrist in a vice-like grip and pulled her forward. "We're going to take a little ride"

"Let go of me. Right now, I mean it."

"Or else what?"

Again, she looked around for help.

"Don't worry. Everyone is fully occupied and out of hearing distance. Screaming will do you no good. So you can walk or I can pick you up. Which is it?"

She tried to jerk her arm away but pulling against Butch was like trying to pull an eighteen-wheeler by herself. He squeezed her arm harder. Tears gathered behind her eyes. She huffed, resisting, not making it easy for him to pull her along. He stopped and glared down at her.

"I mean it. I'll throw you over my shoulder."

Seeing no other option just yet, she followed Butch toward a side entrance. She watched the area and looked for anything she could use as a weapon. She wasn't about to just let him take her. Her eyes darted from side to side, looking and praying for an opportunity, anything she could try to slow down, if not stop him.

His hand was on the door when she grabbed the tab on the alarm beside the door. The piercing noise triggered all the alarms on that one detonator. They screamed. Butch pushed her against the door, slamming her shoulder and the side of her face into the metal. Pain radiated down her entire body and she screamed.

She felt her body being hefted up and thrown over Butch's shoulder. She bounced around, not able to grab or hold on to anything that would keep her from feeling like she would eat dirt any minute. Her body tossed and then landed against more metal.

She groaned as she stopped sliding. Before she could sit up and get her bearings, she was jerked back. Her head hit something solid. It hurt like hell and then there was nothing.

****

Trish tried to move but couldn't. Her entire body felt like someone had slammed her against a cement block and then dragged her across a gravel road for ten miles. She moaned and tried to open her eyes, but couldn't. She tried to move her arms and couldn't. She tried to stand but her legs refused to move.

She swallowed hard and tasted blood. Her tongue felt as thick as an apple stuffed into her mouth. Tears streamed down her face. She tried not to panic but that effort didn't last very long. She wept. That made her headache worse. Where ever she was, it was cold and damp.

Her thoughts were everywhere. How long had she been here? Where was here? Why would Butch do this? Denver? Where was Denver? Was he alright? Was he looking for her? Was anyone looking for her? The weeping turned to wailing. She carried on so badly that she did not hear Butch's footsteps, but his voice made her freeze.

"I tried to make it easy on you, Trish. You brought this on yourself."

He lifted the cloth covering her eyes. Now she understood why she couldn't open them. Her lids were swollen and sore but she made out his face through her tears. He stepped back and looked at her.

"Now I got your attention?"

Trish didn't respond. In her mind it wouldn't do her any good. She had to keep her head. She had to find a way out.

"Why did you have to go and mess things up by marrying that chump? I tried to wait until you were ready, but no, you had to ruin it."

He paced in front of her. She tried, at first, to follow him but it made her eyes throb.

"I didn't want to bring you here but you gave me no choice."

He stopped pacing for a moment then picked it up again. When he moved in front of her again, this time he stooped and touched the side of her face. She pulled back. Both his touch and her movement hurt. Tears silently ran down her face.

"Sorry, darling, I didn't want to hurt you. I... I just wish you would have listened."

He stood and Trish closed her eyes, praying silently. *Please God, help me. Please. I want to see my husband again, see my family.* She swallowed hard again, still tasting blood. He continued his rant but she no longer heard it.

When she stirred again and opened her eyes, it was completely dark and very cold. She shivered and pulled her arms around her. She looked down, able to see them now. She didn't understand why she couldn't move them before. She was also able to move her legs and feet. Everything still ached but at least she could move. She felt around in the dark before she attempted to stand.

CHAPTER 48

It took almost every hand on the ranch to keep him from tearing the tack shed apart. He saw red. At one time he couldn't even stand on his own. His heart had left his body and he no longer cared about anything. He would find Trish or die trying.

It had been a full twenty-four hours since he received the call from the Sheriff. His meeting with Juanita all but forgotten, he had torn ass getting to the mercantile warehouse.

As was customary in these parts, the keys were in the ignition of the van, parked right next to the back-loading door.

They searched the perimeter of the store and the bushes surrounding it as well. It was Dan, the store owner who told them the only other person in the store had been Butch Monroe.

The bottom of his gut had dropped to his toes. He could no longer hold it together. He swore he would kill him with his bare hands if he had harmed Trish in any way.

They extended the search to several country roads in different directions and found nothing. Denver was beside himself when he got home.

He walked, then ran and then walked some more to try and clear his head. By the time night fell with no word, he left to search on his own. Sleep evaded him.

He wanted to wait until they got some positive leads before calling her parents. He hoped to spare them the worry he was consumed with. But his mother called them right away. She thought it best.

They were on their way. He couldn't be at the ranch when they got there. Her father had only turned her over to his care weeks before. How could he explain this to him?

He jumped in the shower. With his head beneath the spray, tears ran freely down his face. He turned off the water and dressed. Before he could get out the door, his mother called to him.

"Den, honey."

"I can't just sit around waiting, Mom. I have to find her."

"We'll find her Den, but in the meantime, you have to take care of yourself. You'll be no good finding her if you don't pull it together. We always have hope, son. We've always had God, yes?"

He nodded and hugged his mother. When he released her, he continued on his way. He rode up and down every country road he could think of. Others had joined in the search but still nothing.

He saw not one, but two trucks when he got home. He dragged himself through the door to the house and immediately caught her mother's tearful eyes.

She rose and grabbed him in a tight hug. He could no longer keep his worry in check. He slumped to her feet, hugging her legs.

"I'm sorry, Madear. I have to find her."

"Oh, Denver, sweetheart. We're going to find her. I'm very confident in God's mercy. Try not to worry too much."

Alvin knelt next to him and rubbed his back.

"We'll find her, Den. Come, stand up."

Denver tried but couldn't quite make it. He felt several hands around him and looked up. All three of her brothers were there. They helped him to a chair. His mother handed Michael a glass of water, which Michael forced into his hand. Denver drank a little, then stared out in front of him. He couldn't look any of them in the eye.

"So, we've been talking, trying to come up with a plan," Travis began.

It was like him to lead. In getting to know her brothers, he had found an instant bond with them, one that helped him fully understand their place in Trish's life. She'd always been protected. But he also knew Trish was a tough cookie. Having brothers had taught her to hold her own.

Denver was restless and left the family gathered in the den.

"Denver."

Trae had followed him. He pulled him into a bear hug. He and Trae were probably the closest in age. He liked this guy. Something about him made Denver believe they were much alike. They walked in silence at first, then Trae asked, "Tell me about this joker, Butch."

"I will kill him, Trae, if he has done anything to harm her."

"You might have to get in line, bruh."

They talked as they walked and by the time he got

back to his quarters, he was able to think a little more clearly.

Denver's sister, Robin, had made it to the house by then, which meant he would bunk with the crew again. She hugged him tight, her tears soaked his shirt. The men moved to the kitchen to make plans for the next day.

Just before dawn, Denver walked into the barn and saddled Winter. Denver took the path he and Trish normally took. She loved the wildflowers there. They would always stop so she could pick a bunch or two. By the time the sun was rising, he turned and headed to the farthest east gate. The grass had grown high, probably as tall as him. He would have to remember to have someone come out and cut it down some.

He was ready to turn around when he heard something. A hurt animal, maybe? None of his herd was kept this far away. Maybe it was a coyote or wildcat?

It was a stretch to see anything like that on the ranch because they sat traps and used other devices to keep them away from the cattle. Still, he heard something. He continued on.

"Careful, boy. I didn't bring the rifle or my cell phone. We might have to make a go of it."

He patted Winter on the neck and eased the horse forward. His heart froze again, this time with disbelief. He hurriedly moved closer and jumped from the horse. He raced towards Trish.

She'd bent over. He picked her up and crushed her to him, tears of joy stinging his eyes.

"Oh, my God! Oh, baby, where did you come from? Are you okay?"

He looked at her. Her face was bruised, her eyes were swollen. She screamed in agony when he pulled her against him.

He tried to be gentle but his hands had to make sure nothing was broken or protruding. She hadn't yet answered him. She was mumbling something but it had not yet registered with her who he was.

"Trish, baby. Look at me."

She shook her head. He tried with all his might not to add to the pain he saw in her eyes when he just touched face. He dropped to the ground and drew her to him, cradling her like an infant.

"Oh, sweetheart. You scared me. I've been looking everywhere for you."

"Den?" A hoarse whisper escaped her lips.

"Yes, baby, it's me. Let's get you home."

He lifted her and whistled for Winter. When the stallion moved closer, he tried to figure out how to get on the animal with Trish in his arms.

"Damn!"

He looked and saw a rock that would help. He headed toward it. Winter followed. Denver stepped up on the rock and with as much care as he possible, sat Trish in the saddle, using one hand to hold her in place while he mounted behind her. Winter seemed to understand the implication and held still until Denver stuck his foot in the stirrup. Then he moved gently. Denver moved Trish closer and they took the most direct path home. The thrill that filled him to have her in his arms made him want to slap the reins to make Winter hightail it home. Instead, he took it slow and steady. He talked to her and leaned down to kiss the top of her head.

When they got on the path directly to the house, he saw the crew preparing for the morning chores. Reve saw him first and stormed toward the house. It didn't take long before everyone came running from the house. He stopped by Travis and lifted his arms, reluctantly handing

Trish down to him. Then he dismounted.

She cried out when Travis crushed her against him. "Careful bruh, I think she's hurt." Reve was there to take Winter's reins. Travis had already started towards the house. Everyone else followed them into the house. Diane was close, and when Travis placed Trish down, Diane sat next to her.

"Give her space, please." She begged.

Beatrice handed Diane a towel. Robin was calling 911.

Denver stood by helplessly again. He should have been there with her. Not on the sidelines. Trish was his charge. When that thought settled in his mind, he pushed through the family gathered around. Diane looked up at him and stood. He sat where she'd been. He gently touched her face and she stirred.

By the time a caddy pulled off, sirens blasting, Trish was semi-unconscious. They weren't allowed in the room at the hospital while the doctors worked to get her vitals and get her hooked up to an IV. They all paced the waiting room. No one asked where he'd found her or how. It would all come out soon, he just knew it.

When she was stabilized, they were allowed, one by one, into the room to see and kiss her. Everyone except the two mothers, who insisted on going in together. While they were with Trish, he stood.

"I found Trish wandering the field at the far east side of my ranch. I have no idea how she got there but I'm going to kill Butch. This I promise you. His ass better leave Texas. And even then, he won't be safe."

"Now, Denver, you can't go getting yourself locked up. That won't do Trish any good, you hear me, son."

Alvin's hand squeezed his shoulder. But Denver wasn't hearing any of it. Butch would pay and pay dearly. He bit the inside of his cheek to keep the words to himself. No one would talk him out of it. He'd already made up his mind.

Travis must have read his mind. He pushed up next to him and whispered. "I got first dibs, Den."

Denver glanced at his brother-in-law who looked like he was ready to chew fire. Travis's jaw clenched and a vein in his temple bulged. Denver nodded in acknowledgement.

He'd given the sheriff his statement about where he'd found his wife. Now he looked up and saw the sheriff and two deputies approach. Everyone stood.

"We went out to your east gate, Baldwin. Looks like you're going to have to shore up that fence again. It would seem that whoever took your wife..."

"It was Butch. And I'm telling you now; he won't make it through the week if I get my hands on him."

"Denver, you can't go off saying stuff like that."

His mother moved next to him and slipped her arm under his. "Den, please."

He glanced down at her before giving the sheriff his attention again.

"There's a cave opening just on the inside of your gate. We found evidence that your wife had been taken there. We'll find Butch for questioning."

"You haven't found him yet? You better before I do."

The man eyed him before moving on.

Denver was the last to go in to see Trish. She looked peaceful. He kissed the top of her head. He picked up her limp hand and pressed it to his lips.

"I'll be back to take you home, my love."

He passed through the waiting room where his family waited. He kept moving and didn't expect anyone to follow. When he glanced back, all three of Trish's linebacking brothers were on his tail.

"We're coming, Baldwin." Travis barked.

He didn't protest. He would find Butch, with or without any help. He was going down.

"Take my truck." Trae tossed him his keys.

Denver had already pulled his pistol from his glove compartment. He tucked it in a holster just above his boot. They sped off in Trae's truck like a bat out of hell.

Denver knew some of the hiding spots where guys took their booty calls for some free ass.

He spotted Butch's truck at the first hidden cove, just beyond a field of tall grass and pulled to the side of the road a couple of hundred yards away. He held his index finger to his mouth.

They all unloaded, slowly and quietly closing their doors.

When they crept up to the campsite, they found Butch asleep. By the time he realized he had company, it was too late.

Denver snatched him up and threw several punches before the man realized what was happening. He grinned widely, using the back of his hand to wipe away blood from his busted lip.

"Yeah, I've been waiting for this."

He took a posture ready to duke it out with Denver. His smile faded when Trish's three brothers stepped up.

"Yeah, when you're done, I'm next. In fact, you stole my spot, Denver. I was supposed to have first dibs."

Butch backed up as he eyed each of the men. "Who the hell are you?"

"You're going to wish you'd never met us. That's who the hell we are." Michael moved ahead of Travis. "Nobody fucks with my sister, you punk. I'm going to teach your ass a lesson."

"I wasn't trying to hurt her, I promise. In fact, I…"

"You had the damn nerve to take my wife and then hide her on my property. You must be crazy!" Denver screamed.

Butch didn't get to say anything. Trae threw the first punch as if to say he was through with this damn talking. He was all about getting it done. Travis jabbed him next, followed by Michael. When Denver jabbed him while he was still bent over, Butch went sailing backwards.

Each man threw blows that knocked him down again and again. It was obvious Butch wasn't smart. He kept trying to get up. He never quite made it.

They filled his body with blow after blow, taking their rage out on him. Intent on beating Butch to a pulp, none of them heard the sirens or the arrival of the law enforcement behind them.

"Okay, guys, back it up. We got it from here."

Butch's face was bloody and swollen. He couldn't stand. Each blow they'd rendered was followed with a swift kick.

Denver wasn't fully satisfied. He had to be detained when he pulled the gun from his holster and pointed it at Butch.

"I will kill you, you hear me," he screamed.

CHAPTER 49

Trish stirred and the beeping noise got louder and louder. She moved her head from side to side, hoping to escape. The pounding in her hand moved up her arm. She lifted it up in hopes of discovering why. When she opened her eyes and looked down, she understood.

She glanced around. There were machines on either side of her. The throbbing came from the areas where tubes were inserted into her skin. The other ends were plugged into machines. Hospital. She was in a hospital. Flashes of her encounter with Butch came to mind and she gasped. The beeping on one of the machines grew louder and faster.

Her hand came down and landed on top of a head. She peeked down. It was Denver. Tears flowed as she stroked her fingers across the top of his head. He glanced up and smiled. She tried to smile. She wasn't sure she was successful.

"Hi sweetheart."

"I'm sorry, Den. I tried…"

Her raspy voice was a whisper.

"Hush. You're fine."

Several staffers came rushing in. They immediately went to the machine making the loudest racket and hit several buttons.

"Mrs. Baldwin, are you in any pain?"

Trish winced but her eyes would not leave Denver. She recognized the worry in his. He touched her hand in silent communication. Still, she waited for his verbal response. She needed to hear him say it.

"We're good. I'm okay now that you're okay, sweetheart."

"Den…"

"Don't worry. Just rest. We'll go home as soon as the doctor lets us."

She pressed her lips together and ran her tongue, which felt like wood, across her bottom lip. She winced again as she felt a surge through her.

"I just gave you a little medicine to help you sleep." The nurse announced.

She finally looked at the woman. She didn't want to sleep. She wanted to be with Denver, to see his face, to feel his touch. She looked back at him to make sure he was still there. He was. Trish squinted, trying to keep her eyes on him. He moved farther and farther away.

"Den, don't leave me, please stay with…"

****

Trish took a cleansing breath and turned her head toward the chatter. The laughter was infectious so she chuckled even though she had no idea what everyone was laughing about. She opened her eyes enough to catch her mother and sister-in-law, Robin's profiles. Robin was always a load of laughter. She had a way of making people smile, even when they didn't want to. Apparently, she'd said something that had them both hysterical.

Trish shifted her body but was limited by the tubes in her arms. Her mouth was full of cotton and her throat raw. Her movement caught her mother's attention. Both women rushed to her bedside.

"Trish, honey. Don't move, just wait. Are you thirsty?"

"Yes, ma'am"

She tried to take a long swig, but most of her drink ended down her chin.

"Go slow, sweetie," Robin coached. "Here, let me raise you up a little bit.

When the bed was up, Trish felt a lot better. The room was filled with flowers and cards. Her mother sat on the side of the bed. She brushed her curl from Trish's face. She felt groggy and stiff.

"What day is it?" She asked.

"Saturday, bae. You've been here a couple of days now."

She touched her hair, afraid that after a day of not combing it, the locks would be a tangled, frizzy mess. But when she reached up, most of it had been piled up on the very top of her head into a bun. She looked at her mother and smiled.

"It's a good thing Robin knows what to do with that stuff up there you call hair. Honey, it was a mess."

"That's what I was afraid of. I'd considered cutting it all off at one point."

Her throat was still sore and raspy.

"Don't you dare cut off that beautiful hair. Women are paying big bucks just to get your hair." Robin stroked her hair at her temple.

"I must have really been knocked out to not feel anything. I'm usually tender headed."

"Yes, you were gone for a minute, little-bit." Robin smiled.

"Mom, where's Denver?"

"Honey, that boy has been here the entire time. We had to threaten him to make him go home to shower and change clothes. He's been gone about an hour."

Robin added, "And if I know him, he just barely ran his tail under that damn water. He is likely to walk through those doors any second."

It wasn't seconds, but he did walk in and stole her breath away when she saw his handsome face and dark eyes. When he entered, all the air in the room was pushed out. He held his hat in one hand and a bunch of wildflowers in the other.

He walked straight to her. Her mother and Robin picked up their belongings and headed for the door. As he got closer, she swallowed him whole with a single glance. It was bad enough that her tongue felt like it weighed a ton. Now she had no way to breathe.

She leaned forward and waited.

"Hello, beautiful. I'm relieved to see you up."

Denver kissed her mouth. His breath smelled like the new mint toothpaste they'd taken to using. She tried to lift her arms around his neck but again, she was restrained.

"I love you."

"And, I love you. These are for you." He placed the bouquet in her lap. "I went to your favorite spot to pick them."

"They're beautiful. I can't wait to get home."

"It may be a few days."

"Den, I still have to finish..."

"You worry too much, my love. The clinic is very aware that you are here. We'll work that out when you're better."

****

It was three weeks now since she'd been out of the hospital. Things had returned to normal. It had taken a little while for her to venture from the ranch. She only traveled from the house to the clinic to the store. Generally, someone dropped her off or accompanied her wherever she needed to go.

Today, she was solo, happy for her freedom and the return of peace and quiet at the house. She hummed her usual song. Today was her day of elevation. Finally, her status would be 'Doctor' and she couldn't be any happier.

She logged into the clinic, pushed her arms through her coat and turned the corner. She paused when she met a hall full of staff and students with balloons, horns and signs. Trish covered her mouth and widened her eyes to consume the entire group.

"Dr. Baldwin, congratulations."

Her professor gave her a hardy handshake. All the well-wishers greeted her, some with handshakes, most with hugs. As the line thinned, there he was, all consuming, all powerfully masculine, the very love of her life.

"Hey, you, what are you doing here?"

"It's a celebration, Dr. Baldwin."

He wrapped her in his arms and kissed her deeply before releasing her. She admired his wide grin and strong arms. She could stay there forever.

"You're always my celebration."

"So, you'll remember this tonight?"

"I guess you'll have to wait and see."

Once the short celebration was over, she got straight to work. Her schedule was full so seeing her husband gave her that extra boost she needed to get through the day, even though he'd already given her a special goodbye before she left the house.

The celebration died the moment she pulled in next to Denver's truck back at the house. Two law enforcement vehicles flanked the side fence near the porch. She stomped up the stairs leading to porch and paused as her hand touched the door.

When she walked in, the room quieted. She looked at Denver first. He stood and walked toward her.

"Come on in. The sheriff was just giving us the report on the fire and on Butch." He kissed her sweetly.

She frowned on hearing Butch's name and the fire in the same sentence. She didn't understand how they were connected. She looked from him to Mom Bea and then to the Sheriff.

"I don't understand."

"Come, have a sit. Unless you're not feeling up to this?"

"No, I want to know. I need to know what's going to happen to Butch."

When she and Denver got to talk about what happened that day Butch forced her from the mercantile, there were still things she didn't know. Denver had told her that Butch had taken her to a cave on their property. She didn't remember anything other than wandering out of a dark place in the middle of the night.

She remembered having to feel her way up what she thought were steps. And once outside, she knew she could barely make her way through a field because her eyes were sore and her head pounded. Trish remembered the stories Denver had told her about wild animals in Texas. Some were small but still very dangerous.

She'd prayed that a wild animal would not get her. She'd tried following the direction of the moon. She didn't remember Denver finding her and bringing her home.

Now, having to relive the nightmare again made her uneasy, but she knew the only way to move past the trauma was to deal with it head on. Sighing, she sat next to Denver, clasping his hand.

"Butch apparently was pretty mad at you when you confronted him in the dry goods store."

The details were shocking. Apparently Butch had been sneaking onto Baldwin Ranch for years. Hearing this made Denver piping hot. She thought they were going to have to haul him away. He'd stolen several of Keith's gas cans, among other things that had mysteriously disappeared. They were all found in the cave.

"You won't have to worry about Butch Monroe for a while."

The announcement didn't make her feel much better, but at least he would be out of Denver's reach. She didn't want *him* to end up in jail. And if he got a hold of the man, that's exactly what would happen.

Fully shaken by the conversation, Trish stood and left the room. She braced the stool at the center of the granite counter. Just as she bent over and placed her forehead on top of her hand, his arms circled her waist. With ease he pulled her into his arms.

"I will never allow him to harm you again, darling. I promise."

Denver lips touched the base of her neck. The heat gently bathed her with a calm she would never be able to explain. The comfort of his embrace offer security but also showered her with love. She had no doubts about how he felt about her or what lengths he would go to protect her. Denver, since knowing him, had been a man of his word. Any chance he got, he would make Butch pay. And dearly.

"I just want him put away for a very long time. I don't

want you to take revenge, Den. Promise me."

He turned away and stared toward the patio door. She felt his muscles tense, saw the vein in his temple leap. He pulled his bottom lip between his teeth and took a very long breath. He did not answer but looked back at her. His eyes were dark and unreadable.

For the first time since she'd known him, he was cold and unreachable. She trembled after a long moment when his gaze remained unchanged. His mouth drew into a tight long line. The crazy energy transferred from his embrace and moved through her. She pushed against his chest to break the hold. But he wouldn't release her and this troubled her even more.

"Den?" She whispered. "You're scaring me."

He released her but instead of consoling her, he stormed out of the side door and slammed it hard behind him. Trish rushed to the door, ready to go after him, but paused. Was he mad at her? If so, why? She had not encouraged Butch, not even before they'd met.

With her hand still on the door knob, she stood and watched Denver stomp away, his back ramrod straight.

CHAPTER 50

Denver moved as fast as his legs would take him. He almost broke into a sprint. He had to get as far away as he could before he said or did something he would regret. He hadn't quite processed all what the sheriff had told them so he knew it was a lot for Trish to handle, considering what she'd been through. But he couldn't quite hold his anger when she seemed to want to spare that bastard.

He sped up the path to the tack shed and hopped on one of the three-wheelers. Generally, he checked to make sure it had gas but he didn't this time. He slammed the accelerator and sped off, looking only in one direction, ahead of him. He sped directly to the east gate, racing toward it like it would vanish any moment.

He ripped down the yellow tape the sheriff and his deputies had tied from one end of the gate to a stake near the cave's opening. He hadn't been there in a long time, even though it was one of the places he used to frequent as a boy.

He paused before entering. A chill ran up his back, so

he stilled. When he finally bent down and entered the dark, damp cave, he placed his hand at the small opening to the right. It was where he used to keep a flash light. Butch knew this. At one time as kids, they'd hung out here together. Sure enough, his hand met the cool metal. He was certain it had been left there by Butch.

He pulled it down and fished for its switch. When he found it, the dim rays flickered at first but eventually became a steady stream of light. With shaky hands he moved forward and with each step a piece of his heart faded. He inhaled the musty scent of the enclosure. Some of the ground was muddy, but for the most part, the red clay flooring was solid. As he drew closer to what looked like a bench, his free arm moved to and covered his nose and mouth to suppress the whimper growing from his gut.

He dropped to one knee, his mind racing. He could only imagine seeing Trish tied up here. The rope was still scattered about. He bolted straight up, his head nearly colliding with the sharp rocks above him. His heart raced so fast, he could hear it in his ears. The heat clamoring through his veins would scald anyone within two feet if they dared approach.

He had to get out, and quickly. Coming here was not a good idea after all. The sight only infuriated him more. With the flashlight still in hand, he rushed through the opening and flung the metal as far as he could. Denver bent, hands on his knees, with his eyes squeezed tight.

"Please, God, don't let me do something that will make my family suffer."

He remained bent over until he heard the galloping of an animal nearby. He still didn't look up or look her way. He knew it was Trish. He just couldn't face her. How had he let her down? He was supposed to protect her. He'd failed not just her father, but her as well.

And as his wife raced toward him, she nearly bolted them both over when her body crashed against him.

"Den?"

He lifted them up and pulled her close.

"I'm sorry, Trish."

"No, Den. It wasn't our fault. Butch had it in his mind. Nothing would have stopped him."

Denver buried his face into her hair as he held her tight.

"I don't know that I can honor your request, baby."

"You have to, Den. You can't let him steal our joy. We have so much to look forward to. I don't want to live without you, honey. And that's exactly what will happen if you let Butch ruin this for us."

He didn't respond for a long moment, just simply held her in a vice-like grip. Only after Lightning walked up and nudged him in the back did he let up and looked behind him.

"What do you want man. She's mine."

He glared at the animal as he nodded his head up and down and then neighed. Lightning did this a couple of times then blew air from his nostrils at Denver. The interaction broke the stifled energy and both he and Trish chuckled at the stallion's intrusion.

Denver eased his hold on Trish but didn't release her until he'd kissed her deeply. Once more, her horse poked him and Denver he turned and gently swatted at the animal's nose.

"You don't run things here."

He moved to the horse's side with Trish's hand still in his. He helped as she put her foot in a stirrup and threw her leg across the saddle. Once in place, he stepped back.

"I promise, Trish."

"Thank you."

He nodded and looked at the busted fence.

"As soon as they finish up, I'm going to have both the fence and this cave closed and locked."

Trish nodded. He took several steps back. "I'll see you at the house in a few minutes."

"You're coming straight home, right?"

"Yes, I'm right behind you."

"Okay."

She headed back toward the house but briefly looked back. He took another look around before he got back on his vehicle. A few minutes later, he pulled up to the tack shed. When he strolled up to the house, he met his mother's worried eyes. She stood arm in arm with Trish as he approached. Trish released her, giving him the space to pull her close.

"It's okay."

"Are you sure?"

"Yes. I love you, Mom."

"I love you both."

Beatrice reached for Trish again, kissing them both on the cheeks before she left them standing and staring at one another. He drew his fingers along Trish's forehead before kissing her.

"Let's go inside, Mrs. Baldwin. We've got some celebrating to finish."

"Is that right?"

"Yes. It's time to back up those words you used this morning."

"What about supper?"

"You are my supper."

The shower was short and sweet. They wasted little time washing one another. After drying her off, he swept her up into his arms and headed to the bed. Trish had lit the candles and pulled back the covers. He placed her in the bed.

"Move back, darling."

She complied. He hovered above her, his lips starting at her forehead and loving on her lush lips until they traveled the length of her body. He granted every stopping point a measure of goose bumps until he reached the space, warm, moist and as sweet as the morning dew. He blessed the insides of her thighs, using her legs to prevent her squirming.

When Denver's tongue met her opening with eagerness, Trish's body trembled in his grasp. Her scream made him move up her body with urgency. He covered her mouth to swallow the cry that was shaking the house.

"Oh, but Mrs. Baldwin, you're making way too much noise," he growled into her mouth.

Trish squirmed beneath him. She attempted to move her legs around him but he still held them in his tight grip. His growing arousal slammed against her in anticipation.

Yes. This was the kind of celebration he'd been looking forward to all day.

And now, with the sheriff and the stifling experience at the cave forgotten for the moment, he would make all they'd experienced in their short journey, worth the ride.

"I love you," he mumbled into her open mouth.

She groaned, attempting to respond. He wouldn't let her. He covered her mouth completely as he drove into her waiting kingdom.

Her eyes flew open and gazed into his. He held her there as he made his sharp entry. He didn't move an inch once he was completely inside.

Denver stared into her teary eyes, trying like hell to convey to her all he felt for her. He wanted her to know that he'd never let another person harm her, ever again. He would give up his life to make sure.

When her tears rolled into her hair, he kissed each lid as she closed her eyes again. He moved his lips to her ear. "I love you, darling."

Her trembling lips met the side of his face.

"I love you, Denver. Always."

With her words, he released her legs and began their song and dance until the final note of their melody silenced both their doubts and fears.

BOOKS BY ANN CLAY

More Than a Bargain
Waving From the Heart
A Fresh Encounter
Cupid's Connection
A Love for all Times
Priceless
Protective Custody
Blue Autumn in the Bayou
Final Play
Beyond the Blue Cypress
A Perfect Blend
Faith in Ordinary Things
Game Changer
Love on the Run

ABOUT THE AUTHOR

An avid reader and lover of positive, strong men, Award-Winning Author, **ANN CLAY** began her writing venture in 1999. She has been duly recognized for her warm-hearted stories, bursting with memorable characters, places and special moments. Venturing into several genres, Ann still prefers her romantic versions of life and living. She resides in Southern Illinois with family and loves hearing from her readers. Check her out at www.annclay.com, by email at annclay@annclay.com or on Twitter @annclaywrites.

Don't forget to check out Ann's upcoming projects, including the Winter Games Series entitled Romance on Ice is scheduled in 2018; and the new series, Durbin Enterprises. Happy Reading!